Acclaim for Arabesques

"This stunning first novel…summons the old vanquished world of Arab Palestine back to life and makes it speak with extraordinary power and grace.…In the best tradition of the great storyteller of his people, Anton Shammas dazzles us.…"

Fouad Ajami, *Washington Post Book World*

"Anton Shammas shows no lack of sophistication in the ways of the literary West: his novel about Palestinians is intricately conceived and beautifully written.…"

John Updike, *The New Yorker*

"Politics aside, it is a wonderful story by a talented and important writer…it is deeply moving and engrossing."

Michael Lerner, *San Francisco Examiner-Chronicle*

"By implication it is the story of all emotional displacement…of connections, not divisions; it is a triumph of the healing power of imagination over the fragmenting force of politics."

Richard Wakefield, *Seattle Times Post*

"By changing scenery and time without diminishing his lush description, Shammas establishes his first novel as a very original means of creating a literary universe that both records the rich heritage of one family and insinuates that of countless others.… With *Arabesques*, Shammas emerges as an interesting and important new voice in Israeli literature."

Sharon Fleisher, *Jewish Week*

Anton Shammas

ARABESQUES

TRANSLATED FROM THE HEBREW
BY VIVIAN EDEN

Harper & Row, Publishers, New York
Cambridge, Grand Rapids, Philadelphia, St. Louis, San Francisco,
London, Singapore, Sydney, Tokyo

Grateful acknowledgment is made for assistance from The Institute for the Translation of Hebrew Literature.

For permission to quote excerpts from copyrighted material, acknowledgment is made to the following publishers:

Alfred A. Knopf, Inc., for "Anecdote of the Jar," Copyright 1923 and renewed 1951 by Wallace Stevens. Reprinted from *The Collected Poems of Wallace Stevens*.

Houghton Mifflin Company for *My Antonia* by Willa Cather. Copyright 1918, by Willa Sibert Cather. Copyright renewed 1946 by Willa Sibert Cather.

New Directions Publishing Corporation for *How German Is It*. Copyright © 1980 by Walter Abish.

Published by arrangement with Michaelmark Books, Ltd., Israel.

First PERENNIAL LIBRARY edition published 1989.

Library of Congress Cataloging-in-Publication Data

Shammas, Anton.
  Arabesques.

  "Perennial Library."
  Translation of: 'Arabeskot.'
  I. Title.
PJ5054.S414A8913   1989   892.4'36   87–45665
ISBN 0-06-091583-8

89 90 91 92 93 FG 10 9 8 7 6 5 4 3 2

NOTE ON THE TRANSLATION

Readers who like to compare texts will notice that frequently both the words and the music of the English version of *Arabesques* diverge from the original Hebrew; together we have added, subtracted or restructured passages with the aim of rendering accessible to readers of English a story originally told in a very allusive and layered kind of Hebrew with equally complex Arabic resonances, especially in the rhythm section.

Vivian Eden and Anton Shammas

Most first novels are disguised autobiographies.
This autobiography is a disguised novel.

Clive James, *Unreliable Memoirs*

PART ONE
THE TALE

You told me, you know, that when a child
is brought to a foreign country, it picks up the
language in a few weeks, and forgets its own.
Well, I am a child in your country.

George Bernard Shaw, *Pygmalion*

CHAPTER 1

Grandmother Alia had never in her life heard of communism, despite the sickle laid upon her belly on Thursday, the first of April, 1954. Since the early hours of that morning, whose chill still scorches my memory, Abu Jameel, the village carpenter, had been working intently, turning the planks from an old cupboard into a coffin. His sense of humor usually covered for his slow work pace, but he was pensive and quiet now. The soft-footed wail of the plane seemed to leap over the shavings curling from the wood, to pad out of the darkness of Uncle Yusef's house, across the courtyard from ours, and rub themselves like abandoned cats at my grandmother's feet as she lay, hands crossed, on her mattress laid upon a straw mat on the cold concrete floor.

She had died the night before, and her belly puffed up, so in the morning my father laid the iron sickle on it. Abu Jameel said something about how tiny she was, that there is no need for so much wood, and really it's a shame to waste the cupboard. From one of the leftover planks he made a low stool, which my mother would later sit on to do laundry or knead dough, and we would all use it for the weekly *hammam* on Saturday nights, when we would place it in the tin tub of water that had been heated on the primus stove. I was four when Grandmother died. They had shooed me away,

3

to no distress on my part, and sent me to watch the coffin being built at Uncle Yusef's. Only the sight of the sickle in my father's hand took my enchanted eyes from the carpenter's work. Abu Jameel winked and said, "The old woman's fooling you—today is April first."

A moth was circling above a dying body twenty-four years after that April morning. It was a miniature white moth, one of those attracted to electric light on summer nights in Haifa. At another time my mother would have called it a *bashoora,* an omen-moth, for good or ill. My mother didn't notice this moth, because her veiled eyes were fixed upon the mouth that would open every few seconds to release, each time more faintly, the years that had been pressed into the body stretched out beneath the moth's flight. A freight train clattered over the railroad tracks a few dozen meters from the house, and the walls, as always, trembled slightly. The rhythmic clatter of the wheels gave the scene an illusory order. Beneath the floor tiles which transmitted the vibrations of the engine to our feet, the roots of the eucalyptus slowly continued to gnaw away at the sewer pipes.

As the priest's hand flicked at the moth, his chant was thrown off its track, but he adapted to this swerve and raised his voice above the racket of the train. For a moment it seemed that the whole scene was taken from some early-morning dream, as if the moth, which had intruded itself so delicately, had tipped the balance, and the whole scene would collapse upon one's awakening. Even when the racket of the wheels had ebbed away, the voice went on in its loud tones to encourage the spirit that was no longer willing to inhabit the weak flesh: "Open for us the Gate of Supplication, Holy Mother." But as the Holy Mother prefers the pleas of those who whisper, he then repeated his words in a subdued voice for the last time, asking the Holy Mother to open the Gate of Supplication for the dying man. The

4

moth flew out through the door, which had been open a crack. My father's head, which for years had been accustomed to a pillow stuffed with bran, now sank away on a cotton one.

Grandmother Alia was the one who had first conceived of stuffing the pillows with bran, during the years of the Great War, when her husband, Jubran, after whom my eldest brother is named, was away on the other side of the world. My father preserved the bran pillow as a memorial less to his mother than to the world that had vanished, as the saying goes, like the chaff which the wind driveth away from the threshing floor of the village he had left behind for the city in the early 1960s.

The place where my grandmother lay was beneath the western window. On its wide sill my mother would place the teakettle, from which she trickled water to wash her face. My father would use the sill to take apart the kerosene lamp every four weeks on Sunday afternoon. He would first close the window very tightly. Then he would turn a stool on its side, and between the rungs he would steady the "head" of the lamp, which held the magical fragile mantle inside which the kerosene turned to light. My father was always anxious that this mantle would fall apart for no good reason. The project of cleaning the lamp culminated in his inspection of the jet of pumped kerosene that sprang through the tiny hole that a very fine needle was responsible for keeping clean. The jet of kerosene made a joyful arc in the air, which would color the circles of light that came into the room through the leaves of the apricot tree that canopied the cistern. The filtered sun wove on the cold concrete floor a dappled rug, which fades whenever my father leans over the lantern to examine the cleaning needle that has broken in the hole.

No sun circles danced around my grandmother now. It was very early, and the sky was dark. As I listened to the muted wail of the plane, I was thinking about the sickle used for the wheat harvest and about the blackness of the women kneeling around the body as I listened to the muted wail of the plane, intent upon preparing the final smooth couch for my grandmother, whose hard years had trickled out of her body through the wrinkles that furrowed her face.

I stood near the table Abu Jameel was using in the same place where at the end of the fall the strings of dried tobacco were brought to be stuffed into a special large wooden box. When they let me, I would pass Uncle Yusef the strings of tobacco already cut in two, which he would arrange artfully in the box. Whenever the box filled up and the tobacco threatened to spill over like boiling milk, my uncle and his son would lay a board over the leaves and stand on it to tamp them down. The smell of the first rain always arouses in me the smell of pressed tobacco sifting into the small square courtyard between our house and my uncle's, the courtyard that was filling up that April morning with wailing women who had come to mourn for Grandmother as she lay there with clasped hands, the hands that held this same sickle during the harvest and held my hand when I went with her to visit my aunt Jaleeleh, who had rejected the hand of Abu Jameel the carpenter.

I so loved the touch of Grandmother's hand that I never complained about holding it for a long time, even though my raised arm would grow numb. It was only when we had gotten to the facade of the village church, halfway to my aunt's house, and she would release my hand to cross herself, that I could circle halfway around her and tuck my other hand in hers.

It was my aunt Jaleeleh's hand that now held the hand of the dying man, usurping from my mother the touch of the hand she had so loved with a gesture which let her understand that even forty years of marriage did not prevail over the years of family ties.

6

Grandmother was said to have been born in the year of the Ottoman law on growing tobacco. My father did not know her birth date. In his notebook, bound in faded leather, he calculated the date by referring to other important events in the life of Grandfather Jubran. But, as I have said, the oral tradition puts Grandmother's birth in the year the Ottoman tobacco law was published. Had I not chanced upon the 1874 volume of the Lebanese journal *Al-Jinan*, I would not have known that my father had actually been correct in his calculations.

The church was the walking distance of a single Ave Maria from our house. So a special relationship developed between my family and the priests, which cost my brothers and me our early-morning sleep when we had to serve at the altar during Matins and Lauds. At the end of the fifties an eccentric priest came to the village, who was apparently the first man to carry an open umbrella on the hot, dry days of summer. The white parasol protected the delicate priest from the ruthless sun but exposed him to many discreet smiles of ridicule and won him a prominent place on the list of eccentrics inscribed in the village memory. Along with the parasol the priest brought a collection of old books and journals, which my oldest brother, Jubran, coveted. Bit by bit this collection made its way to our bookcase, which was embedded in the thick wall. Its olive-colored door was locked with the yellow key that was kept in the cookie dish in the "armoire" that was brought disassembled from Beirut in 1940 in a truck and was loaded on the backs of two camels in the village of Rmeish, near the Lebanese border. Its doors, shelves and drawers were covered by a fragile brown veneer, which had survived the journey, and there was a thick mirror on its middle door. Behind this looking glass was the full cookie dish, kept under lock and key. There was a custom in the family that the key to the bookcase could not be taken until the cookie dish was emptied by guests. However, everyone knew that my eldest brother, the book lover, who was systematically raiding the priest's library, had found a way to loosen the lock by lifting the lower-left-hand corner of the mirrored door.

In time I, too, mastered this trick, which enabled me not only to raid the domain of cookies but also to handle a magical wooden sword with a red-painted blade, which my brother kept in the armoire. He had never returned it to its proper owner at the conclusion of a play that had been produced at the local school. For a whole trimester the pupils had to rehearse it under the heavy thumbs of the principal—the priest before the one with the parasol—and the math teacher. They even had to sleep at the school the night before the performance to guard the props, and it was then that they avenged themselves by throwing ink on the colorful maps of the continents and on the white walls and by giving the priest reason to believe that the water in the cistern under the floor of one of the classrooms, the water that went to the tank on the roof of the school and from there to the priest's rooms on the second floor, was no longer pure. In the play my brother was a sword bearer, and though he didn't have a single line to deliver, he was the only student who had a printed copy of the text. In time many books from the priest's library joined it in the bookcase in the wall. Later these books changed hands in order to blur their tracks, but I still have the copy of *Al-Jinan* from 1874, the year my grandmother was born, in which I found the complete text of the law on growing tobacco.

Grandmother Alia complained all her life of the blind fate that had dumped her in the hands of the wayward Shammas family. My grandfather, who was fourteen years older, left her twice to sail far away. The first time was at the end of the last century, when he went off to Brazil for a year and left her holding Uncle Yusef, a squalling infant, in her arms. Then, on the eve of the First World War, he went to Argentina, where he vanished for about ten years, leaving behind three daughters and three sons, all of them hungry. When he finally returned he brought a large wooden box and a pair of scissors. When his sons opened the box they found it was filled with rusty clothes. Grandfather, for some reason, had hidden a pair of scissors, which had rusted in the box and during the three-month sea voyage had wandered among the clothes, making "crazy patterns," as Grandmother called them.

Seven years after that she said goodbye to her son Jiryes, never to see him again. She preserved him in her mind by telling a story about two dairy cans of milk he had once brought her, which always made her laugh so that she would have to hide her face behind her head scarf. The war also took away one of her eyes, which was ravaged by a disease, and she was granted in its stead the art of staying home and the art of conserving matter. She never threw anything away; instead, she accompanied her things through their metamorphoses. Her shabby dress became the *karah*, the round baking pillow upon which the thin dough is laid in order to set it on the hot tin dome of the oven, and when the pillow wore out it became a *turraha*, a poor man's sitting mat, and when it was too worn for that it became a rag to polish shoes in my father's cobbler shop.

Letters from Uncle Jiryes, whom I never knew, would arrive from Argentina unpredictably. All of them, down to the very last one, which still lies between the pages of my father's missal, concluded, "And to everyone who claims I have not sent him greetings, I hereby send a thousand and one greetings." After my grandmother died, his letters began to reveal an open longing for his birthplace. My oldest brother, Jubran, who was then an apprentice cobbler in my father's shop, tried to squeeze through this opening a request for rolls of Argentine leather. But far from making this gesture to ease his homesickness, Uncle Jiryes instead shrouded himself in a silence that went on for some ten years, until my sister reopened the correspondence in the mid-1960s. By then his letters were like the last signals from a sinking ship. Several months after his last one, we learned from a letter sent to the village by his friend, who had accompanied him on his voyage in 1928, that he had died penniless in an old-age home. Along with enormous debts, he had left behind rumors of a local wife. This would have been in addition to his first wife, Almaza, who had never set foot on Argentinian soil, and had last seen her husband waving from the ship steaming out of Beirut harbor to take my uncle there.

Uncle Jiryes was the only one of my grandfather's sons and daughters, six in all, who inherited the "wrinkle in the mind," as my grandmother called it, that may have been responsible for the great wanderings of the family's patriarch in the early part of the last century. From a remote village in southwestern Syria, called Khabab, he eventually reached the remote village of Fassuta in Galilee, where I was destined to be born. But it seems that our ancestor was driven there less by wanderlust than by his family's fear for his life, which was avidly sought by the Muslim clan in the village. He was still a boy when he set forth on his wanderings, accompanied by his father, who had become a priest after his marriage because he was blessed with a beautiful voice. This voice was finally to be his undoing in one of the villages of mixed religions in the lower Galilee. Some of the villagers there were so delighted by his voice that they tried to make him see, first by gentle persuasion and then by force, that he was wasting his talent in the shabby village church. He could just as easily bestow the pleasures of his voice upon a larger audience of the devout, by transmitting it to all four corners of the village as well as to the heavenly winds, from the heights of the minaret of the local mosque. Thereupon the priest was brought to the top of the minaret, only to find his death at its base. It may be said that he was a martyr who died for the sake of the Holy Name, but just which name that was has never been entirely clear.

Uncle Yusef, who told me this story, was not to be fully trusted in matters having to do with mosques. For in the early years of this century, he and the other villagers of Fassuta were subject to persecutions and torture at the hands of the Muslim inhabitants of the nearby village of Deir El-Kasi, which later was given the Hebrew name Moshav Elkosh. *Bala tool seereh,* or to make a long story short, as my uncle would say, the son was again saved in the nick of time. Smuggled out of that village in the lower Galilee, he came to live with a cousin in Fassuta.

Our village is built on the ruins of the Crusader castle of Fassove, which was built on the ruins of Mifshata, the Jewish village that had been settled after the destruction of the Second Temple by the Harim, a group of deviant priests. It is said that they annulled the commandments pertaining to tithing and the sabbatical year, in which the land must lie fallow, and for this they were punished by four judgments: Plague, the Sword, Famine and Captivity. In the words of the seventh-century Hebrew poet Eleazar Ben Kallir:

> From her land is banished the bejeweled bride
> Because of fallow laws and tithes:
> Quadruply punished for her crimes,
> All her finery stripped aside,
> The Harim of Mifshata.

The son did not rest until he had reached the place with the beautiful view that the Crusaders called Bellevue—as it is written: *Bellum videre quod Sarracenie vocatur Fassove*—and the villagers called Fassu-ta, as a sort of Jewish-Crusader compromise. And he took a wife there and started a family. Grandmother Alia married the son of that wanderer and never managed to extinguish the passion for wandering that smoldered in the breast of Jubran, the heir who fell to her

11

lot, or of her son Jiryes, the only one of her children to inherit that "wrinkle in the mind." She who marries a gypsy, as the saying goes, will learn in the end to hold the tambourine for him. But my grandmother never learned; nor did she manage, when she was nursing Uncle Jiryes, to infuse his body with that serenity which comes from staying home. Her nursing of him became an issue when Jiryes decided to go off to distant Argentina. All else having failed, she told him of how much she had suffered when she nursed him, only to have given him of her milk in vain. My uncle then calculated that the quantity of milk he had suckled from my grandmother was the equivalent of two dairy cans. About a week before his departure, he got up very early one morning, untied Uncle Yusef's donkey and set out with it for the village. An hour later, the donkey came back alone, bearing two dairy cans of milk. My grandmother covered her face with her head scarf and said nothing. Forty years later his younger sister Jaleeleh, who hadn't married the carpenter, would say, "My dear brother Jiryes, as you lay on your deathbed, was there no one near you to give you a glass of water?"

Uncle Jiryes's wife, Almaza, drew back when she saw the water in November 1928. She was not enthusiastic in the first place with the idea of emigration. She stood on the dock in Beirut harbor and watched the ship sailing away as she held in her arms my uncle's firstborn son, Anton, who was nine months old. Six months later my uncle sent her a ticket, but still she wouldn't go. She remained in Beirut with some distant relatives, supporting herself by working as a cleaning woman in the homes of wealthy families. A year later word reached the village that little Anton had fallen ill and died. His death severed the last tie that bound Almaza to her husband and also to his family and to Fassuta, the village of her birth.

At the end of the 1960s Almaza would recall that long

moment on the dock. She had come back by then to the village and was told that in his last letter my uncle begs her forgiveness and calls her "the light of my eyes" and promises to return and see her. When she walks through the streets of the village she holds in her arms the feather pillow upon which Anton had slept. She climbs the fig tree in the courtyard of the house in which she has rented a room. This reminds her of the strip of cloth my uncle had tied around the fig tree next to our house before he departed. He knew that she would stay behind, and he knew that if he should find when he returned that the cloth had become untied, it would be a sign that his wife had been unfaithful to him. Now she tears her garments into strips and winds them around her arms, and she begs that at her death they put only one thing into the coffin with her—Anton's pillow. I, who am writing down all these matters, was named after that child.

It was my uncle Yusef who first told me about my name, as I stood on the boulder in the center of the *duwara*, the garden behind his house, and watched him prune the grapevine. According to legend, this boulder covers one of the entrances to the enormous cave beneath the center of the village. This cave was said to have opened only once, for the villagers to hide in back in the 1860s, when rumors of the religious wars in Lebanon reached Fassuta. At the sight of the piles of golden treasure, which had been buried there in Crusader times, the villagers were so shocked out of their senses that they could not take any with them, and no one believed them once the cave was sealed up again. Several times my cousin Hilweh has seen this boulder gleaming on nights when the moon is full. And she has even seen Ar-Rasad, who is the rooster that the *djinnis* have commanded to guard the entrance to the cave. But the feather that Ar-Rasad leaves behind once every seventy years has never been seen by a mortal, for who is wise enough to know the secret of how the *djinnis* calculate and who is wise enough to know the *djinnis'* calendar?

Except for that wrinkle in his mind, Uncle Jiryes was not particularly equipped to cope with his new life. In his first early letters, except for the anger at his wife, Almaza, who refused to join him, there were only the usual expressions of village emigrants. "I am fine and I lack for nothing except for the sight of your shining faces"—that was always the opening sentence. And the closing sentence always conveyed the thousand and one greetings to everyone who said they had not had greetings from my uncle. The village elders of today still remember the handsome youngster who apparently was the first among them to have suggested the idea of a cultural club. It bothered Uncle Jiryes that the young people of the village showed no interest in the preservation of tradition and folklore. After one wedding in the village of Ikrit (which was destined to be evacuated in 1948 and to become the cause of a great many nostalgic sighs), he was angry at the other young men of the village, who had brought shame upon Fassuta when they could not join in the circle of dancers performing the "Dabkeh Shamaliyeh," the tempestuous northern one, and they returned, hangdog, to our village. That same night he announced he was starting a group to whom he would himself teach the *dabkeh.* He was also the group's only musician, being a wonderful player of the *mijwez,* the double-barreled shepherd's flute that is the Arab version of the bagpipe. Whereas in the latter there is a leather bag, the *mijwez* makes do with the player's mouth.

In his youth my father also gave his breath to the playing of the *mijwez.* He would practice for hours on end, much to my grandmother's distress, though not from the sighing voice of the *mijwez.* For this you must know—that to play the *mijwez* properly you must first put a dry wheat stalk into a glass of water and blow through it. The longer you can make the water bubble, the better your chances are of becoming a successful *mijwez* player. My grandmother

14

thought that blowing air bubbles in a glass of water was a total waste of time. My uncle would undoubtedly have been very sorry to hear that today there is but one *mijwez* player in the village, and even he has been edged out of weddings by electric musical instruments. Uncle Jiryes left his son behind, but he took the *mijwez* to Argentina, and if after all there was someone there to give him a glass of water as he lay dying, did the bubbles of memory rise in his mind?

The scissors that belonged to my father, who had once been a barber, now lay alongside his other instruments in a damascene wooden box inlaid with mother-of-pearl, which had been bought in Beirut in the late 1930s as a betrothal gift to my mother. My father's pocketknife, with the black horn handle, was not in that box, as I had expected it to be. Several days later I found it in his briefcase. This penknife, which I had never imagined I would one day play with to my heart's content, had in the past served my uncle Yusef "to bind the mouths of the wild beasts." Whenever any of the villagers lost a cow or a horse, he would go to see my uncle in the evening, after a day of futile searching, and ask him to bind up the mouths of the wild beasts so that he might rest. My uncle would borrow my father's penknife, pull out the blade, mutter an impenetrable incantation, and return the blade to its place, with the warning that the pocketknife must not be opened before the animal was found. In time I found out that the incantation was nothing but the Christian Creed, which my uncle would mumble backwards over the drawn blade.

Now the priest was reciting it as an absolution, but in his hand he held the missal, and his words flowed from the beginning to the end. My uncle Yusef did not see the moth either, but it was because he had returned to the village the day before. The penknife was not lying in the damascene box inlaid with mother-of-pearl, but there was a lock of graying hair from the head of Grandmother Alia, wrapped

15

in a page of an old religious journal that carried the end of an article in praise of the Inquisition and the beginning of one about the Canaanite woman who believed in Jesus after he exorcised the spirits from her daughter's body. The folded page had been tucked into the inner pocket of the faded leather cover of my father's notebook. Next to the notebook were two small blue velvet boxes, all that remained of the bridal jewelry that had been stolen thirty years earlier out of this same damascene box, where it had been kept by my mother. She had come at the end of the 1930s to Fassuta to teach French and had fallen in love with the man now lying before her. For his sake she had given up her family in Beirut and the memories of her girlhood in the fishermen's alleys of Tyre, and now he was abandoning her to the diaspora of her longings.

On one of the pages of the notebook, among the listings of the workdays of my aunt Najeebeh's son in my father's cobbler shop, which he opened after the barbershop failed, and among notations of the sums owed him by the villagers, my father had written with his *koubia,* the indelible copying pencil: "My mother died Wednesday, the thirty-first of March, 1954, at ten to six in the evening." Now my brother goes over to the cupboard, opens the damascene box inlaid with mother-of-pearl, takes out the notebook, and in the space my father had left under those lines, writes in ballpoint pen: "And my father died on Monday, the nineteenth of June, 1978, at twenty to ten in the evening. He was seventy years old when he died." Many pages of that notebook are still blank.

CHAPTER **2**

"I see three white horses standing near the oak tree by the monastery, guarding the treasure, and that is the place to dig. But now I see only oil." She was looking with downcast eyes at her brother, who presided over the *mandal.* He begged her to look once more into the slick of olive oil floating on the water in the saucer before her. As she stared at the oil she was suddenly slashed by the feeling that the *mandal* had ebbed away, and that she would never again see the worlds that had been unfolding to her vision and folding again like the silken fan in her mother's hand during Sunday Mass at the church across the street, the Church of St. Thomas in Tyre.

Her mother had been widowed when she was only four months in the womb. After her father's death, her mother had transferred the management of the shop to her eldest brother, Elias, who now presides over the *mandal.* At that time he was only twelve years old and swiftly brought the shop to the brink of bankruptcy. Thereupon her mother set her hand to sewing in order to support the four children. The younger son, Shukrallah, set his heart on becoming a priest, and was sent to the As-Salahiyeh seminary in Jerusalem. The eldest daughter, Rose, became a seamstress too, remained single, and died in middle age of a wasting disease.

She carried a scar on her knee, which would bother her every year at the same season, a memento of something that had happened in her childhood, when she tried to get her little sister, Elaine, the one who was now looking into the *mandal,* to give her some of the walnuts she was clutching in her fist. Elaine screamed, and perhaps because she was so small and defenseless, their mother, who had been bent over her sewing since the early hours of the morning, got angry and threw a pair of scissors at Rose, which penetrated her knee. Every year, at the anniversary of this event, when the pain twitched in her knee, she would remember her sister, who could see all sorts of things in the saucer until the slick of olive oil became blank and its revelations were sealed.

Elaine had seen other things before that day with her brother Elias, but she didn't dare allow them across the threshold of her lips or even the threshold of her heart. She buried them inside herself and guarded them as fiercely as she later would guard the cookie dish behind the locked mirror. Until she was about seventeen, she did not even allow herself to think about them. And when she finally did, she could not grasp their meaning. She would see images alternately rising and sinking into the oil slick that writhed and flickered on the surface of the saucer. She once saw a child dying. The child is her own son and also the son of another woman who is her kin, who comes to find out whether all is well with him. He changes shape and grows within her, a dead child grows within her, a corpse twines inside and passions try to root it out until they concede, placated. Then, twenty years later, she sees . . .

"Breathe deeply, Elaine, and look at the oil slick, look hard and concentrate on the slick," her brother says to her now. She does as he bids her, and tries once again to penetrate the sealed world behind the tiny oil slick. But she sees nothing except the saucer set on the embroidered tablecloth, nothing except the oil slick on the surface of the water, nothing except her obstinate brother, who several months earlier had invited a delegation from the Hareesa monastery overlooking Junia in the north to come to their house in Tyre and observe the wonders of the nine-year-old girl who can see into the *mandal*. The delegation observed the wonders and subsequently published in the journal of the order, which my mother now proudly hands me, a skeptical and detailed article about the little girl who could describe minutely whole shelves of books in the monastery's library. But even then she tells them nothing more. She does not tell them that she also sees an olive-colored bookcase, embedded in a thick wall, or that she sees that dying boy removing the books from it, spreading them on the sofa, and selecting from among them the journal in which the article would appear, thanks to her brother, the angry and disappointed brother who now grabbed the saucer and flung it out the door, where it twirled over the railing at the top of the seven steps leading up to the entrance and landed with a crash and shattered on the white limestone paving. The water trickled through the pores in the stone, but the oil stain on one of the paving stones did not fade and will appear nine years later in one of the pictures in the family album that I so loved to look at when I was a child.

Tyre, Lebanon, 1938: Three pretty girls looking straight at the camera. Behind them a wobbly rail protects whoever comes up the seven steps to the door, which is not in the picture. The girl on the left, Marcelle Farah, the daughter of the official in charge of the port, will marry a Frenchman, who will desert her and return to his native land. The very short young lady on the right, Laurice Rizk, who has draped herself over the shoulder of the one in the middle in order to reduce the difference in height, will marry and be widowed and have no children. The girl in the center, at whose feet lies an inexplicable stain, wears black, and she will eventually be my mother.

But now, in the picture, she is thinking about her white dress and about a pair of white doves with red ribbons tied

19

around their necks in a straw basket decorated with white lace. All of three years old, she clutches the basket in her tiny hand and recites for the Patriarch Maximus IV verses her brother Elias has composed in praise of her. When she is done the Patriarch leans over and kisses her on both cheeks, and she will remember the feel of the bristly beard perfumed with that special scent of high-ranking ecclesiastical personages. Then the personage behind the beard accepts the offering of the two doves, which will be sacrificed upon his dinner table that Sunday afternoon, and in their place fills the basket with sweets. When they get home the mother greets the little girl by burning incense all around her and over her head for fear of the Evil Eye, which years earlier had fallen upon her son Joseph, who was born on Ascension Day and died on the same day one year later. Shukrallah, the son who will be ordained as a priest, will choose the name Joseph, in memory of this brother who went up to Heaven in such good company when he was but one year old. Then into the room walked Mlle Sa'da, a nun of sorts, in secular clothing, who managed the patriarchate's charitable enterprises and lived with Elaine's family. She scolds the mother, who still believes in the magic power of incense even though she is a devout Christian. Mlle Sa'da has no inkling then of her own power to determine the fate of the little girl dressed in white.

Thirteen years later, on Friday, the thirtieth of October, 1936, in my father's barbershop in the village of Fassuta, a man sat down, gave himself up to the pleasure of a shave and, with eyes closed, sank into that state of total weariness which makes the mind preternaturally alert. Just as my father finished lathering the man's face, his bloodshot eyes snapped open and he looked out the western window. His trained gaze was aimed at the place where three white horses stood tethered to the gate of the goatshed on the western outskirts of the village. The man's hands tightened around the English rifle poised between his knees. From that distance, no one would have noticed the horses right away, particularly not my father, who despite the chilling presence of the rifle kept a cool head and concentrated upon sharpening his razor on the taut leather strop. The man dozed off. When the blade touched his sideburn, he woke with a start. From the thin cut near his ear a streak of blood unfurled. Then, stung by the alum stone my father pressed against the wound to stem the flow of blood, his hands again tightly embraced the rifle and his gaze focused upon the three white horses. Nothing was heard in the small space of the barbershop but the scratching of the razor against the beard. The man thought about the pita bread, filled with savory *mjaddara*, that was being brought by my father's nephew, whom he had sent to Grandmother Alia. Then the silhouette of a figure passing by the western window caught my father's hand in the midst of drawing the blade across his client's jowl. Looking out, he managed to see the hem of the dress worn by Elaine Bitar, the new teacher, who had been working in the village for the past two months. She is on her way to the girls' school, in the two rooms south of the church, where I myself will go to class twenty years later. As she walks, she dreams about this barber she will marry, whom she saw for the first time earlier that year in Beirut.

Mlle Sa'da, the nun of sorts, came to Fassuta in the summer of 1933, after the Bitar family she had lived with moved from Tyre to Beirut, and after some profound differences of opinion between her and the Patriarch. She was sent to work in the Galilee diocese, which was headed at the time by Archbishop Hajjar, and she continued to work there even after he passed away in the early forties and was replaced by Archbishop Hakim, a handsome man and a controversial figure.

During Hakim's reign Mlle Sa'da was transferred from Fassuta to take charge of an orphanage for girls in Nazareth, the city where Mother Mary learned that she was to give birth to the son of God. She served in this mission for some ten years, until the mid-fifties, when the police opened an investigation into the death of an infant born in mysterious circumstances to one of the girls in the orphanage. The investigation was abruptly closed when its threads led to delicate places best served by silence. Though the case was closed, the orphanage was closed as well. The girls were sent out into the big world, and Mlle Sa'da was sent to Lebanon. At the beginning of the sixties, when my family moved to Haifa, her name came to be mentioned by one of the neighborhood women who had run away from the orphanage for girls in Nazareth, because she could not stand its harsh discipline and punishments. What inspired her to run away was a bath in extremely hot water prepared by Mlle Sa'da herself.

Mlle Sa'da is also the very same woman who had sent my father in January of 1936 to the house of the Bitar family in Beirut in order to deliver into their hands a ten-year-old girl from the village, who had lost both her parents and whom none of her relatives had offered to adopt. The girl, Laylah Khoury, whose blond beauty had daunted her relatives, spent nine months in the home of the Bitar family. About a week after the day he appeared with the girl, the house was full of lice, and Rose, the sister with the scissors scar on her knee, cut off the girl's lavish blond hair, washed her scalp with kerosene and burned all her clothes. Nine months later, on the orders of Mlle Sa'da, the girl is sent to work as a servant in the house of another family in Beirut, though her family in the village is told that she has gone to study in a respectable boarding school for girls in the land of the cedars.

Toward the end of 1948, just after Fassuta became part of the new state, her sister, who remained in the village and has always yearned to bring Laylah home, locates her in Beirut. But once she gets her back to the village, the Israeli Army soon comes and takes her away to the area of Jenin, and there she is expelled, with tens of others like her, who do not have the right papers, across the border to Jordan. After that all trace of her is lost again for about ten years, until rumors reach the village, via the people who have been permitted to go over to Jordan through the Mandelbaum Gate for Christmas, that Laylah has converted to Islam, has completely changed her name, and has married a refugee in a village near Ramallah.

Now Laylah is remembered by Elaine as she walks on to her little school and runs into the *natoor,* the village watchman and messenger, who greets her hastily. He has two things on his mind: Will the *mukhtar,* the village leader, manage to detain the British officer and his soldiers and convince them to stay for the noonday meal, and if so will he himself be invited to eat in the kitchen? Consumed by anxiety, he hurries on to the barbershop, where my father's razor has by now reached midchin. The *natoor* bursts in and addresses the man in the chair, who is cradled in the strokes of the shave. "*Khawaja* Al-Asbah, the *mukhtar* says to tell you that British soldiers have reached the village and they are looking for you." Al-Asbah leaps up, wipes the soap off half his face and springs like an arrow out the door of the barbershop.

Al-Asbah, a native of Ja'ooneh, was the leader of a small group of rebels, which a year later was to fall into a British ambush near the village of Arrabeh in the lower Galilee. When the corpses were examined, it was clear that most of the rebels had been starving. As he wipes the lather off half his face, he remembers the descent of the British upon his village, how they smashed the jars of olive oil and soaked the blankets in the flowing oil that trickled into the earth, then slaughtered all the chickens and called it a punitive action. He does not wait for the return of the boy who had been sent to bring the pitas full of *mjaddara,* who now meets his little brother as he leaves the school. The two of them, the sons of Aunt Marie, stop to talk with the new French

23

teacher, and when she inquires he tells her that he has been sent to bring food from Grandmother Alia's house for Al-Asbah and his two men. As the boys turn to continue on their way, the three of them hear shots from the direction of the goatshed on the western outskirts of the village and see the three white horses fall. Elaine's heart is lacerated by the razor-sharp image of the three white horses guarding the treasure that her brother had begged her to tell him more about that day the *mandal* was sealed. In the barbershop my stunned father still holds the razor and gazes at the place at which Al-Asbah had gazed as he sat there, given over to the pleasures of getting shaved, and where, if he had continued to sit there, he would have witnessed the three white horses fall.

Al-Asbah and his two companions watched their horses from a hiding place inside the goatshed, and when the British soldiers burst into the shed all they found were bloodstains on the black manure. It was not until some seventeen months later, in March 1938, or so said the rumors which reached the village, that the British soldiers managed to kill Abdallah Al-Asbah near the Lebanese border. My father's nephew, when he sees what's going on, takes the three pitas out of the cloth sack and shares them with the teacher and with his little brother, and the three of them stand there and chew and hear the three last shots, which put an end to the lives of the wounded horses.

For all her gift of divination, Elaine did not know that the eight-year-old boy would one day marry her daughter and that his elder brother would have his leg amputated forty years later. But those shots were to ricochet through her memory as she heard the jubilant volleys in her honor fired by the men of the village when she came as a bride upon a white horse, near the place called Ad-Darajeh, which means "the terrace," near the Lebanese border early in February 1940.

The rains that fell that entire week made Grandmother

worry that they were an evil omen for her son and his bride. A delegation of villagers went out to greet them as they came on foot from the village of Rmeish near the border, along with two camels bearing the mirrored wardrobe and the *jhaz,* which is all the things the bride would need in her years of matrimony. In her school Mlle Sa'da drew the curtains so the girls in the classroom would see neither the groom nor the bride. Elaine Bitar had dared disobey her by marrying Hanna Shammas, whom she had seen for the first time in her life in her family's home when he brought the blond girl Laylah Khoury there, at the request of Mlle Sa'da.

That was at the beginning of 1936. The following September Mlle Sa'da brought Elaine to Fassuta to teach French in her school for girls. During the first school year the young teacher slept in the second-grade classroom where twenty years later, for having written correctly in Arabic on the blackboard "And Mary laid Him in the manger," I was awarded a mechanical pencil in whose shaft was embedded a tiny ship afloat in a mysterious liquid. From the window of this classroom it was possible to see where the Shammas family lived, in the southern quarter of the village. Aunt Jaleeleh, the aunt who did not marry the carpenter, made friends with the new teacher and would also sleep in the classroom. My father on his daily walk to the barbershop, which would soon become a cobbler's shop, used to walk past the window and send longing but, as was his nature, discreet looks at the new teacher, who didn't completely avert her eyes. And these were the days of the Arab Rebellion.

In the summer *vacances* of 1937 Elaine returned to Beirut. Her brother Shukrallah, who in the meanwhile had been ordained as a priest, also came home, for his last visit before he disappeared into the black robes. The whole family went on an excursion through the primeval cedar forests in the mountains of Lebanon. This would be the last time Elaine was to see the cedars, and the last time the future priest was

25

to breathe air of freedom. When Elaine returned to Fassuta in the fall, her brother Elias began seriously to ask himself what is there for a young lady from Beirut in an obscure Galilean village, and what, after all, do the inhabitants of this obscure village in the Galilee make of her colorful *chapeaux* and her velvet frocks rippling in the cold Galilean wind? It never occurred to him that it was the man who had come to their house about two years earlier to bring them the blond girl—his hair slicked back, his sideburns precisely trimmed, wearing a brown suit and an extremely courteous demeanor—who was the reason she had come back and not the love of teaching.

During her second year in the village, Elaine Bitar boarded in the home of Abu Habeeb, Aunt Marie's brother-in-law, who was the trustee of the *waqf,* the local church's lands. That was the year my father decided to abandon the head in favor of the feet and turned the barbershop into a cobbler's shop, but he still kept his oar in on Saturdays and Sundays, receiving his customers in the western room of Aunt Marie's house—which stood opposite Abu Habeeb's house—under the watchful eyes of the young lady from Beirut. And these were the days, as I said, of the Arab Rebellion.

Elias married on the same day King Farouk of Egypt wed Queen Farida, at the beginning of 1938, and subsequently, wonder of dynastic wonders, they both became fathers on the same day. Early in September 1938, when the Arab Rebellion was at its peak, Elias objected to Elaine's third trip to Fassuta but did not forbid it. Unlike the previous times, when she had crossed the border at Nakura without any formalities, she had to go first to Tyre to get a passport. There she was delayed because of the skirmishes between the rebels and the British Army in the area of Al-Bassa, west of the village. As it happened, Elias's objection had less to do with the perils of the journey than with the perils of love.

For in August of that same year, to which the last stamp in his British passport bears witness, my father had come to Beirut to ask for my mother's hand and "to put an end to the rumors," as people say. Elias put him off gently, promising him an answer when things calmed down a bit and the situation in the Galilee became clearer. Elaine returned to Beirut because of the perils of the journey to Fassuta. Once there, she did not go back to teach in the village, and did not see Hanna Shammas until my father came at the beginning of July 1939 to the home of the Bitar family, with his uncle Mikha'eel and two Lebanese friends. This time the delegation asked for Elaine's hand, and when they did not get an immediate answer, my father called upon the family every single day, resolutely, as was also his way. His personal campaign continued for a whole week. Elias who had hesitated to let his little sister go, Elias whose heart had hardened, finally agreed that she should go forth, leaving her father's house and her kin whom she loved and her city, and link her fate with the fate of this stubborn barber-cobbler from the village no one had ever heard of, in the hills of the Galilee.

But the matter did not come to pass all at once, for about a week later Elaine, suffering from pains in her back, was told by a doctor to go to the hot springs of the village of Mayfouq. Finally, on Tuesday, the fifteenth of August, 1939, which is the feast of the Assumption of Our Lady, the betrothal took place in Mayfouq. It was the same day that Shahroor El-Wadi, the Lebanese bard whose fame spread far and wide, performed at the café next to the hot springs. The bride was given as a betrothal gift the damascene wooden box inlaid with mother-of-pearl, the box from which the jewels were destined to vanish and be replaced by barbering instruments that belonged to my father, who was not to see his betrothed again until he came to Beirut on the Feast of the Baptism of Our Lord, on Saturday, January 6, 1940, together with his sister Jaleeleh, to purchase the *jhaz*.

The young Catholic couple were married in a village on the outskirts of Beirut. They had to go there to the Church of St. Estefan, a Maronite church, because the priest of the Catholic church in Beirut refused to perform the ceremony for a young man from Palestine. This was on Tuesday, January 30, 1940. Three days later, on the Feast of Our Lord's Entry into the Temple, they celebrated their first Mass as a married couple. On the same day they returned to Beirut. The rain began to fall and the Al-Kasmiyeh bridge was swept away in a flood and the journey of the couple to Fassuta was delayed.

At dawn of the following Monday, which was the first day of Lent, Grandmother Alia, soaked through to her worried bones, came to the home of Aunt Marie, who lay sick in bed. "What are you in bed for?" Grandmother said to her. "We haven't had a word from Hanna since the Feast of the Baptism of Our Lord, and since then I haven't been able to swallow a crust of bread." On the Feast of the Baptism my grandmother, according to Christian custom, always put a ball of dough in a square of cloth and suspended it from a tree overnight so it would ferment and provide leaven for the whole year. The rain had been falling in drops as big as coffee cups, as Aunt Marie would say, and the village looked like a boat in the middle of the sea. But she arose from her sickbed and went forth with my grandmother to the village of Rmeish to find out what had happened to the bride and groom. They crossed the Lebanese border at the Al-Mansoora gate of the fence that had been erected by the British at the start of the Arab Rebellion four years before and was in tatters by the time the state was founded, only to reappear in the guise of "The Good Fence" many fine years later.

By ten they arrived at the village of Rmeish, at the home of Sa'id El-Ma'tooq, a kinsman of Aunt Marie's husband. The two of them were shocked to find his son Fuad consuming a hearty breakfast despite the holy fast, because he was in a rage about his cow, which had been injured and lay at the gate of the house. Aunt Marie asked Fuad to accompany her on her search for the bridegroom, leaving Grandmother Alia in Rmeish. Under clearing skies, they reached the village of Ein Ebel, which boasted the only telephone in the area, and rang up Dr. Mgheizel in Bent Jbeil to find out if the bus was running from Tyre, which was midway from Beirut. He told them that there was no news from Tyre. Nevertheless Marie decided to follow the paved road to Bent Jbeil. There was an unpaved road, which was three times shorter, but they hoped to encounter the bride and groom on the good road. At the Bent Jbeil crossroads they met the bus from Tyre, and the driver, whom Fuad knew, informed them that the bride and the groom would be arriving the next day. "Come out to meet them at Rmeish."

So they turned around and retraced their steps to Rmeish. When they arrived there it was the hour of Vespers, and my aunt went into the church and prayed and fulfilled the vow she had made to light twelve candles to the Blessed Virgin at the moment she was certain that all was well with the bridegroom and his bride. The following morning, even before Matins, she went off alone to our village, arriving at the Al-Mansoora gate before it was open. When it opened she rushed to tell the villagers to come out to greet the bride and groom, who were to arrive later in the day, along with Grandmother Alia and Aunt Jaleeleh, who had been with the couple all this time. When the groom and the bride got to the terrace called Ad-Darajeh, the bride was lifted onto the back of a white horse, and a joyful fusillade of gunshots echoed in the air, which now was limpid after a week of rainstorms, and those were the shots that reminded the bride of the shots that put an end to the lives of the three white horses at the end of October 1936. She was to remember those shots again two days before the Christmas of 1946, by which time she was the mother of four children.

Elias Mikha'eel, an uncle of Almaza who in her old age climbed the fig tree, had maintained the family tradition. He took leave of his senses in the fullness of his days and would run naked through the streets of the village, or else he would take his mattress out into the street and pelt it with stones, cursing it for all the hours of sleep he had wasted upon it. But the act for which he most often bobs up in the flow of the village's memory is connected to his son Nakhleh, who served in the British Police at Tarbeekha station. Late in 1946 the father collected all the tins that were to be filled with olive oil from the late-autumn pressing. After he cut them open and flattened them down, he explained to the fascinated onlookers that he was going to build an armored vehicle for his son, in which he could ride safe and sound to the police station at Tarbeekha.

His beloved son was murdered in his bed two days before the Christmas of 1946. The following day, during the funeral, somebody stole into our house, somehow opened the mirrored door of the cupboard, lifted the lid of the damascene wooden box inlaid with mother-of-pearl and removed from the little blue velvet boxes all the jewelry my mother had been given as a wedding gift by her mother. My father insisted upon seeking the advice of a fortuneteller from Tarsheeha as to the identity of the thief. In the saucer of oil on his table my mother, who had given up the *mandal,* recognized a woman who was familiar to her, but she would not say who it was. Ten years later she was to see the pearl earrings her mother had given her adorning the ears of a friend of that same woman, who came from the city in which the Holy Virgin heard the news that she heard, but my mother remained silent. Just as she would remain silent four years after the theft, when my father insisted upon naming me after the child who had died in Beirut in 1929. But she would remember the saucer of oil and the dead boy emerging from her. I emerged from her upside down, in a breech birth, and were it not for the practiced hands of the village midwife I would have come as an orphan into this world.

On October 31, 1980, I rode with my brother in his car from Haifa to Fassuta, where we would take the olives to the electric press at the village of Horfeish. I had last visited this press twenty years before, in the company of my cousin Wardeh, the sister of the two boys who with my mother had watched the fall of the three white horses. Because of the new electric press, that was the year of the decline of the old press at Fassuta, the press that had belonged to Abu Shacker, whose white horse would plod round and round by the light of an oil lamp. The horse turned the press beam, the stone that crushed and pounded the olives as they groaned dumbly against the nether stone. An old man would sit there all day long holding a can into which the olive growers would pour their donations of oil. And as he sat there he would pluck at his eyebrows and eyelashes and spit on the floor covered with olive husks and repeat his single unvarying curse against the Arab Rebellion.

The van that was supposed to collect Wardeh and me that afternoon didn't appear until late in the evening, because one of Elias Mikha'eel's granddaughters had broken her leg and had to be rushed in the van, the only vehicle in the village, to Malben Hospital, on the outskirts of Nahariya. As it happened, it was the same hospital that my brother and I stopped at on our way to Fassuta in order to visit Wardeh's brother, whose leg had been amputated because of severe diabetic complications.

As we left the hospital, a middle-aged man approached us and asked if we were by any chance heading north, and if so, could we drive him and his aged father to Tarsheeha. Since my brother doesn't usually like to take hitchhikers, I was surprised when he agreed. The old man sat in the back

31

seat wrapped up in his own soul and didn't utter a word the whole way. The son told us that he and his father had crossed over Allenby Bridge into the West Bank to visit his brother in the village of Silwad, which is near Ramallah. There they heard that one of their relatives from Tarsheeha was in the hospital at Nahariya. Now they had decided to continue northward to see the rest of their relatives who had been driven out of Ja'ooneh in 1948 and come to Tarsheeha as refugees. On the outskirts of Tarsheeha, when the old man heard that we were on our way to Fassuta, he shook off his silence and asked, "Whose sons are you, may Allah preserve you?" "We are the sons of Hanna Shammas," my brother replied. He stopped at the square in the center of the village. The son leaned through the window on my side in order to thank my brother, and the old man moved his son's shoulder aside a bit and leaned his head in through the window. He looked at me and said: "Tell your father that Abdallah Al-Asbah sends his greetings, and that he still owes me half a shave." My brother, who didn't hear the words of the father in the midst of the son's profuse thanks, began slowly to pull away. I stuck my head out the window and said to the old man that my father had passed away about two years ago and that rumor had it that he, too, had passed away. The old man, astounded, stopped in his tracks for a moment and then, with a dismissive flap of his hand, turned and continued on his way.

About a month later a report appeared in one of the daily papers about the curfew the Israel Defense Forces had imposed on the village of Silwad, north of Ramallah, in the wake of the third politically motivated murder that had taken place there. Among the reported reactions of the various villagers, the testimony of one woman stood out, the testimony of Surayyah Sa'id, the mother of thirty-year-old deaf-mute twin sons. She told the reporter that ten soldiers had come to her house and ordered everyone to raise their arms above their heads. When she began to explain that the twins were deaf and couldn't hear the orders, they yelled at her to raise her hands above her head and face the wall and shut up. Then the soldiers spilled the contents of two jars of olive oil on the floor. "I told them it was a shame, and they answered me, 'Shut up. Raise your hands above your head.'" She also told the reporter—who was curious about her blond hair—that she was a Christian who had converted to Islam and married the son of one of the heroes of the Arab Rebellion, whose name was Abdallah Al-Asbah.

And the twins stood on the side and, like a pair of mute turtledoves, watched the olive oil seep into the earth.

CHAPTER 3

Many weeks elapsed before I found the courage and took the step to break the silence I had imposed upon myself after reading about the woman with the blond hair. And so one day I found myself, the way you sometimes find yourself in dreams, on the outskirts of the village of Beitin, on the way to Silwad in the district of Ramallah. But here, too, I procrastinated, gnawed by doubts, putting reluctant heel to irresolute toe, afraid that I might stir up from the distant past the dust of memories that during the long years of her exile had been tamped firmly down into the depths of oblivion, afraid that I might with a single sharp, inquisitive stroke cut into the impacted present and release the bitterness of all those years. Even more than I was concerned about Surayyah Sa'id for the trespass I was about to commit against her, I was concerned about maintaining my own ignorance, for if the chapter about Laylah Khoury was a closed one in my family's story, why should I let myself open the diaspora of a past already sealed by forgetfulness? And this compunction was nothing but the tip of the dim, primal knowledge that had taken root in my consciousness and sprouted from the first moment I had heard about the blond girl, until it had entirely taken hold of me. In my heart I was certain that this Laylah Khoury, should our paths be

34

destined to cross eventually, would take her image as sketched by the family and blur it beyond recognition. Indeed, something of this anguished soul—who as a girl of ten was condemned to wander from her home to the land of the cedars and when she wished to return to the scene of her childhood was flung, instead, by fate's capricious hand to scenes which would in due time be exposed (since history loves repetitions), to that outstretched arm which yet again would deflect the course of her life, in 1948, to eternal exile within her own homeland—something of this anguished soul had seeped into my consciousness all these years and had formed relics of doubt, forbidden to the touch.

I also had another uncertainty. What guarantee was there, after all, that this Surayyah Sa'id with blond hair from the village of Silwad, mother of the deaf-mute twins, was indeed the same Laylah Khoury my father had brought at the beginning of 1936 to the home of the Bitar family in Beirut. By my calculations, if she turned out to be the same person, she would be about fifty-five years old. And what would happen if this woman, when she opens her door to me and to my friend the journalist, who has accompanied me on this visit for his own reasons, and introduces herself as Surayyah Sa'id, what if she should defy me, saying that only their similar plights as refugees could have prompted me to suspect the two women of being one and the same? What if I see that this woman, the contents of whose two jars of olive oil Israeli soldiers had poured in the dust, is too old or too young to be Laylah Khoury?

I suffered from still another uncertainty. What, exactly, was I looking for? Yes, there was something in the news story, something in what Surayyah Sa'id was reported to have said, that reminded me of the dialect of Fassuta, which had stuck to this Laylah-Surayyah like a birthmark. But this whole impression was based on just a few reluctant and evasive words, translated into Hebrew, and on a whisper in my mind, which hasn't really enough to go on, yet reiterates over and over again that this Surayyah Sa'id holds the key to certain enigmas in my family's past.

And there was the uncertainty that tantalized me, which had first hatched on that day late in October 1980, during my brief encounter with Abdallah Al-Asbah, who was presumably Surayyah Sa'id's father-in-law. This was the uncertainty which is an advantage that the dead have over the living—the dead who rise to buffet you when you are indifferent to the twists and turns of the present but are made to realize you are still vulnerable to the caprices of the past. I had imagined that this Al-Asbah had made it possible for me to conclude his story the way it had ended in the previous chapter, and with this his role in the tapestry of the story had ended too. But here I am traveling along the road to Silwad holding on to the end of the thread he had spun and interwoven with the warp and woof of my life. Like a weaver I yank at that thread and find myself wondering about the opportunity that has presented itself to me as a result of the new turn of events, and before I have sufficiently considered my next steps, I comb out the unraveled thread and card it again, then turn to impart to it a completely different color and to weave it once more into the frayed tapestry, mending what had unraveled. What guarantee do I have that this act is not a proclamation of liberty on the part of that thread, once it had been unbound? All at once a story that had apparently come to its end is exposed to a capricious thread, which will draw it into unexpected regions in an adventure whose outcome we cannot foresee.

All these thoughts rise to the surface of my mind on the outskirts of the village of Beitin, near the military checkpoint, to the accompaniment of the stonecutters' saws and the beat of the masons' mallets. They swathe the scene in a mysterious veil of primal rhythm as they rise from either side of the road, pitching a canopy of sorts over its length, and the line of cars creeping toward the checkpoint goes under the canopy and blends into the pacing of the sentries and the rhythm dictated by the blows of the stonemasons' mallets. My friend muses aloud about the eternity of the local stone as compared to the transience of regimes. But when he realizes that the voices are flowing above our heads, he, too, blends into the chorus, and he begins to tap his fingers on the steering wheel to the stonecutters' beat.

For forty years Abu Mas'ood's fingers had tapped against the rock in the quarry of red stone on the piece of land called An-Naqqarah. The faint cries of warning, *"Wardah! Wardah!"* sometimes reached as far as our house, and I would fall flat on my face and put my ear to the cold concrete floor, waiting for the sound of the explosion, the preparations for which had been supervised by Abu Mas'ood and his sons for several days. When the explosion came, the windows shook, as did the glazing in the kerosene lantern suspended from the iron bar hanging down from the keystone of the arch that supported the ceiling of our house. On more than one occasion the explosion toppled the pots and pans that my uncle Yusef's wife used to lean against the wall to dry. She would begin her wailing, which was swiftly followed by curses upon the head and upon the name of Abu Mas'ood, for if he kept up his explosions the day would soon come when our houses would tumble down on our heads, and look, there are new cracks sprouting in the walls every time that man gives voice to his warning cry, *"Wardah! Wardah!"* even before the explosion itself shakes the foundations of the house and its voice is heard clearly through the muffling of the earth.

The most imaginative curses of all were heaped upon Abu Mas'ood the time he dared to suggest to my uncle the crazy idea of putting an end, once and for all, to the halo around the mysterious boulder in the center of the *duwara*, the rock upon which I had been standing when I heard for the first time the reason I was given my name, the rock that once every few years—on nights when the moon is full, according to my cousin, who has seen it herself—glows and dazzles the eyes of all who look upon it. Abu Mas'ood said, tongue in cheek, that he had the means of blowing up that very rock in such a way that its fragments would fly no farther than two or three meters, four at most. And if the rooster Ar-Rasad indeed stands guard over the hidden entrance to the cave which lies under the boulder, why now was the time to get him out of his hiding place to recognize that Abu Mas'ood is intimately acquainted with the soul of stones. Then Allah alone, may His name be praised, would determine the winner in the contest between the guardian rooster, who is the handiwork of the dark forces, and the great Abu Mas'ood himself, who had recently donated to the village church, the Church of Elijah the Prophet, savior of the oppressed and defender of the weak, the altar that had been quarried from the red cliffs of An-Naqqarah. Its four pillars, like the four Evangelists, surround a rectangular stone as high as a man's waist, adorned with a cross made of the black rocks of the village of Bkei'ah. The five stones support Abu Mas'ood's pride and joy, a slab of polished stone which is the altar table. Like a giant paperweight, it prevented the other stones from levitating heavenward upon the voices lifted in prayer and upon the puffs of incense all around them.

In time the red rock he hewed near our village dwindled, and Abu Mas'ood had to journey to neighboring Bkei'ah, where the black stones flower. There he was granted the opportunity to make a name for himself by creating what he called the "foundation stone" of his life among the stones, that is, the black tombstone of the prophet of the modern Jewish State. Benjamin Ze'ev Herzl's vision was realized, but it was an Arab, *davka*, who created the giant black slab that was set as a memorial on his grave. The experts who were sent by the Technion to advise Abu Mas'ood of the most likely place to find a suitable slab quickly found themselves embroiled in a heated argument with this stubborn old stoneface. They told him that the rock he needed lay ten meters underground right here, while he in his utter confidence shouted that, no, the stone upon which the Zionists will build would be found over there, only three meters below the surface. Threatening to take the job from him, they went away again. A few days later a mediator who was sent to the quarry found to his great astonishment that the stubborn Abu Mas'ood had been correct in his prediction and had already begun to hew out the rock. There are two great black stones in the world, the late Abu Mas'ood used to say, the black stone in the Ka'bah in Macca, which was quarried by almighty Allah himself, and the black stone on Herzl's tomb, which was quarried by the mortal Abu Mas'ood himself, and both of them are sites of pilgrimage. Allah, however, does not have an official document from the Technion to prove that he quarried His stone.

"Documents, please!" said the soldier leaning in the window to my friend the journalist.

"And what about him?" asked my friend.

"He looks like one of us," said the soldier. "What is your business here?"

"I'm after a story, and my friend here is looking for a relative of his."

"In which settlement?" asked the soldier.

"In Ofra, of course!" answered my friend with an innocent smile, his incriminating mustache stretched between his two dimples.

A boy leaning over a balcony in the central square of Silwad pricked up his ears at the approach of our car and eagerly asked, "Who are you looking for?"

"The home of the family of *Sitt* Surayyah Sa'id," said my friend.

"Ah! *Sitt* Surayyah Sa'id." The boy grinned at him, with mocking stress on the courteous title *Sitt.* "What for?"

When my friend didn't deign to answer, the boy said: "Maybe you have something bad up your sleeve."

"No," answered my friend. "God forbid! We only have good things up our sleeves. I've brought her a relative."

The boy vanished from the balcony, and before we realized what he was up to, he reappeared at the entrance of the building and leapt into the car without a word, as if the exchange with us had been intended only to delay the inevitable pleasure of the ride in the car and the job of guiding these two helpless grownups, and only Allah in His great mercy knows what on earth they really want.

"Did you hear what the soldiers did at Surayyah Sa'id's place a couple of months ago?" asked the boy, without waiting for an answer. "Not only at her place either. Ten soldiers took all the men out of the houses after midnight and collected them in the schoolyard, and left them there all night until morning. In the morning they went into houses and stole money and poured the flour and the rice and the sugar on the floor, and then poured kerosene all over everything. They also hit a lot of people."

The car slowly made its way through the narrow alleys, whose walls seemed to be closing in on it. At the corner before Surayyah Sa'id's house the boy jumped down and began to direct my friend so that he wouldn't scratch the sides of his car on the rough stones. And when we had negotiated the corner unscathed, something within me whispered that here was the last outpost of indecision, and from here on there was no turning back, for better or for worse.

"After we drop him off at Surayyah Sa'id's house," said my friend to the boy, meaning me, "you take me around to all the houses the soldiers came to so we can hear what happened there."

"That'll take hours and hours and hours," said the boy. "But it just so happens that I don't have anything else special to do today, and here is *Sitt* Surayyah's house!"

A woman in her fifties stood there. She was dressed in black; her disheveled hair, the color of ashes, fluttered in the light wind of early April, which also fluttered the smoke rising from the oven improvised from an oil drum in front of the house. The woman was snapping twigs in her hands and throwing them into the oven.

Boolus the Redhead, the son of my Aunt Najeebeh, was the biggest boy in our gang. One Sunday after Mass he promised to show us something our eyes had never seen, even in our dreams. He told us to go to An-Naqqarah, to Abu Mas'ood's quarry. No one would be at the quarry that day since Sunday was Abu Mas'ood's day of rest, so we four boys figured that it had to do with an enormous explosion that Boolus the wild prankster was going to set off in the quarry.

A week before, he had found in the blackberry patch on some land belonging to Uncle Nimr, my grandmother Alia's brother, a pistol and a rusty tin box full of bullets. Since he couldn't manage to penetrate the mystery of how to load the bullets into the chamber of the pistol, he wanted to find out more about the nature of bullets. The following day, after his mother—that is, my aunt Najeebeh—had finished baking her bread on the tin dome of the oven, Boolus as an experiment laid just one bullet from the tin box among the glowing embers. Stunned by the big bang, his mother then rushed out of the house and found Boolus standing there, all white from head to toe, petrified like a pillar of ashes, before the oven, whose tin dome gaped open as if it had been struck by the blade of a plow. For two days Boolus hid out in our house, for fear of the punishment that would be visited upon him by his mother, who was less upset by what might have happened to her son than she was by the hole that gaped irreparably in the tin dome, which had been acquired only a few days before in Akka.

I, who was the youngest of the group, was also the most curious about Boolus's intentions. I had been warned more than once not to get mixed up in his crazy stunts, and as if to tantalize me he said that maybe I shouldn't accompany them on this adventure, and instead should wait for the gang in our grove of figs at Al-Jahaleef, on the way to An-Naqqarah. But when he saw the wet gleam in my eyes he ruffled my hair and said he was only joking, though he doubted I would understand what was going on. There was also a price we solemnly vowed to pay Boolus. After we had seen whatever it was he was going to show us at An-Naqqarah, we had to prepare *areesheh* for him in our fig grove. *Areesheh* is made from ripe figs, which are spread apart and broiled on a slab of stone heated white by burning twigs under it, until the dripping seeds blacken and the skin of the fruit turns a golden brown. After Boolus had eaten his fill, we would be able to have a taste too.

We set out for Abu Mas'ood's quarry. When we got close, Boolus told us to take cover behind a boulder and wait for his orders. Silence hovered over the quarry with its red stone gleaming in the merciless sunlight, and here and there we could see holes chiseled into the rock, which would be filled with gunpowder. Beyond the red stones we could see the shack of the watchman, whose job it was to guard the heavy machinery and the steel cables and the explosives.

The door opened and the watchman stepped out and looked at the sun, and closed the door behind him. "Mass was over ages ago," said Boolus, imitating the watchman's voice, "So why are you late, woman?" Several minutes later he jerked us to attention with a prolonged *Shhhhh,* even though the whole time we hadn't made a sound. Then he hissed confidently: "Here she comes." It was the watchman's wife, carrying a basket with, apparently, her husband's dinner in it. Having listened to Boolus and followed him here, we now did as he told us but were disappointed at finding ourselves tiptoeing after him toward the shack. We reluctantly put our eyes to the holes in the hot tin walls. As our eyes were adjusting to the dimness inside the shack, we heard the teasing laughter of the watchman's wife: Wouldn't he like to eat something first? However, the basket was not the thing his heart was set on, and with no further talk he lightly pushed his wife toward the bed in the corner of the shack. Before we realized what his intentions were, his trousers slithered down and her dress curled up and his naked scrawny behind seemed to sink into a pillow of flesh. Then he begins to push this way and that, faster and faster. Her hands grab the two glistening buttocks, and guide their movements and lead their tempo. For a moment we stop breathing, and the silence is cut only by a single sound, which is repeated with each stroke, the sound your tongue makes when you undulate it inside your wet mouth. The tempo increases and with it the squeaking of the bed, and at the woman's first cry Boolus yells *"Wardah! Wardah!"* We linger just long enough to see the watchman spring up from between his wife's open legs and look about with alarm in all directions. Then he grasps at his groin, and between the fingers clutching his quivering member spurt rhythmic bursts of a thick and shiny liquid. The whole gang rushes off pell-mell, skipping over the rocks and stones toward the path up to Al-Jahaleef, pursued by the threatening cries of the watchman. In the shade of one of the fig trees Boolus flings himself down, huffing and puffing and smiling rapturously. Then he immediately sets us to work preparing the *areesheh.*

We arrange three slabs of slate in a sort of open square that we fill with dry twigs, and over this we lay another slab of smooth slate, from which all traces of earth have been rubbed, and then we gather the ripe figs and set fire to the twigs and wait. When the slate table is scorching hot, we spread each fig apart and we arrange them on the slate. From the lips of the figs comes the sound of the fire sizzling. The fig seeds dripping sweetness and ripeness on the broiling slate make almost the same sound of the suction of flesh upon flesh in the watchman's shack.

On another slab of slate, which has also been prepared in advance, the browned figs pile up, and the juices collect and trickle into the earth. Boolus says that we have done well. But at the very moment he is about to reach out his hand and select a fig, his eyes widen with alarm and he tells us to scram because the watchman is coming. In the confusion I seek refuge among the branches of the fig tree that forms a kind of canopy over the altar of the *areesheh.* The watchman sees where we are, but he stops chasing the other boys, who are running away. Attracted by the fragrance of the *areesheh,* he walks toward the smoke spiraling up from the twigs. When he reaches the slabs of the slate with the figs dripping their golden juices, he stops and turns in all directions and yells after the spoilers of his delight: "I know who you are; you'll be hearing from me." Then with the tip of his shoe he overturns the slate upon which the broiled figs are heaped, nudges them into the burning twigs, and before he leaves he whips out his member and with a kind of sweet vengeance he urinates, deliberately, on the smoldering ruins. The smoke spirals upward with a hiss of astonishment and flutters in the wind. Just as the wind flutters the smoke spiraling up from her oven as Surayyah Sa'id stands there in front of me breaking twigs.

I used to accompany my uncle Yusef's wife when she went to the flour mill. Although she would complain about how many women were waiting their turn ahead of her, I would rejoice in my good fortune in having time to spend in the room where the motor was, under the vigilant eyes of my uncle's wife, lest I get too close to the giant wheel that the motor turned by means of an awe-inspiring black strap.

After a few minutes of gaping at the mighty machines, I would give myself over entirely to the steady thump of the motor, which shook the floor like a rhythmic giant. And as I stood there, I knew that each beat of the motor created a puff of black smoke from the gullet of the chimney pipe outside the motor room. Boolus, whose house was near the mill, liked to amuse himself by putting black ants on the hot metal base of the chimney, which was attached with four screws to a concrete base in the ground, and when he got bored with that he would urinate on the base and observe with rapture the instant evaporation.

One time I tried to partake of this pleasure. In an interval when my uncle's wife wasn't watching me, I slipped away from the motor room and went around to the other side of the building. At a safe distance from the heat pouring out from the rusty pipe, I lifted my eyes and stood there enchanted by the sight of the puffs of smoke issuing from the lofty gullet and by the rhythmic thump of the motor. Its sound was somewhat muffled now by the thick walls, but each thump shook the ground under my foot. Hesitantly I, too, urinated on the metal base, and enraptured by the evaporation, I was tempted to touch the pipe to see how hot it really was. My uncle's wife rushed me off to Aunt Najeebeh's house, and there I sat scolded and tearful, my seared hand dunked in cold salt water.

About two hours later, when I heard the car's horn honking, I left Surayyah Sa'id sitting on her bed, against the backdrop of the square of light that was the western window. Opposite her, in a corner of the dimly lit kitchen, her twin sons were still watching her, deaf and mute witnesses of the story that had unwound in the space of that room. Something in their tortured expression gave me the feeling that it would have been better if the story had remained curled up like a caterpillar in the cocoon of silence forever. But now that the cocoon had hatched and the butterfly of the story, with a magical flick of its wings, had shaken off the webs of years of forgetfulness, the way backward was closed both for me and for the butterfly.

Uncle Yusef used to say, It is better for a story not to be told, for once it is, it is like a gate that has been left ajar.

CHAPTER 4

The cupboard where we kept our mattresses and blankets, the *smandra,* which was the color of green olives, stood hugging the western wall of our house. It concealed the door behind which, in the thick wall, was an archway that led outside. Set in the threshold of that archway was the mouth of the cistern. A grayish metal lid with a ring in its center covered the mouth, and this protected the cool water in the darkness of the cistern from the whims of children and cats and from the falling leaves, which during the days of summer had made the circles of light that seeped through their profuse foliage dance on the sides of the archway.

At the end of fall, with the first rains, came the sound of the water that coursed from the loam roof of our house into the drainpipe leading into the shaft of the cistern and spattered on its clean floor some twenty feet below. After supper my mother would spread the straw mats on the floor and take the mattresses out of the cupboard and arrange them side by side for the night's sleep. When my ear lay close upon the pillow, I could hear the spattering of the water, swathed in echoes, falling down the shaft to the bottom of the cistern. The spatters grew fainter and fainter and shed their echoes as the water level rose in the cistern, until nothing was heard but moans of repletion, rising and surfacing from the throat of the cistern, for the water pouring down threatened to make the swelling cistern overflow. That was the time when the drainpipe was turned away from the shaft to spill its torrent down the winding path to our fig grove at Al-Jahaleef.

This was also the time of year when Uncle Yusef's cat would go into heat and retreat to her hiding place above the lintel of the door leading to the archway behind the *smandra*. Whenever she went into heat, her fur took upon itself in the most wonderful and mysterious way the blue-green tint of turquoise, which seemed to reel in all the tomcats of the neighborhood, whose wailing came through the locked door of the archway. My father spent many hours wheedling the cat to abandon her perch and go forth to meet her suitors in less acrobatic settings, for fear that one of those love-stricken swains, so besotted with lust for the invisible, his nostrils full of the rutting scent that penetrated through the planks of the door, would manage to get the cover off the mouth of the cistern and plunge to its depths. Uncle Yusef, however, was wrathful at the band of suitors, whose serenade reverberated in its clamorous wails through his sleep. More than once he managed to get his hands on one of the band, grab his tail and swing him around and around his head, and then release him like a stone from a slingshot into the prickly pear that grew in the neighbor's yard. And even though the cat would leap from the other side of the prickly pear unharmed, the mighty arm would suffice to convince the band of his companions to keep away from our house until the next day.

At summer's end, when the voices of the water exploding had ebbed entirely from my pillow, and when the bucket that was let down into the cistern too soon in the year touched only the muddy water at the bottom, the house would resound with accusations that whoever it was had turned away the drainpipe too soon. This was also the time talk would begin about the need to clean the bottom of the cistern of the silt and the remnants of the leaves that had sunk into the concavity at the center of its rounded and sloping floor, in order to get it ready for the rainy season, though no one knew on which day the first rain would choose to fall.

I was ten years old when one night as we sat around the dinner table it was said that the time had come for me to perform this task no one else was eager to perform, because of the dubious pleasures of spending his time at the bottom of a deep cistern covered with a slippery layer of dark silt. But with the eager heedlessness of childhood, I immediately volunteered to take on the task early the following morning. I had a troubled sleep that night, anticipating the adventure awaiting me. In my dream I am lowered down into the dimness, pulled up and drawn back into the light, lowered and pulled up, in and out, back and forth, between the anxiety and the pleasure of discovery that lurked at the bottom of the pit.

Since the archway was in the western wall, we had to wait for the sun to slant westward and illuminate in the end-of-summer light the opening of the cistern and a few tiers of stone in the slope of its throat. When the shadow over the cistern has gone, a rope is tied around my waist, and my oldest brother ruffles my hair affectionately before sending me down. I take off my shoes, and standing with my legs spread across the mouth of the cistern, I attempt to adopt a heroic pose for the benefit of Nawal, the neighbors' daughter, who is watching me on the sly and trying to hide her admiration.

I gingerly let down my foot to touch the mossy stone in the highest tier. The coldness of the stone and its greenish slickness set off a shudder in my body I have never experienced before. I hold on to my brother and slide the lower portion of my body down, trying not to hide my queasy reaction to the contact of the slippery stone against my bare legs in shorts. My brother tightens his grip on the rope tied around my waist and braces his foot against a stone at the mouth of the cistern and tells me to release my hold on the metal frame of the cover. My eyes closed, I grasp the rope and let go the tips of my toes from the stones. With some last words of warning and encouragement, and promising that he will not sell me to the Ishmaelites, my brother pays out the rope bit by bit. Temporarily reassured by his steadiness and competence, I shut my ears to the sound of the rope scraping on the frame at the opening of the shaft, and shut my eyes to the sight of the walls of the cistern going round and round, as I twist on the rope, which is taut and released by turns. I breathe in the chill of the mildew and the ancient odor of the stones and the dark scent of the silt rising from the bottom of the cistern, suffusing the space around me with the feeling of porous ground waiting to touch the soles of my feet as I am dropped farther and farther down. The scraping sounds ebb away and I seem to be getting closer to its echo, which rises from beneath me and wraps me in a sort of dim solace. I open my eyes and look up at the square of light receding above me, to which I am still tied by this rope, and then look down at the bottom coming closer to me. I try not to think of the approaching meeting between the soles of my bare feet and the crust over the silt and murky water lying in the pool at the center of the rounded and sloping floor. My eyes have become accustomed to the dimness, and I see my own reflection in reverse rising toward me from within the dark mirror of the pool. Then with a shake of the rope my feet sink into the mirror, which shatters into a myriad of fragments glimmering in the darkness and then begins to build anew the reflection of the square of light that is above my head. My legs sink up to the shaking knees in the mixture of mud, straw and foul water that lies beneath the purity of the water drawn from the cistern during the year that has passed. Now the light dims in the square and I see the silhouette of my brother's head looking down from above me and asking whether I have arrived safely and can I untie the rope. I do so, and without taking the time to tell him, I hasten to wade out of the pool to a surface that looks drier and more solid to me. As the rope is drawn upward I try to maintain my footing in the slippery silt while my feet sink deeper into it. After several attempts I manage to do so. Then I begin to be aware of the enchanted presence surrounding me, and the bliss of solitude permeates my anxiety. But all of a sudden I hear a scream. Nawal is trying to frighten me. Her scream explodes into a host of echoes, and from somewhere within my throat comes a kind of wail, which I hasten to stifle with my hand, stained by the hardening silt.

By the time the rope has wriggled down again from within the square of light above, bringing me the bucket with the scoop inside it, my eyes have become further accustomed to the darkness and my body to the queasy touch of mud. I begin to fill the bucket with the black water which exposed with every draw the nice floor of the cistern. The experience becomes more ordinary as the pool dwindles and I begin to scrape with the scoop on the lower parts of the sloping sides. I soon discover that I cannot reach the whole of its circumference from where I stand, and my feet are no longer able to hold their grasp on the concrete floor that is becoming more exposed with every scrape. I tell my brother of this and ask that he let me come up now. But he yells down to me from within the square of light that he is going to send Nawal down to help me. I am hurt to the quick, not just because of the disgrace if I fail to complete the task I alone had been given. And not just because of my frustration when Nawal would be sure to boast to anyone willing to listen that she had cleaned out our cistern, for Nawal, who was a year older than I, was always tagging after boys and refused to play with girls; she was such a tomboy that she would even urinate standing up. But it wasn't these chagrins that so hurt me but rather the feeling that this whole en-

51

chanted world, which I alone inhabited, a world in which I imagined no one but myself had trod, would come to an end once I, against my will, had to share it with someone else.

Twenty years later, Surayyah Sa'id, in the village of Silwad, is about to do something similar to what my brother did. She stands there by the oven, breaking twigs, and the muscle twitching in the corner of her mouth tells me without her saying anything that she is the Laylah Khoury of the past. For her mouth trembled at the sight of my face, which reminded her of the features of a familiar face from the distant past. In the family relay race I had been handed the exact copy of the face that belonged to Uncle Elias, my mother's brother. For nine months in 1936 it was his countenance that shone upon the ten-year-old orphan in the Bitar household in Beirut, and she had retained it within herself as a sort of death mask of the only father figure who had come her way during the years of her first exile. She looks at the live copy standing before her now and does not know yet how those features are related to the face that rises to the surface of her consciousness from the depths of her memories. A black goat, which wandered up and gently butted the legs of this woman dressed in an embroidered Bedouin dress, and a bony hand that pushed back a lock of hair the color of dust from her wrinkled forehead provided the final touches to the scene.

I introduced myself by referring to both sides of my family. She immediately led me up the path to her house. I said that I would leave for a while and come back when she had finished her baking. She said that she was waiting for the dough to rise and it was only out of boredom that she had lit the twigs. There was a vine arbor over the entryway, and despite the poverty that was tangible in the atmosphere, one quick look was enough to show that everything was very clean. The front door opened into a large sitting room furnished with beds covered with flowered cloth. An old faded wardrobe hugged the wall on the left, and opposite it was a closed door, which apparently led to another room. She asked me to sit on the only chair. As my eyes adjusted to the dimness of the room, I noticed through the doorway to the kitchen the grown twins sitting at a battered table, where they were eating the lentil dish called *mjaddara.* On the other side of the table were piled layers of unbaked pita, with a cloth folded between the layers. Surayyah Sa'id sat down on the edge of the bed by the western window. Again I apologized for coming and interrupting her work, and again she reassured me, in the more friendly voice Arab women use when they are inside their own homes.

"What is it you want me to tell you?"

And despite all the years that had passed, the dialect of Fassuta peeped through the words like a hidden birthmark.

I told her about how I had come across the traces of her, about the stories concerning her my mother had told from time to time, about the report in the newspaper, and about the encounter with Abdallah Al-Asbah in the central square of Tarsheeha. "May Allah bless his memory," she said. "Where the British failed, the Jews succeeded. He was killed in an air raid." And I sensed that one thread in the warp and the woof of the web between us had broken. Instead of consoling her, I found myself asking, "How is it that your family name is Sa'id and your father-in-law's name was Al-Asbah?"

"Al-Asbah is only a nickname, and the family name is Sa'id. And while we're on the subject of names, you told me whose son you are, but you haven't told me what your name is."

I told her my name.

Against the backdrop of the window I saw the *djinni* burst out of her sealed face and hover in the space of that room. All of a sudden I was like someone who finds himself cut off from the sounds and sights and smells that surround him and floating inside a private bubble, until from the kitchen came the sound of a spoon tapping against a plate, and the bubble burst.

"What's the matter, *Sitt* Surayyah?"

"I didn't know that there was anyone else with that name."

"Yes, I was named after another Anton Shammas, the son of my uncle Jiryes and his wife, Almaza. He died in 1929. But how do you know about all this? If my calculations are correct, you must have been only three years old then."

"I'm not sure you're going to want to hear this story. If a madman throws a stone into the cistern, only a thousand wise men will manage to pull it out, as the saying goes. And you don't look crazy to me."

From a tale that was apparently drawing to an end, a new unruly thread shoots out and turns the tale in a startling direction.

Before I could begin to accept my brother's insult and my hopeless opposition to the sentence that he imposed upon me while I was in the depths of the cistern, Nawal's body rippling down crumpled the serenity of the square of light, and every time a bit more rope was released, my shadowy kingdom dwindled. But the sound of Nawal's nervous and thrilled laughter, and the sight of her legs, whose brightness winked out beneath her shorts, and of her hair, which shimmered as it fanned out with each twist of the rope against the light—these tempered the insult a bit. I even began to feel a certain contentment and security, for after all, it was I who gave the orders in my own kingdom. And it was at the moment the bare soles of Nawal's feet tentatively touched bottom that I first noticed the two small cones that quivered against her blouse. And it was just then that she lost her balance, with the rope still tied around her waist. She clasped my arm, and her smooth hair slapped against my face. Then a fragrance, different from all the odors that had enfolded me, spread through the cistern and completely eradicated my opposition to her invasion.

As soon as her eyes adjusted to the dim light in the cistern, she grabbed the scoop from my hands and threw herself up the slope, trying to get as far away from me as possible. But after she had made a couple of futile attempts to balance herself, I found myself supporting her back with hesitant hands, and she, encouraged by the support, made slow progress up the slope and began to bend her knees to steady herself. My hands shift downward as she lowers herself, and by itself a mutual position comes to pass in which it is convenient for her to control the movement of the scoop and convenient for me to concentrate upon the touch of my hands on her waist, and with every few scrapes I hold her farther down in order to provide more traction. Finally I find my two palms cupping her two buttocks, and she turns her head toward me and smiles. I feel the movement of the scraping hand transmitting itself into the muscles of her body, and the vibrating of her flesh passes into the palms of my hands and transmits itself through my own body and jolts against the place where my outstretched leg is trying to improve its hold. Very slowly the cistern melts away all around me, as does the sound of the scraping, while my clasping palms fill with quiverings and her body, which has stopped swooping, maintains its twisting movement and the quiverings break in the soles of my feet and turn around again and race through my body and explode in the palms of my hands, which have now locked into the converging buttocks which flinch with a shudder along the back that has arched itself into a taut bow.

And then everything melted away again into the echoing voice of my brother asking why we were taking so long. Once the floor was exposed all around, my brother dangled the rope down. I tie the rope around Nawal's waist with a concentration that helps me to evade her look. Before I know it her face bends swiftly toward me and her lips flutter against the corner of my mouth. And still not knowing what it all means, I watch her rise, and her foot draws a muddy gray line up the length of my thigh.

Two years later we moved from the village to Haifa, and in all that time Nawal never exchanged a single word with me.

"But," says Surayyah Sa'id, "it looks like I'm the one who is crazy."

The secret she had guarded, like the knife Uncle Yusef used to bind the mouth of the wild beast with, had weakened during the course of the years, the years which had taught her that the ways human beings travel twist and turn, and only Allah in His infinite mercy will requite them for their deeds. She is not even sure anymore that the man upon whom she had wished to take revenge in 1948 is the right one, because it is possible that any other villager might have done it. She recalls the events of those two days in 1948, which found her in the home of the Abyad family in Al-Ma'rad Street in Beirut. She learned that her sister was looking for her, to bring her back to Fassuta, on the same night that the parents of Michel Abyad, who was twenty years old at the time, announced to their son that he must go to America the very next day. She felt that the last chain connecting her to her exile was broken, for in her final conversation with Adèle, the laundress in the Abyad household, the latter revealed to her the gossip that was circulating among the servants' quarters of the houses on Al-Ma'rad Street. The secret had lifted its head from where it had lain coiled under twenty years of vigilant safekeeping and threatened to strike at the Abyad family, which was why they were rushing to send their only son overseas.

As soon as she returned with her sister to the village, she asked to talk to someone from the Shammas family or from Almaza's family, because she had something to reveal. Instead, two soldiers from the Jewish Army came to expel this refugee who thought she could deceive the authorities and prove that she was a citizen of the new state. Before she had time to reveal the secret even to her sister, she found herself in a truck full of people from the surrounding villages who had not succeeded in outwitting their fate as wanderers. Among them was an imposing young man, who the women whispered was the son of Abdallah Al-Asbah from the days of the rebellion. He told them about the collaborators in the villages of the north, who had led the soldiers to all the houses where the passengers in the truck had been hiding. He told them to memorize their names for the day of vengeance and retribution, and she heard, but did not believe, the name of Fareed Mikha'eel, the brother-in-law of Almaza, the abandoned wife of Uncle Jiryes.

Two years pass in the refugee camp near Ramallah before the son of Al-Asbah finally convinces her to convert to Islam and marry him. She gives birth to twin sons, and with the passage of time and misfortunes the secret withers in her heart and is forgotten. It was only in recent years, after her husband was imprisoned for "belonging to a hostile organization," that she once again began to think about that Michel Abyad, whom she had loved in the submissive silence of an orphaned servant. From news that reached her from Beirut she had learned that this same Michel, now known as Dr. Michael Abyad, came every so often from the United States to work in the Palestinian Center for Research in Beirut.

"This is the story of a rich couple that was childless," says Surayyah Sa'id, "which Adèle the laundress told me more than thirty years ago."

One day, when their friends could no longer bear to look upon the Abyads' suffering, a certain doctor came and suggested that in return for a sum to ensure the silence of those concerned, they could adopt one of the children in St. Joseph's Hospital, where he worked. The choice fell upon the baby of a servant, who had told the doctors that she was forced to leave his bedside for a week in order to earn enough money to pay for the expenses of his hospitalization.

When she comes back a week later, they tell her that she is too late, that her son came down with typhus and died and was buried three days before. She asks if she can have the pillow upon which he had lain during his last days. From then on she cradled the pillow in her arms and sang lullabies to it in the streets of Beirut.

Twenty years later one of the workers at St. Joseph's appeared at the home of the Abyad family and demanded twenty pounds in gold for him not to reveal to their son that he is the son of a Palestinian maid, and also not to reveal to his real mother, whom the worker had managed to locate, that her son, Anton Jiryes Shammas, is alive and well.

"The refugee wisdom that I've acquired over the years has taught me that this Michel Abyad would do well to retain that name. What have I gotten in return for changing my name? A husband in jail and a pair of poor souls at home."

On the way out of Silwad, after my friend had related to me what he had learned about the incidents of the past winter, he asked if I had heard what I had come for. I answered him, "More than I wanted to hear." I then said, in reply to his inquisitive look, "What would you say if you were to hear that the man whose living double you are, the man you were named after, the man in whose shadow you have lived and whose memory you have carried—what would you say if this man turns out to be the hero of an Arab soap opera?"

A revenge like this Surayyah Sa'id had never imagined.

Deep inside me a cistern gaped open, and I am again a ten-year-old boy far down inside it, alone in my dim, enchanted kingdom, rejoicing in the musty smells and the bewitching sights, and now the silhouette of Laylah Khoury, framed in the square of light way up at the top of the cistern, coils the other Anton Shammas down to me and jerks away the rope.

This was at the beginning of April 1981. On Thursday, April 16, I went to visit my mother in Haifa, and my brother Jubran's wife told me that the whole morning they had tried in vain to inform me of the death and funeral of Almaza. That evening when my mother returned from the village she told us that Almaza's condition had worsened during the past week. She had begun to rip every piece of cloth that came her way and wind the strips around her body. She had also washed herself with kerosene and burst naked into the streets. Afterward she made her sister-in-law, the wife of Fareed Mikha'eel, the one who may have betrayed Layla Khoury, swear that when she was laid in her grave they would put only one thing in her coffin with her: the pillow upon which her son, Anton, had laid his head during his last days in Beirut, fifty years before. "We turned the whole place upside down today," my mother said, "but we couldn't find the pillow."

CHAPTER 5

But in fact I never set foot in the village of Silwad, and the whole trip to see Surayyah Sa'id is just a tale.

The truth is that my friend the journalist and I did get as far as the village of Beitin, that we did pass through the imagined canopy of sounds of stonecutting and sawing, that I was indeed heading for Surayyah Sa'id, despite all my procrastinations, but the soldier with the walkie-talkie in his hand who was at the checkpoint had received an order from whoever it was who gave the orders not to allow journalists into the area. And since my friend's face was well known throughout the occupied territories we were stopped politely but firmly and sent back in the direction of Jerusalem.

On Thursday, the sixteenth of April, 1981, my friend the journalist sent me word, via an acquaintance, that I should meet him at the Pie House in Jerusalem at two that afternoon. He had visited the village of Silwad, and he had something important to tell me concerning Surayyah Sa'id. A few minutes after I hung up, my eldest brother's wife called me from Haifa to inform me of Almaza's death. The funeral was to be in the village at four that afternoon.

The last time I saw Almaza was early in 1981, a few months before she died. She was walking down the main street of Fassuta with her niece Hilweh, my uncle Yusef's daughter, the one who on nights when the moon was full had seen the gleaming of the boulder in the middle of the *duwara,* and the one who claimed she had also seen the regal Ar-Rasad strutting around that same boulder, even though he never left behind a single one of his feathers as a sign. Almaza was wearing a thin gray dress despite the piercing cold of the Galilean winter. Her hair, however, was carefully combed as always, a remnant of her having worked in the homes of wealthy families in Beirut, but now her hair looked like a thin kerchief of sanity.

"Who is that?" she asked my cousin, when she saw her greet me warmly.

"Have you already forgotten Anton?"

And Almaza froze on the spot, scrawny and almost transparent, an icicle of suffering.

"But Anton died a long time ago!" she whispered to herself, and gazed at landscapes that she thought were in Lebanon.

"Don't pay any attention to her; she's gone completely mad. Last week I took her to the physician of the Welfare Office, thinking he could convince her to live in some sort of institution. She was sure that we were in Lebanon, and was amazed by the poor Arabic the doctor spoke. She wouldn't hear of an institution, and all I can do is try to keep her out of trouble. She doesn't sleep at night. I don't know if she ever sleeps. Drugs don't help. If she slept, they would come to take her away in her sleep, she says."

"Who?"

"The people who took Anton from her, poor thing, fifty years ago."

"But Anton died of a disease!"

"Now she says that she never saw the body. The doctors in some hospital in Beirut told her that he died and that they had to bury him. But she never saw the body. They gave her the pillow he slept on."

Like the dreamer who senses that consciousness is beginning to gnaw at his sleep and expose the tip of his dream to the chill of wakefulness, and who hurries to cover it with sleep and take refuge again in his dream, Almaza came awake for a moment at the sound of the word "pillow" but quickly covered the breech and mumbled again, "But my little Anton died a long time ago."

Some fifty-five years before, in 1926, Grandmother Alia lay in bed with sores all over her body, and her eyelids felt like two heavy coins. For a whole week she tossed and turned on the thin edge that separates sleep from wakefulness. Even when she was covered with compresses and bandages smeared with all sorts of ointments that she had asked for, she was not cured and even had no relief from the pains. When she saw that her herbs had failed her, she asked her daughter, my aunt Najeebeh, to sear a certain place on her ankle with a white-hot nail. But even this scorching of her tortured skin was of no avail, and she remained imprisoned in her dazed suffering.

It was just at this time that love blossomed between Jiryes and Almaza, after she had left her cousin Saleem for my uncle, the same Saleem who at a later stage in that opening and closing circle dance of love was to marry Aunt Najeebeh. "I was in love with Saleem from dawn till noon," said Almaza to those who chided her for the whims of her heart, "but ever since noon I have been in love with Jiryes A-Shammas." The truth of the matter is that the match was made by Wadee'ah, Almaza's sister, who had married Uncle Yusef in 1920, and who wanted Almaza for a sister-in-law. But Grandmother Alia, who thought that one of these sisters was more than enough, opposed the match, which of course only made the flame of love burn all the more brightly.

Four years earlier the family had moved out of the house attached to the north side of the old church in the center of the village and had come to live in the house in which Grandmother Alia is now lying, stricken by the illness that neither the potions nor the white-hot nail could overcome. The new house had been built with money that Grandfather Jubran had brought back after the First World War from his second, and last, stay in South America. The new house was the lowest one on the southern slope of the village and only a single Ave Maria's distance from the new church. The path that went past it wound its way to the valley below and then through the fields of red loam till it reached its center, the plot called Khallet Azamel, and there it intersected the road that ran along the length of the valley and climbed up to rocky Al-An'oor and finally vanished at the horizon, which was the end of the world of my childhood. I used to gaze at the end of the world through the south-facing window we called *bab es-sir*, literally "the door to the secret"—the name that is given in Arab architecture to the back exit for emergency use, a sort of low-silled window without a grille over it, through which in times of danger it is possible to escape.

On the wide sill of that window I would sit and muse over the movements that break the stillness of the landscape as seen through the window. A flock of goats goes out to pasture, like a shimmering black stain, getting farther and farther away, growing smaller and spreading out again and dwindling until it vanishes over the horizon, leaving a wake of dust. A man on his donkey is crossing the valley. A woman walks with a large bundle of fodder on her head, which she has pulled from among the tender tobacco plants. A farmer plows his field with a double-shafted plow hitched to a horse, and goes from one side of the field to the other. Furrow by hidden furrow, he gets nearer to me. Despite the distance I interpret the motion of the farmer and his plow and his horse as a sort of self-assigned homework that I am doing for Uncle Yusef, who when he felt like it would take me down to the field with him and teach me the secrets of working the land, and the names of the parts that make up the wonderful plow. And even now as I sit at my desk in Jerusalem and write these things down I feel with one hand the chill of the windowsill and with the other hand I count the parts of the plow, as a prayer of sorts to the memory of Uncle Yusef, and as an act of reconciliation with the memory of his red horse.

My uncle had a red horse, but he wasn't red in color. We just called him that. He was a weary and aged horse, whose color was faded brown. Late in the spring of 1957, during the tobacco-planting season, I accompanied my uncle and his horse across the valley to the plot of land called the "church field," to help him with the planting. The horse was loaded with crates of seedlings and kegs of water, and my good uncle promised me that at the end of the day, if Allah in his great mercy so willed, he would let me ride the horse home. The day was hot and long, but the promised ride on the horse was like an arbor over my head. Finally all the seedlings are planted upright row by row, along the furrows, and the backbreaking work is done. And just then the ancient horse, which had stood still the whole day in the shade of a tree, fills the cavities of his equine lungs with the breath of a long-lost vigor, breaks the reins with a jerk of his neck and races off toward home.

To the right of that *bab es-sir* was another secret door, the door of the bookcase embedded in the thick wall, the key to which my mother would deposit in the cookie dish hidden behind the thick looking glass of the wardrobe. When I got home from the "church field," the longest journey of my childhood, I opened the bookcase with the yellow key I had to steal from behind the mirror and took out the volumes of the Egyptian magazine *Al-Hilal.* Then I stole a red pen from my brother's schoolbag, sat down on the south windowsill and paged through the magazines, looking for pictures of horses. Each horse that I found I then netted in a thick tangle of red lines while I cursed the red horse. My father, who unexpectedly came home just then from his cobbler's shop, pinched my ears for the terrible vandalism I had committed. Later Uncle Yusef's youngest son, who had come home that day on vacation from his teaching job in Nazareth, saw my guilty ears and realized how miserable I was, so he promised that the next time he came from Nazareth, that city of miracles and wonders, he would bring me a bicycle made of candy that I could ride and taste to my heart's content. But Ameen was not to return to the village for twenty-five years, and then without the candy bicycle. The red horse's days were numbered after that deed; the marvelous gallop was his swan song, as it were. On the day he died I got together all the magazines that had suffered the vengeance of the red pen, laid them on the windowsill and prayed with great fervor that the horse might be resurrected.

Back in those days Uncle Jiryes would hover like a sleep-walker over Grandmother Alia's bed, wringing his hands and praying for her recovery, but then turn around and set about his courting. Aunt Najeebeh, his sister, had inherited the secrets of folk medicine from Grandmother Alia, and now that she had observed the failure of the herbs and the fire, she decided that the mysterious sickness was the result of a secret written curse composed by someone who wished Grandmother ill and with the help of the forces of darkness had made the curse into an amulet and placed it near the bed. "But who would want to harm this saintly woman," asked Aunt Marie when she came to visit her mother, "who never in her life even raised her hand against an ant? A cat could steal her dinner right out of her hands." Najeebeh's hypothesis was not well received, and she was accused of shooting in the dark. But she did not concede. And wonder of wonders: in a thorough search of the house she discovered in the pocket of one of the jackets a slip of paper carefully folded into a nest of triangles, and when it was unfolded Aunt Najeebeh saw exactly what she had feared—a mysterious design composed of unintelligible twisting symbols joined together in the shape of a heart. The jacket belonged to Uncle Jiryes, who freely confessed, as if a weight had been lifted from his heart, that in his effort to get his mother to like Almaza, he had gone to a holy man, Sheikh El-Bi'nawi of the village of Tarbeekha, who had prepared this amulet. He had no idea that the effect of the amulet would be so severe, and he was ready with all his heart and all his might to do whatever was necessary to restore his mother's full health.

There was an eccentric priest in the village at that time, called Father Sim'an. A pious soul and a true believer, he did not hesitate to enter the world of the occult and regarded himself as an expert in deciphering amulets and counteracting their effects. Therefore Aunt Najeebeh went to him with the inscription in hand.

28 September 1968

To *Sitt* Josephine Shammas, at the sound of whose sweet name all eyes light up!

Many greetings and blessings to all my dear family and to anyone who asks you about me, and that's all. As for me, God be praised, I am fine and I lack for nothing but the sight of your shining faces. My darling niece, this is to inform you that your precious letter reached me with its news of everyone's good health and that is what I wish for you always, and that's all. Niece, this is to inform you that the minute I sell the shop I will think about the voyage home even if it is the last hour of my life. Because every time I receive a letter from you I can do nothing but weep. This is my life, this is my fortune, this is my fate. Ah, it is all in the hands of Allah. But I left behind my life's companion, *Sitt* Almaza the light of my eyes. Woe is me. Please give her my best regards, and that's all. I beg Allah, may His name be praised, to allow me to see her face once again even in the last hour of my life. Kiss your father and

66

mother's cheeks for me. And to everyone who claims I have not sent him greetings, I hereby send a thousand and one greetings. That's all. End of letter.

May you live and be well.

> Wishing you long life,
> Your loving Uncle,
> Jiryes Jubran A-Shammas

Don't forget to reply at once.

Father Sim'an was wrapped up in his soul that particular day, because of what his cat had done. For years he had been devoting himself to the composition of a history of the Catholic Church in the Holy Land, for which purpose he had purchased in distant Beirut a special notebook, splendidly bound in leather as black as the souls of sinners. On its first page he had inscribed, in his best calligraphy, the title of the book to be written therein, *The Cock Doth Crow in the Catholic Church.* He had also attached a bookmark, a scarlet ribbon that had been plucked in a moment of weakness from an antique missal that was in the church. On more than one occasion Father Sim'an had suffered sleepless nights and pangs of conscience over this deed. Sometimes, to the inquisitive meows of his cat, he would descend from his sleepless bed to the church door, fingering the scarlet ribbon he was about to return to the missal. But then he would be swayed by various reasons why he needn't do so, the leading one being the loftiness of the purpose for which it had been borrowed. It was serving, after all, a unique and unparalleled work, which would glorify the Catholic Church among all the Arabic-speaking peoples. Also, once he had completed the text and prepared it for publication, he was going to return the ribbon to its rightful place.

It sometimes happened that an early-rising rooster would crow and disturb his vigil, for he would recall the words of Our Lord that He spake unto Peter, saying, "The cock shall not crow, till thou hast denied me thrice." Then Father Sim'an would say unto himself in the words of Saint

Peter, "I will lay down my life for Thy sake, but I will not deny Thee in any wise, and I will return the ribbon unto its place." But in time the origin of the ribbon slipped away from his conscience. The sentences of the text had long since taken their final form in his ornate Arabic calligraphy, and even though the work of editing and correcting had long been completed, the ribbon still lay between the pages of the notebook, peeping and spiraling out of it, its fringe caressing the shelf.

Directly under this shelf stood a large crock into which the villagers would pour as much of their virgin olive oil as their spirit of generosity moved them to give at the end of the pressing season. Now, on that particular day, Father Sim'an had decided to take the tiniest bit of oil to add to the dish he was preparing in his meager kitchen. As he was returning the cover to the crock, he noticed that it hadn't been washed for some time. He took it and went back to the kitchen, where he found his cat sniffing around the simmering pot. Father Sim'an in his wrath loudly scolded the cat and expelled her from his kitchen. The cat, still salivating, slunk into the other room. And there she sees on the shelf above the open crock of oil the glistening tail of a mouse. Instantly the cat leapt up and pounced upon Father Sim'an's notebook and struggled to claw her way between the pages. As she scrabbled and kicked and pulled and scratched, she pushed the notebook straight into the jar. Father Sim'an returned with the rinsed cover in his hand, and threw his habitual glance over toward the notebook, as if to assure himself of its well-being, and lo! the twice-frustrated cat lay there in its stead. With rancorous eyes he looked into the jar and spied a dark patch in its depths. He rolled up his sleeve and drew out *The Cock Doth Crow in the Catholic Church* and discovered that the calligraphy which had adorned the pages of the notebook had returned to its liquid state. Father Sim-'an laid the dripping notebook on the shelf and tore out the scarlet ribbon in order to return it to the church at once.

Just then Aunt Najeebeh knocked on his door, as he stood there with the bookmark in his dripping hand. He tried to persuade her to come back the next day. But Aunt Najeebeh said that her mother was dying. So Father Sim'an took the amulet and looked it over hurriedly. "It's very easy," he said. "For the flesh, that is. The course of her soul will be difficult to reverse."

Aunt Najeebeh took the paper and went back to Grandmother Alia. When darkness fell, she put the paper into a glass of water, as Father Sim'an had instructed, and left the glass on the boulder in the *duwara* all night long, exposed to the starlight. At dawn she put the cup to my grandmother's mouth and told her to drink. "This tastes like ink," my grandmother said. "I can understand that, but where does the taste of oil come from?"

They buried the amulet by the enchanted boulder. And wonder of wonders, Grandmother Alia came to love Almaza with all her soul, as if her hatred had been nothing but letters written upon a slick of oil.

Thus after the passage of a year Uncle Jiryes took Almaza the light of his eyes to be his wife.

12 March 1970

To My Beloved Niece Josephine Najjar, May You Live and Be Well.

Warmest greetings to all the family and the relatives. As for me, my health, Allah be praised, is fine and I lack for nothing but the sight of your shining faces. Secondly, this is to inform you that I have already received three letters from you to which I have not yet responded to date because I am consumed by worries as I have put the shop up for sale at least twenty times but— And this is what is worrying me, because the Argentine these days isn't worth a thing, and the new ruler has begun to change the currency, and that's all. And as Easter is just around the corner I am asking you to take my place and give my best wishes to all the family and the relatives, and especially to

Sitt Almaza the light of my eyes. And I am hereby making every possible effort to save myself from the Argentine because Allah has sent His wrath upon me for having left behind everyone I had. I cry Brother and there is no brother, I cry Cousin and there is no cousin. This is what is written on my brow, but I have great faith in Allah that I shall return and see Yusef and Hanna and Marie and Jaleeleh and all who are the flesh of my flesh and blood of my blood. Alas, will this ever come to pass? Woe is me, and that's all. And to everyone who claims I have not sent him greetings, I hereby send a thousand and one greetings. Pray take no notice of the frequency of my letters, *Sitt* Josephine.

> Wishing you long life,
> Your Uncle,
> Jiryes A-Shammas

On Saturday evening, the twenty-first of January, 1928, Anton, Uncle Jiryes's son by his wife, Almaza, was born. His birth opened a new chapter in the relationship between Wadee'ah, Uncle Yusef's wife, and her sister Almaza. Jealousy rots the bones, as Solomon said, and he was certainly right about the two sisters. At the request of Aunt Marie I shall refrain from revealing the source of that destructive jealousy.

I shall mention only this: The day of Anton's birth was the day when Uncle Jiryes first conceived the idea of going to Argentina. In vain Grandfather Jubran, gray-haired and himself wise in the ways of traveling, tried to dissuade his son. In vain he recited to him his misadventures and reminded him that his uncle Elias, Grandfather Jubran's brother, had died on the way to Buenos Aires thirty years earlier, on the ship that carried the three brothers Ya'kub and Jubran and Elias, in addition to their uncle Nimr, who was their mother's brother. The sea, Uncle Jiryes said to him, is satisfied with one victim from every family.

The *mukhtar* of the village agreed to serve as his guarantor to the authorities. When everyone saw how determined he was, they tried to convince him to take his wife along and not abandon her. But Almaza was in agreement with her husband. It would be best, they both said, for him to go there first and establish himself, and then send the *nowloon*, the ship's ticket, for his wife. Several other men from the village set out at the same time as Uncle Jiryes. They all spent several weeks in Beirut waiting for the ship. At one point Uncle Jiryes had a change of heart and returned to the village, together with another man from the group. But the *mukhtar* was displeased by their irresolution, and he sent them back to the ship. That was in November 1928.

On Thursday, April 16, 1981, I met my friend the journalist, and did not attend Almaza's funeral.

"What would you say if you were to find out that you have a cousin who is also called Anton Shammas?" he asked before I even sat down.

"I really did have a cousin like that, but he died in Beirut fifty years ago. Are you trying to tell me that Surayya Sa'id really is who I think she is?"

"She told me that her father-in-law, one Al-Asbah, told her, on his way back to the Sabra camp in Beirut, about how he had met you. One of the old women at the camp who heard the family name remembered a rumor that had circulated in Beirut at the end of the 1920s, when she was a laundress in rich people's houses, about the Abyad family's adopted son, and about his Palestinian mother, who was from the Shammas family. The son, Michel, was smuggled later on into the United States, but he came back a few years ago and joined the Palestinian Center for Research in Beirut. That's all she knows. But tell me, wasn't this Al-Asbah somebody in the Arab Rebellion?"

"I'm not really sure there ever was such a person."

"But your uncle's wife will be very happy, won't she? After so many years!"

I was tempted to say: I doubt that there's room enough for such joy in a coffin.

For even after I had looked through the gate that has

71

been left ajar, had seen what was on the other side and had succumbed to the temptation of opening the gate itself, I never imagined that I would find myself, like the heroes of *A Thousand and One Nights,* confronted by an infinite number of doors, and that every door concealed behind it additional doors. Through the gate of fantasy I had entered into the tunnels and secret places of the past, and in my imagination the partition between what there is and what was hidden had already fallen. And now I find that what I had imagined to have been only a web woven upon the warp of reality with the woof of fantasy was no longer obedient to its maker, that the net of memory that had been cast had caught the fisherman.

Not one of Laylah Khoury's few relatives to whom I told her story was keen to renew the connection. Nor was she enthusiastic either. In fact, the possibility that the other Anton was alive and well was deeply doubted by my family. How can it be, they said, that this rumor which winged its way through Beirut never reached Almaza's ears? And if it ever had—why did it never pass her lips before the day she died? True, in the fullness of her years she had gotten a little demented, and had begun to imagine all kinds of stories about what had happened to her son. But that can be attributed to the Elias Mikha'eel family, several of whose members from generation to generation lost their minds in the twilight of their days. And even if there was some truth in the rumor, why hadn't this Michel Abyad, who is closer than we are to its source, why hasn't he tried to verify it and attempted to get in touch with us as we are trying to get in touch with him? No, this is nothing but delayed revenge on the part of Laylah Khoury, who is trying to get back at the Mikha'eels for having turned her in in 1948. Most of all, why would anyone want to learn that for the entire fifty years of his life he has really been somebody else?

Two months later I received word, via an acquaintance of mine in Europe, a childhood friend of my eldest brother, who worked in the Palestinian Center for Research in Beirut, that there was indeed someone called Dr. Michael Abyad who had been associated with the center, but that the connection had broken off several years earlier.

In the September 27, 1982, issue of *Time* magazine there was a photo story about the slaughter in the Sabra and Shatila refugee camps in West Beirut. Among other matters, there was the account of a man who said that his father had gone for fifty years unharmed by the bullets of the British and the bombings of the Israelis, only to be finally felled by the sign of the Cross which the Phalangists' knives had etched on his breast. After that came the testimony of one of the workers at the Palestinian Center for Research, who on the morning after the slaughter had ridden his bicycle through the streets of the Sabra camp. To the right of the column in which these two witnesses appeared were three pictures of the slaughter. In the foreground of the bottom photograph was a horse, which had collapsed in the midst of drinking. His head was still resting as if trapped on the edge of the barrel. Above it was a picture of two children lying in the dust. And at the top of the page was the picture of a man on a bicycle looking to his left and seeing two corpses next to the sidewalk. The caption beneath the picture said: "Dr. Michael Abyad, American writer and researcher, observes the victims of the slaughter in the Sabra camp."

Sometimes they burn the tongue, the red candies of memory.

PART TWO
THE TELLER: Père Lachaise

Dresses of beautiful women, in blue and white.
And everything in three languages:
Hebrew, Arabic and Death.

Yehuda Amichai

1. Third Person

For weeks after she left their apartment, her red hair, like sudden fires, would turn up in the most unexpected places. Mornings, he'd find a bit of it still entangled in the hairbrush she never admitted she used or caught in the tangle of electric cords lying on the carpet near the bed. He'd spend hours hunting for hairs, on the carpet and under it, in the folds of woolen blankets which had been put away in the cupboard, among the pillows on the sofa, in the puffs that bloomed anew every morning under the bed, between pages of books she had read or had not read, as she lay on the bed beneath the bookshelves. It came to haunt him, her hair. It declined to leave him, declined to leave him alone. It entangled him, strangled him, stranded him in the strands of her life. . . .

And his.

He sits at a small wooden table and writes about her hair. Hôtel Vaneau, room 62. Framed by the window, far from it all, in the morning light of Paris, a tarnished rooster on the weather vane of a church spire. A clock with Roman numerals under the rooster strikes a quarter to nine, and a red sun pops in from behind the hoary buildings. To his left, a wardrobe with austere carvings around the mirror of its door. Behind him, a rumpled double bed, a woman's black hairs scattered between its sheets.

2. Nadia

She stood leaning on the railing of the window, on the fifth floor, and watched the gesticulations of the proprietor of the *fruits de mer* shop. From that height it was possible only to see the movements of his lips persuading and his hands gesturing expansively, most probably in praise of the *huîtres.* The customer pokes an indifferent finger into the ice, and passes it along the edge of the crate of tightly sealed crustaceans, and shakes his head from side to side, puffs a bit on his pipe, and wipes the tip of his finger on a sky-blue handkerchief. He moves off into the flow of shoppers streaming through the market.

Its buzz rose up to the window where the woman was standing when she heard a dull thud followed by a sharp cry. She knew without turning her head that the orange juice she had prepared in the small kitchen and had slapped down in front of the boy was now trickling over the carpet that had saved the glass from shattering. Nor did she turn her head when the cry turned into another of the crying fits that had lately come over him. And as usual came the perfunctory blows on the other side of the wall as if detached from the fists of the two Lebanese students, friends of her brother-in-law, who were most likely studying for some exam. Even the sentence she muttered sounded to her as if it had been spoken by one of the shoppers in the market and then disintegrated into meaningless sounds and got lost in the hubbub below. As the thump from the other side of the wall receded, her eyes followed the owner of the sky-blue handkerchief, until her glance fell upon a different man, who was in a hurry and cleared a way for himself with the help of the shopping bag in his arms. He lifted his head and seemed to look at her window, when he bumped into an old man and the bag was almost knocked out of his arms.

She leans over the rail, her face in her hands, and her elbows suck up the chill of the railing and her black hair wafts in the breeze, which is saturated with the smells of the market. Instinctively she presses her palm to the top of her blouse, and then the realization flickers through her that she is not leaning on her windowsill in Abu Dhabi; a smile of pleasure flutters up and settles on the corners of her mouth. "You don't need to hurry," she whispers toward the man. "Your child is no longer trapped inside my body."

Even when she heard the jangle of the keys on the other side of the door she did not turn her head. Three different keys were inserted and withdrawn. With the fourth one she turned away from the window and went to open the door. Now the ringing of the bell joined the other sounds.

"Didn't you see me in the street?" he asked, and set the shopping bag on the kitchen table. But she had drifted back to the window. He stuck his head out the kitchen door and called to her in a voice that tried to penetrate through the boy's crying to where she stood.

"Nadia, didn't you see me down in the street?"

"Maybe you can get Elias to be quiet. I can't hear what you're saying."

He went over to the child and picked him up in his arms. A hot tear fell onto his arm. "Daddy's home," he said into the child's ear. "Daddy's here." His sentence echoes inside her, and her eyes go back to look for the man with the sky-blue handkerchief.

3. Amira

Am Sayyed, the caretaker of their house in Alexandria, comes toward her. His face lights up and his eyes, which had been two dark slots, beam at her. She doesn't even ask how the gift of sight has been returned to him, as though she takes it for granted. Nana comes down the steps, wiping her hands on her apron, but something of their cold dampness sticks to her cheeks when Nana kisses her. "Oh, Amira, Amira," Nana says to her in Arabic. "I could sing for joy at seeing you, but the forty days of mourning aren't over yet." Amira thinks that it should be only the Jewish thirty days. Suddenly they are all in the Jewish cemetery in Alexandria, near her father's tombstone, but her father is standing next to her, holding a camera. He asks the three of them to stand in front of the tombstone so that he can take a picture. His finger presses, but there is no click. He presses again and the camera turns into a green lizard. He holds it out to Am Sayyed, who brings it up to his right eye, and the lizard escapes and disappears into its dark slot.

4. *Yehoshua Bar-On*

The reception clerk tells me that my Jew has not called and there are no messages for me. At the foot of the spiral staircase I watch the smoke rings curling out of my pipe and think about what he would say if he knew that in speaking to myself I call that proud Palestinian-Arab-Israeli "my Jew." I think it over as I head toward the exit from my Hôtel des Écoles and go back out into the Rue Delambre. My finger is still spiced with the scent of the *fruits de mer,* which is what had brought me out into the street. Let your fingers do the walking, Yosh Bar-On; their stride is no less *pathétique.* From across the street, from the thousands of gleaming colored marble rectangles of the facade of the *école maternelle,* waves of children's cries roll toward me. I float on them toward the Café le Dôme, accompanied by the gurgle of the water washing the curb from the spouts of *eau non potable* on the sidewalk.

Le Dôme is nearly empty of customers but not of the smell of the previous night's Gauloises. I loathe cigarette smoke, particularly stale cigarette smoke. The nose accustomed to the fragrances of the pipe is sensitive. I deliberate and decide to sit inside. The decision to sit on the canopied terrace, open and defenseless, has more than once left me susceptible to the preying pests of Montparnasse, who fall upon their victims like a pack of hunting dogs that have caught a whiff of home. But this thought prompts me to ask what I am doing here. I would not be sitting in this place at such an early hour if I had not been led here by my finger, still redolent of the brinish smell of the ice. I stand in the doorway and watch a waiter polish an antique gramophone. The floor spreads out behind him, and the kitchen's dumbwaiter belches and squeaks. A flock of waiters descend upon it and unload stacks of gleaming plates sprinkled with all the colors of the stained-glass window soaked in the morning sun of Rue Delambre. Variations on the Descent from the Cross, my Jew would undoubtedly comment. Opposite me is a glass clock, its digits red and black dots set above pots of flowers, perhaps real, perhaps not. At eye level are the pictures of celebrities who have frequented this place.

I select a seat at one of the tables in the front, veiled from the inquisitive eyes of the passersby of Montparnasse by lace curtains, above which lamps with pink shades hang down. In the depths of the room, a couple sit by a table similar to mine, swathed in their love. "So let us not speak ill of our generation," as the French writer who now gazes out from a wooden frame once said. Or is he Irish? It is doubtful whether that waiter, who keeps me waiting out of principle, has ever heard of him. When he finally approaches my table, he takes my order with a stone face and haughty nostrils. He, too, scents my Israeli accent, which is satisfactory or even a bit better, according to the opinion of some of my French friends. He goes off. Even to me my order sounds weird, suitable to neither the hour nor the season. But what would be suitable to this hour? Here they will not serve me a demitasse of cardamoned coffee, which would suit this blessed morning hour. A demitasse of cardamoned coffee! I should jot that down in my notebook. Far better than "a cup of black coffee." Small details of little obvious value but of the greatest importance to the delineation of the character. But does empathy suffice, I muse, as some Israeli writer once claimed; will empathy suffice to grant this character I am creating a place of honor (ah, honor) in the studies that are being produced on "the figure of the Arab in modern Hebrew literature"? This time I'm going to sculpt a well-rounded character. A nice hefty Arab, human and warm. A demitasse of cardamoned coffee, with all that it implies. Cardamoned, and not "bitter," an adjective that lacks aroma and has negative connotations. My Jew happens to drink *thé au lait,* as if he were ducking me and blurring his tracks. But he does not know that it is difficult to blur his aromas, if not impossible. Not only the clothing is soaked with them, but also the skin. And I have a very keen sense of smell. You have let your fingers do the walking, Yosh Bar-On, and look where they, tracking a smell, led you. "Memory's associations are wondrous indeed." Who said that?

And here come the twelve *huîtres* slapped down on the rim of their stand. Wonderfully precise on their bed of ice, as if they were the *Ding an sich.* Extinguished pipe in pocket, I set about enjoying the delicacy.

5. Third Person

Yesterday in the morning, after a night of packing, he left Jerusalem. What does one pack late in August for one day in Paris and several months in the American Midwest? What does one pack from among the clothes that have been carefully inspected to remove her hairs from them?

The plane landed in Paris at twelve fifty-five, local time. And it was only at four that he gathered the courage to give up on his Lebanese relatives who were supposed to meet him.

Two hours later he stands in the shower and curses the French, who do not provide hot water to travelers worn out by their relatives. In a sort of wet revenge he does not towel himself dry, and slips dripping between the sheets. That's what Shlomith used to do, coming back from her shower, to vex him just at the threshold of sleep.

At ten, local time, he opens his bleary eyes, and the August twilight, still lingering outside, mocks his senses. He dozes off again, thinking about the relatives who are waiting for him to phone, and Yehoshua Bar-On as well. Well, they can just wait, his relatives. The writer too. At 2:00 A.M., by the light of the lamp on the chest of drawers, he notices the first of the hairs on the pillow. It brings him totally awake, and he takes apart the bedding. Hairs are scattered between the sheets. A sort of French revenge. He rushes to the shower. But confronting the sole faucet, the distress of the freezing water of the earlier hours, he makes a discovery: when you turn the faucet to the right, it emits hot water as well.

The wonders of the human brain, as his father would have said.

6. Amira

"What brings you here so early?"

"I haven't gone to bed yet."

"What happened?"

"It's a shame I didn't bring the camera in for repair then. The session was wasted."

"Damn. And yesterday I looked great."

"How many times do I have to tell you that when I photograph you against the tombstones you have to let the tombstones look great. In these pictures you're number two, Amira. Not like in my life."

"He hastened to add, with a photographer's quick reflexes."

"I'm serious. The whole idea is to let the dead come alive."

"He hastened to add, with an undertaker's professionalism."

"Amira, please!"

"Are we going out, or shall we have breakfast here?"

"A broken lens makes me hungry."

"I really should write down all these pearls of yours. They're good for my dialogue."

"Now you tell me, after all these years. Well, the Americans will give even better pearls to use."

"They're just a bunch of Midwesterners. They spend all of their time watching the corn grow."

"Maybe you can get them to watch an exhibition of my photographs."

"Maybe so. They could use a historical sense of death over there. Their tombstones are so much newer than ours. They'll just eat up an exhibition of death with some tradition behind it."

"When did you last visit your father's grave?"

"It's strange that you should ask that. I dreamt about it last night."

7. Yehoshua Bar-On

What do Arabs dream about? asks the painter, who as expected had sat himself down at my table. "What do they dream about? The twins Aziz and Khaleel after they appear in Hannah Gonen's nightmare in *My Michael*," he adds, developing the subject, his finger poking into the cold plate. Have I picked up a new *Galut* habit? I can't forgive myself that in a moment of weakness I told this fellow about the novel I'm writing—this *Yored* who left Israel ages ago with his parents but still insists upon calling himself an Israeli. He came in to use the telephone, so he says, and spotted me. I'm regretting even more the whim that brought me at this ungodly hour to Le Dôme and exposed me naked and helpless to that waiter's disdain and to the conceited bleat of this blabbermouth, who hardly had sat down before he informed me, in French, that no true connoisseur would touch *huîtres* during the four months of the year whose names have no *r* in them. Not to mention this early hour of the day. Clearly another example of the notorious gluttony of Israelis. And then what does he do? Saying he's an Israeli himself, he calls the waiter over and orders an empty plate to share them. Nonetheless, I have spared myself one other humiliation. I thank Allah the merciful and the almighty, as my Jew would say, that I had put my pipe away in the pocket of my jacket. Because the last time I was here, in this accursed place, this same needling nudnick had bestowed upon me another of his friendly put-downs. "Why do you insist upon smoking a pipe?" he teased. "Why do you insist on this image of the Palmach generation, which is still visible in those pictures they publish of its writers in anthologies and literary supplements? Pipe in one hand, the other thoughtfully supporting their chin as they gaze at posterity. I mean, you're too young for the Palmach generation and too old for the State one. So keep a low profile."

He's telling me.

8. Nadia

The boy, exhausted from crying, falls asleep. But he will undoubtedly wake up when the phone rings. And the other child, if you can still call it that, has left his space, an astronaut detached from the umbilical cord that ties him to the mother ship, and has fallen forever into the enchanted state of weightlessness. What were the features of his face and the shape of his buttocks and his hands? His tiny hands, the doctor told her, could have killed her. Almost did. Kamal, calm as usual, snaps her out of her musings.

"He didn't phone, your cousin."

"I'm not worried. I know he's arrived already."

"Your father used to say that his sister was blessed with your ability to see things that other people couldn't, so why didn't you guess that the plane was landing at one in the afternoon instead of one in the morning?"

"My powers have been playing tricks on me lately, not to mention my fallopian tubes."

"I'm sorry to remind you of that."

"But there's nothing there anymore," she said.

9. Third Person

And now, at two in the morning, in a strange city, he stands before the small mirror over the basin and lathers his face. "Who else uses a brush these days?" the security man at Lod airport had said, in a tone that managed to combine curiosity, suspicion and condescension. "My father does," he answered, deliberately using the present tense, his only retaliation against the searching.

When the security man's searching fingers happened to touch the erect hairs behind his right earlobe, he felt, for the first time, humiliation gush and spread through the pores of his forehead. Those were the hairs that in his childhood in the village would be offered up to the blade of the razor in his father's hand at the end of the haircut, the razor that made lines straight, rounded the arc above the ear, regulated the downy hair.

This was usually on Sunday, before Mass. The church bell would already have rung for the second time, to announce that the priest had come down from his quarters to put on his vestments by the niche behind the altar. The brush, which had been bought in Beirut in the forties, scattered the hair, prickly as the stubble in the fields, from his neck and face. Then out came the razor for the finishing touches.

After the family moved to Haifa, when he was twelve years old, his father stopped cutting his hair. No razor ever again touched the line of erect hairs. Sixteen years later the roles were reversed when he began to cut the hair of his stricken father and to shave his beard. The intimate places of his father's body were now within his reach, turned over to the touch of his fingers: his father who had never embraced him as a child. First he would touch his earlobes, to move them out of the way for the scissors, which had been taken out of the mother-of-pearl damascene box. Then he would take the nose between his thumb and forefinger, and give it a slight lift so as to shave above the upper lip. And the more the cancer gnawed away at the liver and the body grew limp, the more it opened to him, replete with its disappointments, sated with its tribulations. They would sit together in silence, the father and he, the youngest of his sons. His mother, who did not know about the cancer, wrapped the house in her compassion. Her love, which had blossomed like the cedar, was now withering like moss. There had already been between them, the father and his son, the closeness of long nights by lantern light, when they had stayed behind in the village until the rest of the family could try to establish itself for the second time, in Haifa. Now the long night of slow dying lay before them, like the fading of a lantern put to shame by an electric lamp.

10. Amira

"Have you noticed that you always bring me back to the dead?"

"I'm not bringing you anywhere. I'm just placing you between me and the tombstone."

"But you're also using me as a buffer."

"Amira, why can't we just see it as photography? We've talked about it more than we've done it. We spend ten times more time on arguments than on work."

"Your work. Don't forget that."

"But the idea, if you remember, was yours."

"It was a way to stay in touch with my father. Now it's become something else."

"My idea hasn't changed."

"Maybe it has. Don't forget the project was different at first. This was supposed to be a rehearsal for it. Instead of dragging your celebrities to Père Lachaise and running around with them among the tombstones, you could use me as a sort of trial model."

"I've already given up on the celebrities."

"In practice, maybe, but not in theory. You still see me as some other person. Which drives me out of my mind. I reach my father only in my dreams. When I'm with you he's distant, somewhere behind me. Maybe he can touch me, but I can't touch him. I'm busy looking at you most of the time, and this has nothing to do with my father, with Alexandria, with the old house."

"You're blaming me as if I were responsible for your dreams."

"But don't you see, that's the point. You really are responsible for my dreams. And that's what scares you, being responsible for my dreams. You've been running away from that ever since I've known you. To the extent I know you at all."

"You know me. You're not my wife."

"I only know that you're protected there behind your wife and behind your camera. And I'm exposed. And my being exposed is what you want to show in your pictures. A grave that's closed and sealed, against a woman who's exposed and defenseless."

"Do you love me at all?"

"I love Père Lachaise."

"And what about me?"

"You're my alibi; Père Lachaise is yours."

11. Nadia

There was no reason for the blue mood. Apparently, at least.

In Abu Dhabi, where they had gone after finishing their degrees in computer science in Paris, the doctor reassured her, after his diagnosis, that the problem could be easily handled by a surgeon in Paris. The fainting spells became less frequent, and the pain that had swelled within her receded. Their place was taken by the gut knowledge that somewhere in her left fallopian tube a tiny fetus was stuck and would stay there until it was plucked out by the surgeon. Where would it go from there? That was as far as her thoughts took her; beyond them was the silence of the unknown. The silence between sob and sob. It's the sobbing that isn't noted in the medical history of the problem. That's why the doctor in Abu Dhabi didn't take account of it. How can she explain the spell of crying that has come over little Elias, as if the fetus whose fate was sealed in her abdomen wished to transmit to her a secret message in a primal code, traces of which were still in the possession of its brother, stumbling through this earthly life.

"It's a romantic explanation. I'm prepared to accept it only as a compelling reason to have the operation right away," said Kamal.

But it was exactly the sort of explanation he normally would have adopted if he had been the one who proposed it in the first place. This was one of his character traits, his own kind of egocentricity, which she loved but was embarrassing to him. It was like the thought that the two of them overlapped from time to time, which made him anxious and soothed and fascinated her. She never told him this difference, for fear he might panic and strike the reins of their love from her hands.

She had held the reins ever since the day at the entrance to the American University in Beirut when she had handed him, an anonymous passerby, a flier from the Syrian Social Nationalist Party. He had glanced and smiled at the mimeographed page, then raised his eyes. His smile flooded her, and she knew that this was the man who was meant for her and that he was a party member. By the next day they were old friends, whispering secrets in a corner of the cafeteria, which was as noisy as a beehive. When he had finished telling her the story of his father, who had spent many years in jail on charges of membership in the SSNP, she said to him, "Come over to our house this evening and ask my father for my hand." He came and asked and Elias Bitar consented. They went to Paris to continue their studies, and here their eyes were opened to the fascist side of the SSNP. Especially his eyes; nearly all of her attention was given over to their firstborn son, who was now sitting at the table beside him, both of them drawing pictures.

She goes to the window, and the scar from the operation pulls to it the warmth of her body by cords of pain, and a chill makes her shudder, and she closes the window and thinks there is no reason for the blue mood. Apparently, at least.

12. *Third Person*

He remembers the dream he dreamt before he woke up suddenly and saw the first hair on the pillow. He is sleeping in his bed in the apartment on Sabbath Square in Jerusalem and is trying to wake up from a nightmare. Then he is at the window that looks out over Mea Shearim. He wants to call for help in Hebrew, because who would think of calling for help in Arabic in Mea Shearim, but the word he is thinking of isn't the right one. He opens the window, still hoping to remember the word. On the balcony opposite, a door is open into a room, and a woman whose head is piously covered in a scarf stands before a mirror. She notices him in the mirror, curls off her dress, rolls down her panties, and she wiggles her snow-white magnificent behind as if she were a village woman expressing her disdain in the most expressive way that nature has put at her disposal. On another balcony, another woman, whom he knows, is completing a transaction with two Arabs wearing *abayas* and *kufiyas*. She takes bank notes from them and gives them two parcels. As they leave he suddenly remembers the right Hebrew cry for help and shouts after them, *"Hatsilu!"* They freeze in their tracks, drop their parcels and raise their hands as if hoping not to be shot.

13. Yehoshua Bar-On

My Jew will be an educated Arab. But not an intellectual. He does not gallop on the back of a thoroughbred mare, as was the custom at the turn of the century, nor is he a prisoner of the IDF, as was the custom at the turn of the state. Nor is he A. B. Yehoshua's adolescent Lover. He speaks and writes excellent Hebrew, but within the bounds of the permissible. For there must be some areas that are out of bounds for him, so nobody will accuse me of producing the stereotype in reverse, the virtuous Arab. He might be permitted the *Kaddish,* as it were, but not the *Kol Nidre.* And so on and so forth. A real minefield.

I can't remember where it was I read about the Arab as a literary solution. But it will come, ah yes, it will come. Some lurking critic like a mole planted in my path will accuse me, in a learned and rigidly reasoned article, that my Arab is nothing but a solution to my personal problems and not to the problems of fiction. So where does that leave us? In A. B. Yehoshua's phrase, "the continuous silence of the writer," as someone is bound to write, "was broken, which is a pity." Then the ambitious young reporters, the girls with their first jobs at the yellow journals, will come, eager to rub shoulders with even an obsolete author. Perhaps at my son's instigation, they will bring up some detail or other and ask me to comment on it. That's the most frightening question— "Could you comment, please?" That is, someone has passed judgment on you, and all you can do is mutter a few words of comment. And I'll be strangled and entangled, entangled and strangled, as the poet says, and *après moi* a deluge of gossip: "Let all the snakes that lurk in the mud hatch out." A metaphor for the new loneliness. A wife who left. A son who got in trouble with the police. Not necessarily in that order. The story he published on how I did and did not raise him. And all the poems in his drawer after the arrest. Perhaps that's the subject I ought to write about: all the drawers I never even knew existed. But there wouldn't be any aesthetic distance. Or interest on my part either.

There has to be an Arab this time, as some sort of solution to some sort of silence. An Arab who speaks the language of Grace, as Dante once called it. Hebrew as the language of Grace, as opposed to the language of Confusion that swept over the world when the Tower of Babel collapsed. My Arab will build his tower of confusion on my plot. In the language of Grace. That's his only possible redemption. Within the boundaries of what's permissible, of course.

He will fall in love with a Jewish woman. With red hair. Married. To an army officer, maybe. An army officer's redhead. "One shore beyond desire," one David too many. A love that from the start is pregnant with the seed of its own self-destruction. A love that will never be realized. That's the initial premise. And when the forbidden fruit is revealed, the wounded husband will rage and, like Solomon, will make the woman choose: either the love split in two by the sword or the living child. And here, too, there will be a trial, at the end of which it will be decreed that everyone must return to his or her place. The living child will return to its mother, the dead love to the obtuse side of the triangle, and life to its usual course.

I'm thinking about a motto for the whole thing. I once saw a movie that began with the sentence: "Only the loneliness of the tiger in the forest is greater than the loneliness of the Samurai." Then it came out that this wasn't an old Japanese saying, as it was purported to be in the movie, but rather an invention of the director's, who managed to fool even the Japanese themselves. I'll write about the loneliness of the Palestinian Arab Israeli, which is the greatest loneliness of all. With the skill of the veteran Samurai who is still remembered for a few precise and devastating sword strokes of prose, among the best in Hebrew literature.

Now it's coming to me—a possible opening line for the first chapter: "Having come to Jerusalem from his village in the Galilee, he learned that, like the coffin, the loneliness of the Arab has room enough in it for only one person." I doubt if my readers are any smarter than the Japanese.

14. Amira

"You know, I'm half Arab," Amira says, "because the creative side of my mind comes from Alexandria. I love you in a Jewish way, but I write about it Arab style. I used to write to my father in Arabic, and he would answer me in French. But you could sense the smells of the beach at Alexandria behind his words. Also the smells of my mother's kitchen. I didn't understand everything he wrote, but the dried-up stream of his Hebrew somehow flowed into my Arabic. Do you know that the Hebrew letters that were fastened to his tombstone were stolen? An Arab stonecutter came and carved them into the stone. I was surprised to see Hebrew letters on it, because he lived his life in Arabic. So why should his death be in Hebrew? Come to think of it, maybe that's why Hebrew is the language of death for me."

"That, as you know, the camera can't catch," he says.

15. Third Person

The night porter was curled up in his armchair. At his feet stretched a pregnant cat, her eyes glowing in the dim light. The porter grumbled with the ill temper of one who is roused from a French dream, but did as he was requested and opened the locked gate. And there was Paris spread out before his eyes at three in the morning, up the Rue de Sèvres to the burbling of the fountain in the wall of the Hôpital Laënnec: an Egyptian man with a plump waist, holding two tipped jugs, and from their corked mouths the water flows in two thin jets. On the back wall of the Hôtel Vaneau, a faded advertisement for Dubonnet: A seated man, in three different poses, successively raises the bottle to his lips forever. Empty streets, and late August in the air.

Uncle Yusef, now lying on his deathbed in the village, would banish all stories at this hour and grant admittance only to dreams. He would protest that he never had enough waking hours to recount the dreams that visited him in his sleep or that stumbled through the veils of his naps. Now he no longer remembers the magic word that would return him to the narrow world. For now he is being gathered unto his dreams. "This is the last time we'll meet," Uncle Yusef said to him when he went to say goodbye, "unless the grace of Our Savior's Holy Mother shall will it." Uncle Yusef loved Her, and perhaps She loved him. And he loved Shlomith, and she loved him, but they had no savior. He stands forever at his window wanting to cry for help, but never remembering the right word, or in what language to say it. When he cared for his father on his deathbed, he wrote her letters. In Hebrew. After he had accompanied his father to his burial in the village and returned to Jerusalem, he discov-

94

ered that the letters had proved to be an absolution of sorts. The husband had discovered the correspondence, and the secret, so terrible in its beauty, was gone, and the world reverted to its former state of "Hebrew, Arabic and Death."

A band of three young people bursts out of one of the alleys up Saint-Germain and blocks his way. The girl, who cannot control the laughter that has overwhelmed her, grabs his sleeve and explains in French what they want. The two boys look on expectantly. He explains to them, in English, that he doesn't know what they are saying and what they want. In vain. The girl wraps her arm about his neck and drags him into a café, followed by the two boys. Cries of joy greet them inside the café. Some people even applaud. His embarrassment begins to melt as he delivers himself into their hands and allows himself to be swept along by their mood. An English-speaker who comes over to their table manages to explain to him, in sentences that mostly get lost in the racket, that for the past hour or so an argument has been going on about the question of whether one human being can act like God or any other Supreme Being, to divert the life path of another. The three who have blocked his way believe that any abstract idea has no existence without its concrete realization; and he is being used to prove the thesis that it is possible to divert the life path of another person.

One evening during his first years in Haifa he went out for a walk in the city. Suddenly a car crammed with a noisy bunch of people pulled up alongside. A girl sitting next to the driver stuck her head out the window, smiled at him and asked in Hebrew, "Want to come to a party with us?" Then she pulled her head back in and the car sped off. He stood there quivering with anger and incomprehension. He had been so happy on his little walk through the little village world he carried in his pockets and in his head. Then all of a sudden this girl, some Marinka, appears, and without asking leave she flings into the air around him promises of a different world on the other side of the fence, as in Bialik's story. Then without even waiting for an answer she disappears as suddenly as she had appeared.

Years later he went into the Bet Ha'am lending library in Jerusalem, looking for the Hebrew translation of Willa Cather's *My Ántonia*. Along comes a redheaded librarian, whom he had never seen before, and stops next to him to return a book to its place on the shelf. Suddenly she turns to him and says, "Maybe you would like to read this book?" She shows him the cover—*The Life of the Bees*, by Maurice Maeterlinck—and he, who has never had any interest in bees and their lives, stands there gazing in wonder at her face. Recognizing that she has trespassed, she tried to retreat, laughing and mumbling an apology, as she returned the book to the shelf and went to her place behind the lending desk. After he found what he was looking for, as a gesture of delight he took *The Life of the Bees* off the shelf and went over to the desk. Though he knew the price of honey, he borrowed the book, for here it was, the party that had been promised.

At five in the morning he asked the girl, with the help of the interpreter, to accompany him this time. Tipsy from wine, the two of them arrived at the river. Lights twinkled in the ripples that softly licked the bridge they stood on. The smell of the water awakens a momentary longing in him. His glance is drawn away from the water and scales the dark wall of a building that resembles a camel kneeling in the darkness. "You must visit Notre Dame," she says to him in English. And he answers her in Arabic that Uncle Yusef would now want them both to go into the church and light candles at the feet of Our Savior's Mother, but that he would do so tomorrow.

Near a green gate to her house in the Rue de Seine she kisses him goodbye, and the two of them go back to being strangers whose solitude can be concealed only by the darkness of the false dawn.

Calmed, he continues on his way. At five in the morning the city begins to awaken. First in hot breaths puffing and rising out of grates in the sidewalks. Then in the garbage trucks pausing by locked gates. Two North African sanitation workers walk along the sidewalk in silence, the sound of their brooms on the steep asphalt trailing after them, and from time to time the hesitant dawn is split by the sound of their scrubbing at last night's dog droppings. He walks by the Sorbonne, which is immersed in gloom, and past the northern wall of the gray Luxembourg Gardens. Going down the Boulevard Raspail, he turns right into the Rue Delambre and lingers by the entrance to number 15, the Hôtel des Écoles.

He imagines Yehoshua Bar-On, Yosh to his friends, opening his eyes and peering at his watch. "Who the hell wants to see me at this hour!" But he relinquishes the nasty idea and continues on his way. Even if he were to present himself at the door to Bar-On's room, the big shot would not recognize him. They had never been introduced, but he knew Bar-On on sight, and once, before Bar-On's famous silence, he had even attended a ceremony at which some literary prize was awarded to this writer whom none of the critics knew how to deal with, nor did they know in which pigeonhole to file him. His hair, still thick and reddish though he was now in his late fifties, aroused jealousy in the hearts of several critics, who had not been so blessed and had to conscript hair from elsewhere to cover their disgrace. Bar-On, who was leaving for Paris before him, had telephoned him and suggested that they meet there, for they would be flying to the United States together. He later would call Bar-On instead of the relatives who had not met him at the airport as promised.

At the corner of the Rue de la Gaîté there is a bakery van. A teenager in a white smock opens its back door and takes out tray. The smell of the fresh croissants catches his senses with a line of silk, and the whole street rises like a wake of fluff following the tray up the Rue de Montparnasse. He walks behind it, and in his imagination a file of smells unfolds like a fan. The smell of the croissants kisses a different fragrance, which he used to breathe in the nape of Shlomith's neck after they had made love. The fragrance that separated the smoothness of the nape from the red hair.

Since breakfast in the airplane, he has not eaten. Now that the lift of the wine has ebbed away, he is lured by the tender wake of the baking. He arrives at the Vaneau just before seven o'clock, and the porter who had grumbled crossly at him in the middle of the night greets him with smiles as he places a saucer of milk before his turquoise cat, who rubs her belly over his bedroom slippers and purrs with the refined sensuousness of a pregnant cat.

16. Nadia

Judging from the pictures, he is an unrefined version of herself. But he does not call, and the day is drawing close to the hour when the scar comes to life and leads her through the paths of the afternoon to another night of restless dreams. She wants to see him, to speak to him, to hear about his mother, of whom she is an exact copy. But not here, not in the presence of the child, not in the presence of her husband. She wants the encounter for herself, face to face, without any other faces around, no matter how much she loves them. Three weeks ago she lost a child, and now she may be finding a relative. That word, too, would make Kamal anxious. She can already sense the nerves churning under his skin, at the prospect of meeting some relative who will force himself between them. His anxiety, which she knows inside and out, makes her feel as if this wished-for meeting had an element of betrayal. That's how it feels to her as she makes a silent effort to dull the ripples of pressure that have begun to spread in the curves of her belly. As if it were an illicit meeting, to which the telephone call that doesn't come adds a nuance of deviousness.

And now little Elias begins to sob again, after a long nap. She picks him up in her arms, despite Kamal's objections, and hugs him. His sobbing diminishes and his flesh, still girded in sleep, soothes her own and warms the chill in her body. She realizes how much she has missed this warmth during the past weeks. This special primal warmth that children have. She gives herself over to it, until the telephone rings.

17. Yehoshua Bar-On

The clerk at the front desk at Des Écoles tells me without lifting his head that my Jew has not yet called. I'd best go up to my room and have a rest—which is one of the things my character wouldn't do. These are the best hours for him to be disturbing the naps of the other characters. Though it would be amusing to hear my Jew talking about the *Schlaf-stunde.* Though perhaps, like the mourner's *Kaddish,* we are now invading territories that are out of bounds. Maybe I'll call it "The Restricted Zone of Language." That's what I don't want him to infiltrate. Because if he does, he might get out of my control. And who knows how an Arab behaves in a restricted zone? But leave it; I've gotten quite far with him today, and it's definitely enough. Now to rest. Even real Jews aren't allowed to disturb my sleep.

The telephone rings.

He did it on purpose. Because why else did he decide to disturb my sleep exactly now, just to tell me that he is going to see his Lebanese relatives and won't be able to meet me today? And why don't I pick him up tomorrow morning and we'll ride out to the airport together. I wouldn't waste my anger at the Lebanese who have brought the battlefield here too, were it not for his suggestion that I pick him up in the morning. This exceptional self-confidence will also have to be taken under consideration. Well, so much for the taken-for-granted Arab, who in earlier circumstances would have gone to the trouble to order a taxi and would have called to tell me that everything is all arranged and that I need do nothing but wait in my room until he comes and has the clerk call me. I knew that a new generation was springing up right under our noses, but it never occurred to me that this generation, with a Sabra-like shrug of the shoulders, had divested itself of the tradition of respecting its elders. Even though I'm not exactly elderly.

But now I'm simmering down, and drowsiness once again weights my eyelids. And if I thought I had finished dealing with my Arabs today, both characters and fellow travelers, I'm likely mistaken. I really and truly would like to know whether there is a single Arab writer who dreams about his Jewish characters while he sleeps.

"Relatives from Lebanon," he says. It's probably another way of saying PLO.

18. Third Person

On his way to the Rue Daguerre he goes past some of the streets he had walked before sunrise. Maybe he had even passed the building without knowing it. In the air was the smell of dying things: the market day that had ended; the withering foliage of late summer; the gasps of the metro through the grates in the sidewalk, puffing into the streets the thick fragrance of Paris, which wavers between *l'air du croissant* and *vent du clochard;* the summer still lingering in the cemetery of Montparnasse; and finally this feeling of the city's outskirts, the feeling that here ends the pale of the special and the famous, and now begins the daily grind, which the tourist guides ignore.

According to the map, in whose folds tiny mouths already gaped, this must be the Rue Daguerre. The smell of shellfish smites his nose. Crustaceans, the likes of which he has never seen in his life, repose on beds of ice. And he muses about what his grandmother would have said about the way they were cooked, if they were, and about the way they tasted, if taste they had, and about people who bought them and even took pleasure in eating them.

The door of the elevator closed behind him on the fifth floor, and he is enveloped in total darkness. He pats the wall behind, searching in vain for the switch. He opens the door of the elevator again, and the shaft of light that springs out of it cleaves the darkness and falls upon the opposite wall, in the middle of which glows what appears to be an illuminated switch. His eyes sweep the darkness in search of some object he can use to prop the door open, but he finds none. He allows the door to slam shut and immediately hears the plummeting of the elevator. He moves in the direction he assumes to be correct and succeeds in putting his finger on the pale button, but the light does not leap on at his touch. The previous shaft of light had sufficed to inform him that he was surrounded by a multitude of corners and turnings, which were swallowed up in the darkness.

On his left he hears the double click of a lock, followed by the sound of Arabic voices, with a Lebanese accent. Two silhouettes stand in the illuminated rectangle of a doorway, and before they close the door he addresses them. "Yes, this is their apartment, on the right. Maybe you could take their child for a few hours and go for a walk?"

He does not understand their laughter and turns to the door on the right. For a moment he thinks that the two Lebanese have tricked him, but finally his hand lands on the doorknob. He slides his other hand along the wall, seeking the bell, and his ear discerns the velvet serenity of a female voice on the other side of the door. He knocks on the door and waits. There is no reply. He knocks again and the door opens and he is dazzled by the light. He freezes to the spot and blinks his eyes, then shelters them with his hand. A man stretches out his hand to him. The silhouette of a woman comes toward him out of the square of light, a child clutching the hem of her dress. He greets them, apologizing for his momentary blindness as he shakes Kamal's hand. Nadia takes on shape and raiment and stands before him, her face a magical mirror that reflects a refined image of his own features. He clasps her outstretched hand between his own and kisses her twice, on this cheek and that, and she kisses him thrice. "It's the Lebanese custom," she says.

Seating him in a chair by the window, she vanishes into the kitchen. Kamal apologizes and explains the misunderstanding about the flight's time of arrival. Gazing at him with tear-filled eyes, the boy draws closer to his father. Their embarrassment recedes when Nadia reappears, bearing a glass of orange juice in her hand. "You are probably thirsty from the road," she says, still holding the juice. She goes to bring a small table, and sets the juice on it and carries the improvised tray over to him. The leg of the table bumps into his leg and the orange juice spills into his lap. There is no end to the words of apology, until she runs to the closet and pulls out a pair of Kamal's trousers. "Go change; it looks like you're both the same size." In the bathroom he puts on Kamal's pants and smiles to himself over the obvious symbolism.

They sink into an exchange of information about the health of the family members on both sides, until the conversation gets to the story of her operation. Kamal, who from the first has sensed the circle of intimacy tightening around them, leaving him on the outside, offers to go down to the cleaner's next door to see what can be done about the wet trousers. The child, sniffing the possibility of an outing, pushes his father toward the door. But Nadia promises him a different outing, to someplace lovely and far away, if he lets his father go by himself, and the boy agrees.

"He's crazy about cemeteries," she says, "and I think you'll also fall in love with the place."

"Where?" he asks.

"Père Lachaise," she says, "the most beautiful place in Paris. What have you seen of the city?"

So he tells her about his nocturnal wanderings in the

company of the anonymous girl and about Notre Dame in the darkness and the trail of the croissants. He sees a twitching in the corner of her mouth, like a charming twinge of jealousy over the fact that it had not fallen to her to lead him on his first night through Paris.

"And how did you part from her?" she teases.

"With three kisses," he says.

She laughs. He realizes that he has not noticed that Kamal has already gone out, and he can't remember if he said goodbye to him. He wonders whether Nadia hadn't asked that he leave the child with her as a meliorating presence against the flowing closeness. And suddenly he is conscious of a spark of hostility toward the little boy. He has no great affection for children in general, but for this particular child he feels a special kind of enmity, as if the boy were a trigger of his consciousness of the mighty outstretched arm that had separated him from his mother's family all his life.

The three of them descend the oily stairs to the Denfert-Rochereau metro station. He takes the small hand in his and presses it in reconciliation as he helps the child hop down the stairs. The train to Nation pulls in, and the passengers bursting out of it separate them. The child runs toward his mother and bumps into a man, who knocks him down and hurries on like everyone else. A short scream winds through the station and Nadia rushes to Elias and picks him up. He joins them now, eaten by remorse for the enmity he had felt toward the boy in the apartment, and he encircles the two of them with his arm even though the platform has already emptied of passengers. The three of them manage to slip into the carriage before the doors close.

19. Yehoshua Bar-On

Apparently I fell asleep. "Tomorrow, when I wake, or think I do, what shall I say of today?" Who said that? Whoever it was, it sounds a bit too large for me. That's what my wife used to say: "You're too big for me." One can remember the words, but how is it possible to remember the tone in which they were said? One launches a sentence into space, say . . . how many years ago? Eight, nine years? Eight years ago. The sentence barrels along in time, accumulating various intonations. I'm no longer certain even if that's exactly how she put it. A sentence that began as defiance and was intended to end up in the same tone, but suddenly swerved from its path and went into a different orbit. Like a comet, which is drawn by gravity and expelled by it. At the second or third word, when the mind already anticipates the rest of the sentence, the defiance turns into irony, which borders on disdain, and from there it's but a short distance to outright jeering, sharp as whetted knives, to the absolutely firm and incisive opinion, from which there is no turning back and no escape or refuge, which now she has declared in a few syllables, the opinion that she confined in her gut all those years. Confined in the small habits of the shared household and the financial obligations and the joint accounts and the eve of the Passover Seder and what café to sit in on Friday afternoons and who to invite for the evening and have you finished reading the supplement? and why do you leave the newspaper open on the floor and every fingerprint on the light switch and her favorite position in bed, the position that brought her to orgasm because she never said "come," and the squeezing of the tube of toothpaste in the middle and the splashing of lather from the brush onto the mirror and her Q-Tips smeared with makeup in the soap dish and the half-empty box of tampons on the shelf in the bathroom even though her period—she never called it the "curse"— had not visited her for years and the sheets she insisted upon having starched even though I suffered from insomnia because of it and the imaginary dust I would brush mechanically from my desk when she came to breathe down my neck and to see what in heaven's name I was doing at the desk if I wasn't writing—and *then* she utters the final sentence like a bolt out of the blue, she hurls the thunderbolt that I'm too big for her.

And now, before the mirror in this bathroom, where I am free to splash lather to my heart's content and don't do it, now I know that we were two congruent bodies right down to the pinkies. I was not too big for her and she was not too big for me. The worn-out *macho* now raising his head from under the shaving lather and the graying hair on the chest, which while it certainly is no longer a he-man's nevertheless retains traces of the glory that was: this *macho* whispers to me that there is also a certain comfort in this sentence—I am too big for her, as she sometimes complained, though not very often, because I hurt her in bed. Is it possible to discover the slightest tinge of this opposite intention in the sentence? I wonder. In other words, almost certainly not.

What drives me crazy, though, is what on earth impelled him to include in his story the scene where he stands behind the ajar bedroom door and spies on his parents fucking— meaning what his mother calls making love. You figure it out. Friends at the café didn't mention this point after the story was published, but who can tell what they were thinking deep down? I would arrest him for that and not for what he was accused of by the police. My Jew, too, while we're on the subject, I'd also put in jail, for his phone call just when I was dropping off, if I knew what he looked like. If I were the chambermaid's husband, I would have divorced her ages ago for the way she places the toilet paper. People can't understand how things like this, no matter how trivial they seem, can drive people out of their minds. I should also jot that down in my notebook: As Amichai would say, there are two kinds of people in the world, the p's who set a roll of toilet paper so that it unwinds outward and the q's who turn it inward toward the wall. I am of the former persuasion. The chambermaid and my wife do not realize that they share a disgraceful habit. I wonder what my Jew's feelings on this matter are, if any. Since he is always in a defensive position, I imagine him in the latter group. Like the Arabic saying we used to quote: "Stick close to the wall and say God help me." It sounds better in Arabic, of course.

20. Third Person

As they approached the main gate the boy ran ahead and waited under the quintet of wooden wreaths carved into the lintel of the hoary entrance. His face radiated joy, the founts of his tears had all dried up. He impatiently hopped from foot to foot with a kind of vitality that didn't know in what direction it would flow next. He opened his arms out to his mother, then dug his heels into the paved walk and refused to budge until Nadia picked him up. He suggested that the boy come into his arms, but the boy insisted on his mother's, despite her excuse that she wasn't feeling very well. "I have a big sore on my tummy," she told him. Elias wanted to see it at once. He said to Nadia, "Our little Saint Thomas will believe it only when he thrusts his finger in your scar." Nadia rolled her dress up a little bit and pulled Elias under it, took his hand through the clothes and guided it up the slope of her belly. A small cry of surprised delight burst from under the dress. A couple came through the gate just then. They stopped and looked on in amusement at the scene. Then the man brought out his camera, but just as he focused it the boy shot out from under the dress and ran up the boulevard.

"Does it still hurt you?" he asked.

"Tell me about Shlomith," she said, "about your scar." As if it were permissible now that the child was out of hearing.

"What do you want to hear?" he asked.

"Tell me about her hair," she said, "about her eyes and her body and what she has inside her body."

He laughs in embarrassment. "Her hair is red," he said, "but now it is all extinguished. The fire has gone out and is no more."

"I will take you to the appropriate tomb," she said.

The sun dropped behind the trees, and a cool gust of wind began to play with the hem of her dress. Her black hair lightly brushed against his face and her fingers hesitantly held his elbow and guided him in the right direction. The child hopped along behind them, plucking flowers from faded wreaths on tombs that still had visitors to lay on the graves of those who had returned to the anonymity of the forgotten. Little stone cherubs knelt and prayed with great fervor. And from time to time a cat drowsing in the late sun opened veiled eyes at them, and then sank back into its memories.

Enchanted, he walked beside her on the winding paths, until they reached what looked to him like the Jewish section. He wondered why she had brought him here.

"Look over there, at the end," she said. And there soared a tomb, a cathedral in miniature, with triangular arches supported by thin columns like a roe's legs. And the two lovers, their hands clasped, lay supine on the tombstone, and all around, a wrought-iron fence protects them in their sleep. The boy asks who lives here. *"Abélard et Héloïse,"* says Nadia.

"What have they done?"

"They loved each other," she answers.

"More than you love me?" he asks.

"And more than you love me," she replies.

"Then bye-bye, Abu Louise," he says.

And what will he tell her about Shlomith?

If she were here she would be walking among the graves, brushing dried leaves off them, straightening the wreaths that had slipped out of place, as if she were walking among the bookcases, straightening what the readers had jumbled. An upside-down book. A shelf that has gotten out of order.

A breach of alphabetical order. But what has all this to do with the dead?

"I already know you," says Nadia. "You won't tell me if I don't show you my scar."

He looks at her as if he can't believe it. She is not even smiling. Now they were by Molière and La Fontaine, higher than the other graves and fenced into their own plot.

"Don't worry; you're too big for me to put you under my dress." Then she takes his hand in hers and lays it gently. "Here, feel."

And fingers, as if they were not his own, brush softly along the raised scar. And with pity his other hand gathers her to him. Suddenly she looks over his shoulder and whispers, "Where is Elias?"

A trumpet blast rends the air. It is six already and some impatient guard has declared it is closing time.

They cannot remember when they have last seen him. The thought that the cemetery was now closed, and all the guards were about to go home, increased their feeling of helplessness.

"I'll go back over the paths we followed," he suggested in a calming voice, which attempted to cover up his sense of guilt.

"No, that's not a good idea," she said. "He always runs ahead of me. I don't think he has had enough time to get to the grave of Victor Noir. It's too far. Or to Proust's tomb either, his favorite. Let's try Allan Kardec."

"Who's he?"

"A spiritualist from the beginning of the last century."

They crossed the Transversale No. 1 and turned north. When they came to the edge of Division 44, they saw a group of women standing around a grave heaped with flowers. One woman stood by the carved bust, with her hands spread on its smooth chest, her eyes closed and her mouth uttering silent words.

Beyond the tomb they saw little Elias in the arms of the

woman they had met at the entrance in the company of the photographer. His head was hidden in her shoulder, and his shoulders were heaving with silent sobs. For a second they stood frozen to the spot, and then Nadia raced over to the woman, who was comforting him in Egyptian Arabic, and took him from her arms. A bloodstain remained on the woman's shoulder. Nadia lifted the boy's head above her shoulder and examined his face. Three parallel scratches along his left cheek were bleeding. But despite the blood and the tears, a splendor touched the boy's face. The photographer told them that he had noticed him through the lens of the camera—even though it was forbidden to photograph near Allan Kardec's grave—lying at the end of the path that leads from the tomb into the midst of the plot. He was lying there frightened, his face smeared with dust and his body trembling like a feather in the wind. And in his hand he was holding an astonishingly beautiful feather, crimson in color. The couple could not explain where the feather had disappeared to.

On their way to the metro station, after they had managed to find the side exit to which the photographer had directed them, she said to him that perhaps it had been a wild cat that had attacked the boy, one of the cats that were part of the scenery at the cemetery. Tomorrow she would light a candle at Notre Dame. He wanted to tell her that on his way to see her he had stopped there and stood at the feet of the statue of Our Savior's Mother in the left aisle of the cathedral and lit a candle and asked Her, even though he had not done so since the day he left the village, to intercede in Her great mercy and allow him to see Uncle Yusef once more. But he did not tell her about that, and instead wondered aloud what had happened to the feather.

"Probably blew away in the wind, as feathers will," she said, and lifted Elias's little head, which was hidden in her shoulder, to check if the bleeding had stopped. And he smiled at her and lovingly ruffled her black hair.

I should stay here, in the place I love, and not set out for an unknown country in the middle of nowhere. Because now the words are beginning to flow and I feel that trembling in my fingertips, the trembling of the end of silence. And *davka* now I have to get up and leave. Get used to a new bed and a new pillow. To dealing with new people. Just when I'm beginning to feel the first strands spinning themselves around me as if by their own accord, here in the Café le Sélect. Across from the snobs of Le Dôme and La Coupole. Here behind the glass facade that doesn't hide a thing from the eyes of the passersby of Montparnasse and the metro passengers of Vavin. Here with an obstinate defiance I sit and write. But not at such a late hour, when the place is thronged with blabbermouths and parasites, and the noise is too much to bear.

Now I realize that the entire evening I have hardly taken my eyes off the profile of the woman at the next table, who is sitting with her husband or lover or friend. Skin like honeyed amber, as the poet says, with a blush of red wine. From time to time she laughs aloud, and her eyes glitter with delight. Her companion swears again that he didn't want to tell them because no one would have believed him. Yes, he knows that there are only cats in Père Lachaise, but what he saw through the lens of his camera when he noticed the boy lying on the ground was not a cat but a rooster with a splendid crimson tail, strutting with regal steps away from the child.

Maybe there's a subject here. Just maybe.

PART THREE
THE TALE CONTINUED

Taxi, taxi, take me for free—
Had not the Welfare saved one in three
They'd all be dead, the refugees.
Taxi, taxi, take me for free.

> Palestinian refugee song

CHAPTER 6

I see myself at the entrance to the olive press. I can smell the olive husks from the distance of many years. It is a thick smell that warmly embraces your senses and then withdraws when a breeze blows touched with the edge of autumn. I stand there while the sweating horse plods in timeless circles around the stone press beam, which crushes and squeezes the olives as its shaft is pulled around the upright axle set into the hole in the center of the understone. The mashed olives rise in a great tide and threaten to over-flow the stone banks, until the scoop comes along and re-strains their spill. The olive press is so small that it seems as if the circular motion of the horse is what holds up the walls, preventing them from tumbling down around the axle of the press beam. As I stand in the entrance I hold in my hand a crisp loaf baked moments ago on the tin-domed oven a few houses away. I watch the shadow of the horse cast by the weak lantern on the walls and on the heaps of olive husks, and my soul goes out to my father, whose hands now grasp the handle of the press and carefully lower the iron plate that squeezes the oil through the groaning sieves, set around the gleaming upright axle of the press. The oil then flows into the sump, from which I can take a bit of oil to dip my bread into.

Abu Shacker, the proprietor of the olive press, stands beside me. His gnarled hand, saturated with oil, prods me to cross the path of the horse, and when he senses my hesitation he ruffles my hair. The skin of his hand, rough as olive husks, scrapes like a file down the nape of my neck. I try to catch my father's eye, in a muteness of embarrassment, but he, at the distance of many years, is absorbed body and soul in the craft of squeezing. The golden stream of oil glows in the lantern light, and I, gazing at it, attempt to get free of the hand at the nape of my neck. The rustle of the crispy bread I am eating fresh from the tin-domed oven distracts Abu Shacker to another realm of pleasure, and he breaks off a handful of the loaf and brings the crustiness to his mouth. I throw a last glance at the shadow of the horse plodding around the walls, at my father standing outside the circle, and escape into the night, cheeks burning. I throw the rest of the loaf into the heaps of olive husks and wipe my tears with a shrug of my sleeve.

Abu Shacker is the man who had brought to the village late in October 1948 the news of the advance of the Jaish El-Yahud, the Jewish Army. The Jaish El-Inqad, Kaukji's rescuing army, several hundred of whose soldiers had taken up positions on the slopes of the western hill of the village during the months which had preceded that October, was now retreating along the path that linked the eastern outskirts of the village to the Northern Road. The path, which eventually would be called Khat El-Hazeemeh, that is, Retreater's Way, was built by the sweat of the brows of many men from the nearby villages, who were forced to volunteer. It was intended for the coming of the Arab armies, wreathed in victory, on the day of the liberation of the homeland from the thieving Zionists.

This same way of Victory and of Retreat twisted through the eastern slopes of Tal Hlal, touched a valley also named after the same tribe and wound along the edge of the terrace called Khallet Zeinab, in memory of the woman whose life and death had inflamed the imaginations of the Galileans at the turn of the century. Uncle Yusef used to recount how the Hlal tribesmen, returning from their conquests to their homeland in the Arabian peninsula in the early days of history, had passed by the village. And as they were exhausted from their conquests and the view was pleasing to their travel-weary eyes, they pitched their tents here at this place for a few days of rest. When the valley was covered in a colorful encampment decked with the banners of victory fluttering in the Galilean breeze like the smoke rising from the campfires, the glorious heroes unstrapped their Yemenite swords and left them, gleaming and streaked with blood, in the dimness of their tents, and went out to the border of the encampment to shake the dust of the journey from their raiment and their boots. So great was the number of the horsemen of the tribe of Hlal that before long the dust that was shaken from the boots of the warriors, the dust and the seeds of the legends hidden within it, made a high pile of earth rise up in the shape of a hill. And even before the tribe set off on its way once more, the hill became green, covered with wonderful foliage, enchanted grasses, bushes of astounding bloom and wondrously delicate trees, with birds dwelling amongst their tender branches, chirping songs of longing for distant lands and laying their eggs in the nests that grew with the trees. And the villagers, who were not accustomed to such happenings, raised their eyebrows at the sight of the nesting birds and decided to bestow the name Hlal not only on the *tal* but also on the valley where the warriors had encamped, and they called it Marj Hlal.

As for Zeinab, after whom the *khalleh* was named, her story is utterly different from that of the warriors, though as time passed, the villagers tended to combine her chronicle with that of the tribe of Hlal, because of their being neighbors and because of the well-known village tendency to enfold in one and the same garment a tribe that created a legend with the dust of its boots and a woman who created one with her underpants.

At the turn of the century, Zeinab was the most beautiful woman in the Galilee. Folk poets spent many long nights rhyming songs in her praise. Men from all over the Galilee made their way up to Sa'sa', the village of her birth, to behold if only for a moment her rare beauty. But the men of her village did not look kindly upon the beautiful woman, and they began to spin the web of her death. First they spread rumors about the fiery lust between her legs and said that there was no man alive who could satisfy her appetite. Then they decided to prohibit her from walking through the greening fields lest the crop wither from the rut of her lust. Then they said that its shame would pass from their village only if her passion was extinguished. Thus the elders gathered one night to consider how to put an end to the scandal. At dawn several young men of the village burst into Zeinab's house, dragged her from the bed of her husband and brought her to the outskirts of the village. There they bound her hands and her feet, lifted the hem of her dress and poured gunpowder into her underpants, inserted a wick in her private parts, lit it and ran for their lives. And to this day the place is called Khallet Zeinab.

The Way of Victory, which became the Retreater's Way, meandered through these memories of the past, and the footprints of the defeated imprinted themselves on the same earth that had borne the footprints of the Hlal warriors. Now, late in October 1948, it bears the footprints of Abu Shacker, upon his arrival at the village to warn the inhabitants of the soldiers of the Jews who were on their way to conquer it.

Two weeks earlier Israeli planes had dropped bombs on Tarsheeha, just to the south of Fassuta, to which Al-Asbah's relatives had fled from their conquered village of Ja'ooneh. It was the season of the olive pressing, but it had been a bad year, said the olive growers. For in a bad year the olive withdraws into itself and does not attend to the sticks of the beaters and the hands of the harvesters. Also, that year the olive harvesters would stay home in fear of the bombs that blurred the horizon with spirals of smoke. The inhabitants of Fassuta withdrew into their houses, or sought shelter in the church or in the caves scattered around the village. They had no fear—or hope—of encountering the legendary Ar-Rasad guarding the entrance to one of the caves, for the figure of Ar-Rasad had vanished from their memory in those days. The only roosters that were seen in the village walked about in a fearful state and would flee for their lives at the sound of the dull explosions that shook the ground under their claws, rushing to their coops to assuage their alarm by ruffling the feathers of the hens, who clucked raucously as if they, too, could sense the danger in the air.

The rooster belonging to my uncle's wife would strut around the inner courtyard with lordly deliberation, taking care not to be surprised on the nearby dunghill by the onset of a bombing raid. The turquoise cat would observe him from the place where she lolled, following with eyes that saw what was coming, and knowing that the end, when it came, would take no account of cautionary strutting, knowing that Death, when it visits Allah's creatures, has no care in its black heart for the grief of widowed hens.

And so it came to pass that in the latter half of October my uncle's wife's rooster took leave of his senses in the face of the accumulating tension. With cockscomb erect and wattles atremble, he attacked the scrawny donkey who stood tied in the courtyard sunk in his own worries and suffering the pangs of hunger. For half a year he had not enjoyed a meal of barley because of the lean harvest, and here comes this deranged rooster and takes out upon him the anger with which the rooster had been stricken at the moment of losing his mind. He flings out his feathers, spreads his wings and pecks the donkey's nape, and out of hazy and barleyless self-respect the latter shakes the rooster off his back and kicks him with his rear legs. The turquoise cat looks on indifferently as the rooster plunges and falls nearby, after having banged into the wall behind her, and she knows that she will get his head.

My uncle's wife, who came outside at the sound of the commotion, stood there at a loss, not knowing what to do first, whether to wring the rooster's neck or to beat the donkey.

The turquoise cat watched from the place where she lolled and saw my uncle's wife raining blows upon the scrawny donkey, in a sort of rehearsal of what was to come to pass in the near future. Then she wrung the rooster's neck and threw the head to the cat. And the cat retires to her corner in the nether regions of the courtyard, with her teeth sunk into the impetuous cockscomb. And the whole time the line of refugees from Tarsheeha wound along the Way of the Retreater, toward the Lebanese border.

As the Jews' army was making its way along the road winding up to Deir El-Kasi, Abu Shacker was looting its houses. The inhabitants of Deir El-Kasi had not waited for the convoy to arrive. They were already across the border. And Abu Shacker, who had felt their outstretched arm upon his back in the days of the Arab Rebellion, now entered the home of Mahmood El-Ibraheem, who had been the regional commander in the days of the rebellion. The gate to the courtyard was open, as if the inhabitants of the house had just stepped out for a moment to visit a neighbor. Abu Shacker entered through the gate and shut it behind him as if he were trying to preserve, if only for a moment, the vanishing past, and he stood in the courtyard, in the very spot where he had stood ten years before.

Except that then he was beaten and injured and degraded, and now he straightens his back and inhales deeply all the smells of the house, which formerly swept through his soul transmitting fear and trembling. Now everything is

118

wide open and abandoned and given unto his hand like ripe fruit. A loose donkey ambles along the path outside the gate, and his sudden bray frightens the hens pecking at the stray barley that has fallen from some unraveled sack during the commotion of the flight. He moves closer to the front door, left ajar, and pushes it gently, and with two steps is inside the house of the man who imposed his will upon the inhabitants of the region during the days of the rebellion. He sits down upon a stool and begins to compose in his head a list of all the things he wants to take.

The *smandra* stood with its door gaping open, and within it was a stack of mattresses, of which the uppermost had been slightly displaced by a hesitant hand that had been about to take along a mattress or two but reconsidered. On the opposite wall hung a picture of Haj Ameen, the *mufti* of Jerusalem, and above it gleamed the outline of a scimitar stamped onto the dull and faded wall with the patience of years, and now exposed to the disappointed gaze of Abu Shacker, this being the sword that he had come here for, with the alacrity of one who seeks vengeance. And then he saw a frayed sack of olives standing in the corner of the kitchen. Trailing out of its bulging belly were green olives, which had spilled onto the kitchen floor, their thin glistening skin seeming to be on the point of exploding from the pressure of the oil held within. This sight caused the tears held within Abu Shacker to flow down his cheeks and wet the stubble on his cheeks. He went back to the bench in the hall and plopped down on it and sobbed like the smallest of his children. The frayed sack of olives made tangible what he himself could expect within just a few hours, for his fate and the fate of Mahmood El-Ibraheem were the same. Then he wiped the tears with a tug of his sleeve, laid the sack in which he had collected booty from the other houses down on the floor, rose and went out into the courtyard. The hens were still pecking at the earth.

This was the moment when he saw the three jeeps and

a squad of soldiers winding their way along the road on the slope of the wadi. He stood at the gate, his head empty, his back to the indifferent flock of hens. A black tomcat crossed the path next to him, and instinctively he bunched his fingers together and crossed himself. He immediately regretted having taken the Savior's name in vain by asking him to bestow his grace upon him in the face of a black cat, and then the fury guttering within him flared up again, because he had been wasting his time on such thoughts when the convoy of soldiers was coming closer and closer to him from the bottom of the wadi. Before he had managed to weigh his next moves, he turned and went back into the house, dumped out the contents of the sack that had been lying on the floor, folded it hastily and stuck it under his arm, rushed out the gate and fled for his life back to the village.

It was Saturday, October 30, 1948.

Except for Abu Shacker, all the men of the village had left at dawn for the fields surrounding the village, in search of places to hide until the fury of the conquerer had passed. The women and the children took refuge in the shadow of Elijah the Prophet, the patron saint the church was named after, and wound their voices in supplication to the Virgin Mary to preserve her faithful from the bitter cup of wandering. The old men, who were too frail to run and hide in the fields but too young to sit at home awaiting the judgments of blind Fate and too cynical to pray with the women, sat in the priest's parlor, the priest who was the predecessor of the one with the parasol, upon whom the schoolboys impressed as actors would take revenge the evening before the production of the play *Merciful Is He in Whose Hands Lies the Power*, about six years after these things had happened.

Abu Shacker opened the door of the priest's parlor without knocking and stood in the middle of the front room, with the jute sack still under his arm. "What's happening?"

asked my uncle. "Couldn't be worse," said Abu Shacker. "They're on their way."

The priest rose. After him the rest of the men. An ox goad, which had been prepared in advance, was taken up by my uncle, who walked at the head of the delegation to the eastern outskirts of the village. And when they got to Al-Mahafer my uncle took his white *kufiya* off his head and stuck the cloth onto the tip of the ox goad, and handed the flag of surrender to the priest.

A burst of bullets was heard from the other side of the hill, behind which the road curved out and became visible to them. The priest raised the ox goad, and the *kufiya* fluttered in the wind, as *kufiyas* do. Major Nimr, who sat in the vehicle at the head of the convoy, saw it and ordered that a second burst be shot into the air. He was a Jew from this region, and knew these village elders. He also knew that there would be no resistance, and that the capitulation would be offered by a priest in black, hoisting a white *kufiya*. He had already seen the delegation in his mind's eye when the convoy had gone past Tal Hlal. The inhabitants of Deir El-Kasi who were active members of the Jaish El-Inqad of Kaukji had already departed on the Retreater's Way, and the new way of the Jaish El-Yahud would reach its end in Fassuta before the end of the Jewish Sabbath.

As Major Nimr stepped down from his vehicle and his feet touched the ground of Al-Mahafer, the delegation approached him, and the priest began to deliberate inwardly about what he would do with the ox goad and into whose hands it would be most seemly for him to deliver it. My uncle swiftly snatched the *kufiya* off the ox goad, thinking about his wife's grumbling when she would see the hole that had been made in it by the prod. An old man standing next to him observed the cloud of anxiety spreading over his face and said, "There's no choice; that's the price of defeat." Nearby, the men who had fled to the fields in the morning began to gather, as the rumor reached them that the capitulation had proceeded peacefully. And thus they stood, the soldiers of the Jaish El-Yahud on the one side and the inhabitants of Fassuta on the other, until from somewhere a *mijwez* was whipped out and to its strains the men who had come back from the fields arranged themselves in a semicircle and their feet responded as if of their own accord to the rhythm of the melody. They broke into the "Dabkeh Shamaliyeh," a wild Galilean *dabkeh,* which had in it something of the joy of those who had been passed over by a fatal decree, and something of the pleasure of submission by the weak, and something of fawning before the stranger, and something of the canniness of the villager who draws the most unexpected weapon at the most unexpected moment. It also had in it just plain capriciousness and frivolity. One way or the other, by the time the feet tired of the dance and the capriciousness of the defeated had cooled down, all those present at the ceremony were covered with a thin white layer of dust, and as is the way of all dust, it did not distinguish between the conquering soldier and the conquered villager. After which the official part of the ceremony began, and the celebrants were gently commanded to hand over to the army any weapons in their possession, including the ones concealed in the haystacks and the ones stashed in the fields.

Em Shacker came home and saw that the dough she had kneaded hastily that morning had risen and was threatening to overflow the basin. She hurriedly made balls of the dough, laid the tin dome on the hearth in the courtyard, spread out a length of cloth called the *mayzer* at her feet, and on it she laid the *tabliyeh,* which is the low table upon which the balls of dough are flattened. Then she took the patty of dough and threw it from hand to hand in a circular motion until it was as thin as a round tablecloth, and her practiced hand spread it out on the cushionlike *karah* to flip it onto the tin dome of the oven.

Soon the air was filled with the fragrance of the crisp bread torn by Abu Shacker's hand and dunked in a saucer of oil, which does not reveal to the man who is dipping his bread what will happen to him on the morrow.

The next day, after a hurried Sunday Mass, Abu Shacker will stand with all the other men of the village in front of the *mukhtar*'s house, at the place called Al-Balat, which is an outcropping of white rock, like a sort of foundation stone. Two buses will be waiting there, intended for an unknown destination. The commander will sit on the porch of the *mukhtar*'s house and supervise the proceedings. About two dozen men will be selected by the commander and ordered to board the buses. Abu Shacker will be the last of those selected. The rumors that have made their way to the village about the conduct of the Jaish El-Yahud leave little room for doubt as to their fate.

Like everyone else, the tobacco growers were worried that year. The clusters of threaded leaves went on dangling from the ceilings of the houses, and hope dwindled in the growers' hearts. Mr. Eli Faraji, the representative of Karaman Ltd., said that he would come at the beginning of October, but four weeks went by, and the farmers began to wonder whether they themselves would have to smoke their excellent crop of tobacco. Ordinarily my uncle would smuggle the tobacco to the villages of southern Lebanon and exchange it for rattling crates of bottles of Arak Zahlawi—a high for a high, as it were—and he would distribute them in the villages of southern Palestine. But that year the times were out of joint, and you couldn't cross the Northern Road, so those who were circumspect waited patiently for the evil to pass and for life to return to its established routine, since haste is the devil's work. That was precisely how Mr. Eli Faraji of Karaman Ltd. felt too, which is why he was hanging back that year. Most probably he was waiting for the village to empty itself of its inhabitants, and then he would come to determine the fate of the leaves. So thought Abu Shacker as he climbed onto the bus.

The officer started his vehicle and led the two buses away. Those who remained at Al-Balat gazed with wet eyes after the passengers in the buses as they disappeared in clouds of dust. My uncle left the shocked group and took himself to the outskirts of the village, to the place where he had stood the previous day, his punctured *kufiya* again bound to his head.

The departing buses approached the "church field," the spot where the road went round behind the hill and disappeared from the eye of the beholder. A small vehicle could be seen waiting there, and its driver stood next to it, his figure radiating the confidence of a man accustomed to authority. He waited for the approaching convoy, as though those who led it would help him fix whatever was wrong with his car, a blue '47 Morris. The officer gave the order to halt the convoy, descended from his vehicle and approached the man.

"Mr. Faraji," said the officer, "what are you doing here at a time like this?"

Mr. Faraji, after the fashion of the Jews, replied to the question with a question: "And what are you doing here at a time like this?"

The officer smiled, with some embarrassment. "Following orders," he said.

Mr. Faraji looked in the first of the buses. Its passengers were familiar to him, he having more than once sat with them over a demitasse of coffee in their homes. Suddenly he realized that the whole time, his hand had been poised protectively over the contents of the inner pocket of the beautifully tailored jacket upon which grains of dust were now beginning to settle. With an instinctive gesture he dusted off his left shoulder, and then realized how inappropriate this gesture was for such an occasion.

He had known the officer since the latter was a little boy,

and now as he stood before him he felt as if all the years that had passed since then had never been, and that two opposite poles were coming together right at that moment, before his very eyes. The little boy he had known was leading a convoy of men doomed to wander. He wrapped his arm around the officer's shoulder with the familiarity of an old acquaintance, and the two of them disappeared behind the hill, at the edge of the "church field." Hopes that had withered like the threaded leaves that were awaiting Mr. Faraji began to sprout again, like the soft shoots of tobacco at the beginning of spring. The officer returned to his vehicle, and the soldier who sat next to him went over to the passengers on the buses and ordered them to return to their homes.

"God strikes with one hand and protects with the other," murmured the elders, and nodded their heads. They did not know that a second blow was to fall.

The very next day, Monday, November 1, all the men were ordered to gather at Al-Mahafer, where they had danced the *dabkeh* of surrender. All the women crowded into the store that belonged to Uncle Nimr, my grandmother's brother. Upon the orders of the army, the doors to the houses were left open. The men were ordered to stand in rows. Then a man whose head was covered with a burlap sack walked down the rows and examined the men through two holes in the sack. The first time, he went along all the rows without pausing near anyone. The second time, he stopped by Abu Shacker and directed his gaze at him from behind the burlap mask. Abu Shacker's heart creaked in his chest like the iron plate of his olive press, which squeezed the oil from the folds of the sieves, and sweat dripped from the folds of his forehead and burned his eyes.

He recognizes those eyes staring at him—he could identify them anywhere. But are his senses playing tricks on him—is this not a hallucination after sleepless nights? Is it possible that the man peering at him through the holes is Mahmood El-Ibraheem himself, the man who had been the regional commander in the days of the rebellion twelve years before and was now one of the commanders of Kaukji's Jaish El-Inqad, which had taken the Retreater's Way only a few days ago? He had been sure that these awful times would leave him unscathed, and that he would no longer be subject to the torments of Mahmood El-Ibraheem and his men. But now, as in a nightmare, this famous rebel and military commander turns his coat like a burlap sack and hands over to the Jaish El-Yahud people who he indicates have collaborated with Kaukji's army. But why should Mahmood El-Ibraheem, if indeed it was him, pause by Abu Shacker, who has given support neither to the Arab Rebellion nor to the rescuing army? The seconds stretch out, and his nerves stretch, and his knees shake more than they ever have in his entire life. And then the burlap head continued on his way, and passing quickly through the rows, he went over to the officer and shook his head.

Once the man and the soldiers had climbed into their vehicles and departed for their headquarters in Deir El-Kasi, the village that would eventually be called Elkosh, the men who had been lined up crowded around Abu Shacker. They rejoiced with him in his deliverance when he seemed so close to the edge. But even more, they wanted to know why the burlap head had apparently chosen him, of all Allah's creatures, and afterward changed his mind. What had Abu Shacker done in secret? What had he wrought on the Army of the Jews?

But soon they began to shake their heads in sorrow and pity, for this was the man who ten years earlier had been cruelly beaten by the rebels, who suspected him of having collaborated with the British. And ever since then he had been peculiar and was said to have visions. For now he is swearing by all he holds dear that the man behind the burlap is none other than Mahmood El-Ibraheem, for whose head in a burlap bag both the British and the Jews had offered substantial rewards. Even though the villagers have no particular affection for this Al-Ibraheem and have suffered at his hands, there is nevertheless a limit to fantasy—to accuse him of collaborating with the Jews he hated! "There is no way, Abu Shacker." But Abu Shacker insists.

That night he cannot sleep. In the early hours he slips away from his house to the olive press, and from its hiding place in the shaft of the grindstone he withdraws his famous pistol, which he would tie around his waist with a rope, so that the pistol was known in the village as *fard abu-maraseh,* the roped pistol.

At daybreak, rumors fluttered their wings noisily through the village. There were those who said that a patrol of Jewish soldiers had heard a shot from the direction of the abandoned house of Mahmood El-Ibraheem in Deir El-Kasi. When they rushed there they saw Abu Shacker standing at the gate with his pistol in his hand, and hanging on the iron pole in the front of the house was the body of Mahmood El-Ibraheem, swinging back and forth. On his chest rustled a sheet of paper, upon which was written: "Thus Shall Be Done to Traitors." But there were those who said that the Jews suspected Abu Shacker of having executed Mahmood El-Ibraheem for collaborating with them. But there were also those who said that it was the Jews who had hanged him, once they had gotten what they wanted from him.

Abu Shacker returned to the village after being held for a week. His lips were sealed like the mouth of the cave that the *djinnis* had sealed and put under the guard of Ar-Rasad. After the fashion of village rumors, those about Abu Shacker soon flew away. But the villagers went on turning over the chronicle of the day of the burlap head, for they had come home to find that the soldiers had looted whatever came to hand. "That's the price of remaining in our homes," said the elders. They didn't know that another day of reckoning was yet to come.

On Monday, November 15, my mother stood in the kitchen, preparing stuffed tripe. It was the custom of our family to have stuffed tripe for dinner on Mondays if we had been lucky enough to acquire the entrails of a goat that had been slaughtered the previous day at the butcher's. If it had not been for the tripe, it is doubtful that my mother would have remembered that day and its events.

Grandmother Alia was, at that moment, on her way to the home of Aunt Jaleeleh, in the center of the village, and she'd just walked past my father's cobbler shop, bent her head, wrapped in its black scarf, made blinders of her hands, the better to see in through the windowpane, greeted my father, who was deep in his work, and continued on her way.

Aunt Jaleeleh stood in the doorway to her house, her apron dangling from her hand and her mouth open wide in shock. She had just been told of the rumor that the ax had fallen and that the commander stationed in Deir El-Kasi had ordered that all the inhabitants of Fassuta must abandon their village on that day before sunset.

Grandmother Alia covered her face with the edge of her head scarf and turned on her heels without a word and went to tell my father. As they hurried through the courtyard of our house, the starving donkey threw a weary bray at them, knowing that it wasn't from them that his next meal would come. When my father reached the kitchen door, he told my mother to leave the tripe. The turquoise cat began to rub against his legs, and he took the tripe from the table and threw it all to the cat, silencing my mother's protests as he explained to her what the situation was. The seams of the blanket and pillow covers were quickly opened and stuffed with whatever we could carry on the roads. My father took down the jar that was strictly reserved for very important guests at our house, the jar in which white balls of *labaneh* cheese were preserved in the purest olive oil. Then he pulled a pile of wafer-thin bread from under the straw lid of a copper basin and spread the *labaneh* over each piece and then rolled it in the shape of a scepter—*"labaneh* brides" for the road.

Suddenly all eyes turned upon the gaunt donkey who stood there patiently, as donkeys do, in the courtyard of the house. For he was now to lead the refugees to a safe haven and carry their worldly goods. From its hiding place in the stable, my uncle's wife took a full measure of barley, which had been put away for an emergency like this one, brought out the dough basin, laid it before the donkey and poured the barley into it. With a fullhearted curse, she commanded the starving donkey, who for long months had not tasted barley, to eat to his heart's content. The donkey stared as if he couldn't believe his eyes, flared his nostrils and prepared for a miraculous feast. The turquoise cat paused a moment in the relishing of her tripe, looked alternately at my uncle's wife and at the donkey, and with feline wisdom went back to her own last supper.

The village priest meanwhile had gone to appear before the commander in Deir El-Kasi, to speak to his heart and persuade him to rescind the terrible decree. When he returned, the *mukhtar,* who was waiting for him at the outskirts of the village, was shocked by the exorbitance of the ransom demanded—forty pounds. In the village at that time there were only the twenty pounds that had been in the inside pocket of the jacket of the tobacco buyer, Eli Faraji. And even if you had searched with an oil lamp and a wick, as the villagers say, you wouldn't have found more than perhaps a few additional pounds. But these had been hidden inside pillows, for even worse occasions than this, when all other alternatives might be sealed off, and the owners of these pounds would rather wander to the ends of the earth than hand them over to a rapacious officer. Therefore they set out for the village of Rmeish on the other side of the border to hire camels for the journey.

Again the priest went forth and came before the commander. He laid an envelope on the table and said to him, "That's all there is." The heart of the commander was sufficiently softened by the twenty pounds that he did not banish the inhabitants from their village. A message was sent to those in Rmeish that the decree was annulled. The mattresses and the pillows and the quilts were returned to their covers.

But by the time the message reached my uncle's wife it was too late. She ran to the basin to rescue what was left of the precious barley. The basin gleamed in the twilight, the donkey still snuffling at the bottom in case a grain or two remained. My uncle's wife went to the stable and took a stick. She went back to the voracious donkey and began to beat him, first with blows of rage because the family's supply of barley was gone, then with blows of anger at herself, for having rushed to pay the beast for work he hadn't done, and finally with blows of stifled sobbing because of the Arabs and the Jews and the rebels and the soldiers and the wars and the refugees and pitiless Fate and poverty and her bellyful of it all, and especially because she wanted to stop beating him and she couldn't.

And then winter came, a complete surprise, as if waiting for the war to pass over our village and for peace and quiet to return to our homes before it sent down upon us its own lightning and thunder. But the world did not return to its previous state, for the order of things was disturbed. The bird that my uncle called the *tatamus,* who would come to the village from the cold fields and seek out warm nooks in the walls of the houses, so that my uncle would know that the snow was on its way—this time the *tatamus* came to the village even though the cold edge of approaching snow was not yet in the air. The fireflies whose twinkling lit up the summer nights invaded the village out of season and gathered at the entrance to Abu Shacker's olive press, to which were brought the sacks of olives for the pressing that had been delayed.

Abu Shacker, who was still keeping his mouth shut, watches the fireflies and turns over his memories of the events of that night in Mahmood El-Ibraheem's house. Again and again he sees himself drawing his pistol and firing at the cigarette flashing in the darkness, and by the time he realizes that it is nothing but a firefly, the soldiers of the Jaish El-Yahud have grabbed him and are taking him to their commander. And behind him, under the cover of darkness, swings the body that just a moment before kicked away the stool and now flutters with the last gasps of one who could not bear the humiliation of exile and the shame of wandering.

The face floats up into the pale light of a lone firefly and sinks down again into darkness.

PART FOUR

THE TELLER: Mayflower I

Still, writers are not terribly reliable as witnesses for either the defense or the prosecution. They are also not to be relied upon as lovers. They lack patience. They seem to have certain difficulty in taking pleasure from what they are doing. Like chess players, they are inwardly preparing themselves for the inevitable end game.

Walter Abish, *How German Is It*

Iowa City, September 2

I left my room at the Hôtel Vaneau only to visit Père Lachaise. Nadia and her husband, as I later found out, hadn't
come to the airport because she had been hospitalized that
day for a suspected ectopic pregnancy, and she underwent
surgery the following day while I prowled the paved walks
of Père Lachaise. In my search for Proust's tomb, I arrived
at Division 85, as it was marked in the map of the cemetery
given to me by the guard at the gate. Skirting the colum-
barium, I found myself near what at first glance looked like
a small Muslim cemetery, surrounded by a green hedge.
Two layers of black marble, the work of Lecreux Frères,
formed the tombstone of one Mahmoud Al-Hamshari, a
PLO representative, who—according to the gilded French
engraved on the marble—was born in the village of Em
Khaled the twenty-ninth of August, 1939, and died in Paris
on the ninth of January, 1973. A verse from the Koran at the
head of the tombstone promised, in elevated Arabic, eternal
life in the world to come to those who died for their country.
Beyond the hedge, ten graves to the west, Marcel Proust lay
buried. It must have been the French sense of humor that
granted both of them, the man of the lost country and the

135

man of the *temps perdu,* nearly identical graves: Lerendu Cie. had bestowed upon Proust, about fifty years before the death of Al-Hamshari, two simple layers of shining black marble. Fifty years separate the two lost times, the two darknesses. But both are equally lost under the flowers of remembrance.

I stood there by the green hedge and thought about Yehoshua Bar-On, whom I had called from a café not far from the main gate of the cemetery. I had apparently disturbed his *Schlafstunde.* I thought about Shlomith, and about the two of us, as possible protagonists in a story by Bar-On. Two lost characters whose fate, on paper and otherwise, is in his hands, at the mercy of his whims. But he will never put himself at my mercy, because he is off limits for me, beyond the limits of my life and my writing. A restricted zone of sorts. Then I imagined a parting from Shlomith, and I said to myself, Well, everything has come to the end that was destined by its beginning, and nothing but a squeezed honeycomb separates the beginning from the end. And under the black marble lay the two lost men, each in the darkness of his own tomb, a Jew of Time and an Arab of Place. And apart from the almost matched graves and the avenue of trees reflected in the smoothness of the black marble, they appeared to share nothing at all.

The next day, on the way to the airport, I picked up Bar-On at Des Écoles, and we shared the cost of the taxi. Last night, he told me, he had come to the conclusion that he just couldn't cope with being all by himself for several months in a strange environment, or deal with new people, new loneliness. He likes to write surrounded by his books, sitting at his antique desk, by the light of the antique lamp he had bought, together with the desk, in the flea market in Jaffa, and with his favorite paintings on the four walls. At teatime his wife sinks into the armchair on the other side of the desk and listens to what he wrote the night before. As I gazed out the window at the streets of Paris flooded with light, a dubious envy washed over me. Later, on the plane to Chicago, he confided to me the real reason that, despite it all, he was traveling to a godforsaken town in the Midwest.

"I'm writing a new novel. With an educated Arab as its hero," he told me. "I don't think I'll ever have this kind of opportunity again—to be under the same roof with a person like that in ideal conditions of isolation."

I regarded him with astonishment and said, "We have one little problem. I don't think of myself as what you people call 'an educated Arab.' I'm just another 'intellectual,' as you call your educated Jews."

He laughed and puffed at his extinguished pipe.

"In addition to which," I said, "I hope you won't be breathing down my neck the whole four months."

He immediately began to apologize that he hadn't expressed himself properly. "All I want is to get to know you from up close," he said, "while at the same time preserving a certain amount of aesthetic distance between us, for the sake of objectivity, you know."

"I shall try my best not to disappoint you."

Then he fell asleep.

I thought, Maybe before he wakes up I'll prepare an imaginary autobiography for him, a tale convincing enough to shield me from his critical eye. And when he opened his eyes and asked me why I was looking depressed, although in truth I was in high spirits, I said maybe I would let him use some of my yarn to spin his tale.

I fabricated for him a parting from Shlomith, upon which I embroidered several heartrending details. He whipped out his notebook and began to chronicle my love for the redheaded wife of an army officer, who was in the throes of a legal battle with him over the fate of their son. And as the story grew longer and more intricate, I became more and more aware of the delights of dissembling, the joy granted those who take the liberty to enchant with their imaginary lives. And Bar-On, pleased with the clear under-standing we had reached of our respective roles, said he hoped we would enjoy this experience equally. While all this was going on, I was thinking about Proust and Al-Hamshari, and about how livid the man sitting next to me would be if he knew what odd twinnings and pairings were running through my mind.

As for me, I doubt that I would have gotten to Iowa City were it not for Willa Cather's *My Ántonia,* the first novel I ever read, which I found in our olive-green bookcase, em-bedded in the thick wall. This was a hefty volume, in a soft turquoise cover, decorated with a black-and-white drawing of a boy and a girl, their backs to the reader, facing what was supposed to be an endless ocean of red grass on the prairies of Nebraska. It was in an Arabic translation, whose opening I used to know by heart:

> Last summer in a season of intense heat, Jim Burden and I happened to be crossing Iowa on the same train. He and I are old friends, we grew up together in the same Nebraska town, and we had a great deal to say to each other. While the train flashed through never-ending miles of ripe wheat, by country towns and bright-flowered pastures and oak groves wilting in the sun . . . During that burning day when we were crossing Iowa, our talk kept returning to a central figure, a Bohemian girl whom we had both known long ago. More than any other person we remembered, this girl seemed to mean to us the country, the conditions, the whole adventure of our child-hood. . . . "From time to time I've been writing down what I remember about Ántonia," he told me. . . . When I told him that I would like to read his account of her he said I should certainly see it—if it were ever finished.
>
> Months afterward, Jim called at my apartment one stormy winter afternoon, carrying a legal portfolio. He brought it into the sitting room with him and said, as he stood warming his hands, "Here is the thing about Ántonia. . . . I suppose it hasn't any form. It hasn't any title, either." He went into the next room, sat down at my desk and wrote across the face of the

portfolio the word "Ántonia." He frowned at this a moment, then prefixed another word, making it "My Ántonia." That seemed to satisfy him.

In Chicago we were wait-listed for the flight to Cedar Rapids, north of Iowa City. We sank into two red plastic seats, the ones closest to the reservation desk. Bar-On was alert and full of vitality after his good sleep on the plane, and he delved into his notebook, while I, my times jumbled, sank into a twilight slumber, to the extent the hard seat permitted. Half asleep, I heard the tapping of heels coming closer, and as one man we whipped around to gaze in her direction, he from his notebook and I from my slumber. Bar-On leaned toward her, clutching his knees, his eyes glistening with enthusiasm. "Let's hope that she's also going to the International Writing Program," he said.

There was about her something distant and inaccessible, something that tautened her body like a bow between the torrent of her hair and the tapping of her heels. And the profusion of her body, trapped in a gossamer blouse and a severe skirt, threatened to burst forth at every tap of her heels and flood the terminal. Bar-On began to recite: " 'I placed a jar in Tennessee/And round it was, upon a hill./It made the slovenly wilderness/Surround that hill.

" 'The wilderness rose up to it—' But clearly we're talking about two jars here."

"But only one wilderness," I said, meaning him. He smiled forgivingly, pocketed his notebook and took out his pipe. I sank back into slumber.

In the plane it so happened that I sat next to her, and Bar-On sat two sighs away, across the aisle. As the plane took off, her mouth opened as if she wanted to say something but changed her mind and went on sitting there with her mouth ajar. The stewardess approached her and said, "Is there anything I can do for you?"

"Uh-uh," she said with her mouth open. The stewardess

went up to a passenger a few rows ahead of us, who, even before the captain had turned off the No Smoking sign, had lit a cigarette, the smell of which raised a great many eyebrows in the seats nearby. The woman replied to my curious glances with an apologetic look of her own. "Air-pressure problems," she said.

I stared out the window. Neatly ruled golden-yellow squares and not a hint of the red grass the color of wine stains.

Two students were waiting for us at Cedar Rapids. Bar-On was a bit put off by their casual reception and threw a withering glance at a cocky man in a tight summer suit, who was waiting for the woman with air-pressure problems and hustled her out of the airport. It turned out that several writers had been on the same flight with us. A Palestinian writer in a haze of Paco Rabanne shook Bar-On's hand with obvious reluctance. Liam, a restless young Irishman, observed this encounter with amusement and asked what was new in the Middle East. And out of the pocket of his tight trousers a Filipino poet drew a pack of Indonesian cigarettes and offered everyone a clove smoke that relieves all hostility, real and imagined. "Paco" remained reluctant, Bar-On kept faith with his pipe, and Liam and I were ex-smokers. The passenger lounge blurred in puffs of clove instead of the familiar tobacco.

Meanwhile night is falling, blanketing the midwestern prairies spread outside the window of the minibus, into which we squeezed, valises, suitcases and all.

I tried to go to sleep, but the jolting made me bite my tongue. . . . Cautiously I slipped from under the buffalo hide, got up on my knees and peered over the side of the wagon. There seemed to be nothing to see, no fences, no creeks or trees, no hills or fields. If there was a road, I could not make it out in the starlight. There was nothing but land: not a country at all, but the material out of which countries are made. No, there was nothing but land—slightly undulating, I knew, because often our wheels ground against the brake as we went down into a hollow and lurched up again on the other side. I had the feeling that the world was left behind, that we had got over the edge of it, and were outside man's jurisdiction. . . .

But not outside the jurisdiction of the cloud of cloves, which wafted us into the Mayflower, an eight-story student dormitory, at the northern edge of Iowa City. It resembled a huge reversed lowercase *h* lying on its side along North Dubuque Street, which stretched alongside the left bank of the Iowa River, amidst lawns and maples. They brought us to the back entrance of the building to make it easier to unload the suitcases we had brought, except for the small, compact duffel carried by clever Liam, who hadn't come like the rest of us, laden with all the baggage of the Third World. When the back door opened, our noses were assailed by a smell, the smell of most houses in the Midwest, as we later learned. Here it was still pristine and piercing. It was the mingled smell of synthetic wall-to-wall carpeting and of the glue that fastens it to the floors and seems to scorch whatever it touches. Bar-On stood on the threshold and said, "Fine. I'm going home." Mary, a member of the IWP staff, who greeted the newcomers and cast a net of warm smiles under them in order to soften the impact, asked what he had said, and he said it again, but in English. "Welcome aboard," she said to him. "You're the twelfth writer who has said that today. The twelfth out of thirty-three."

Around midnight all the newcomers gathered in Mary's apartment, on the first floor of the building, for a late supper and a preliminary briefing. Though Bar-On's plan to leave looked at first like the impulsive response of a pampered man, he subsequently became firmer about his decision. I tried to persuade him to think it over for a few days. But his spirit continued to sink into complaints about the quality of the place we had gotten ourselves into, about the bare walls, which gave rise to painful longings for his own four walls.

141

In my heart I was relieved that I was going to be free of the grasp of the hand recording notes in the fateful notebook and of the stern eye examining, from without and within, the guts of his Arab hero. The ardor of my attempts to convince him cooled. Mary joined the conversation. "Next week you'll feel so much at home that you won't want to go back to your country in another four months."

All of a sudden a wail sliced through the space of the room. The smoke detector had not withstood the input of the burning cloves.

The next morning, on the stairs leading to the entrance to the Mayflower, all the members of the program stood around in groups, exchanging names and first impressions. Across North Dubuque Street, on the banks of the river, workmen in blue overalls laid strips of sod over the black earth with muscular and precise movements. On the way to the center of town, we saw white houses on either side, their tiled roofs sharply pointed. Before them lay wide lawns, with a narrow walk extending down to the sidewalk and the tree-lined street. Squirrels rushed about at the feet of the trees, their tails erect with midwestern pride. "The Moral Majority," said Liam. We rode the bus alongside the river, which flows southward serenely, like someone who has been assured that sooner or later he will meet the Mississippi.

The floating names have begun to attach themselves to the faces, faces of every hue and race and age, a Tower of Babel of confused grace. Bar-On, who has attached himself to me, mutters a few grudging words at the quiet beauty of the town and the serenity of the white houses. I sense the hairline cracks in the shell of his resistance growing wider and reconciliation beginning to permeate them. Now only "Paco," the perfumed Palestinian, distresses him, and it's clear to him that their first clash is only a matter of time. Meanwhile I worry the Palestinian who worries him. The three of us in any case are still under the influence of the haze of Paco Rabanne, which blurs our senses and accompanies us like a mysterious nimbus from the East when we go into the First National Bank on the corner of Washington and Dubuque. The vice president of the branch attends to the new clients in person as they open their accounts, and he showers them with his card. Like an incantation, he spells his name, "Mister Sevick—Vee, I, Cee, Kay," with relentless friendliness; and ceremoniously, as if we were being inducted into a secret order, he allows us a glimpse of his golden heirloom watch, with the name "Old Abe" engraved upon it.

A winding path leads to a hilltop, and the maples on either side accompany the falling night with dried pods that spiral down and land with gentle murmurs on the first blankets of red autumn leaves, which have begun to cast their spell on Bar-On and muffle his plans for departure. Liam speaks of his first long walk today in City Park, across the Iowa River from the Mayflower. They have extraordinary mosquitoes there, he says, but the river is beautiful. Some local folk whom he met invited him to have a glass of wine with them. He wants to organize a rowing trip down the river, he and Bjørg, the Norwegian writer who has just arrived today, and now as she walks up the path she says she hopes the fall here isn't contagious. From afar we hear the voices of the local guests who have already arrived, and we see the house at the top of the hill where the reception is, the house of the Engles, who administer the program and the writers. The two-story house floats like an ark on the red flood of maple. Every squirrel's dream, says Bjørg.

At the entrance of the house, in the dimness of the forecourt, Paul Engle and his wife, Hualing Nieh, stand and greet the guests as two by two they ascend from the enchanted wood. Richard, henceforth Rick, presents them to their hosts. In a high, melodious voice, Rick pronounces the names as he tautens his body upward on tiptoe. Already fluent in the minutiae of the guests' biographies, he proceeds to outline the distinction of the bearers by carefully selected high points, as if he were a Chinese painter who all summer long had been making preparatory sketches of the characters, and now with a few swift strokes of his brush captures the essence of each one. Each of these portraits floats up into the canopy of leaves above the forecourt, while eliciting great delight from the Engles, and lands at the feet of the squirrels rushing about here and there in the twilight that has invaded the wood. Paul Engle, tall of stature and high of voice, in an embroidered silk shirt, puts on his face the mask of a sharp-horned gnome, and presents his wife as if he were showing a treasure—a woman elegant in a red silk robe and restrained in her delight, as if she were the Chinese definition of art.

A thickly carpeted wooden staircase creaks and crackles up to a huge living room on the upper level. Once again, the carpet smell of the Midwest hangs in the air, along with the scents of exotic cooking. The length and breadth of the walls are covered with a rare collection of masks, of all colors and races, from India even unto the land of Cush, from China even unto Peru. Masks that had been left behind by participants in the program are reviewed now by Paul as he displays them to the newcomers. Next to the fireplace is an antique Chinese tea table, with carved women tripping down the garden path. On the mantelpiece over the unlit fireplace, a large tray, inlaid with mother-of-pearl, is flanked by Chinese demons in ivory and gold, mute sentinels of some occult secret. And all around, the voices intertwine in murmurings and embarrassed giggles, languages blending, hesitating near one another, sorting and fingering and touching first acquaintance.

Bjørg asks what brings me to this out-of-the-way place. "Willa Cather," I say. Hualing passes in front of us to the far side of the room and returns with Paul Engle in tow.

"Look what a coincidence," she tells him. "Willa Cather, whom I translated into Chinese, has brought this nice Jewish writer to Iowa City!"

"You know," said Paul, "I was born in Cedar Rapids, and when I was a boy I was a Shabbes goy for some of the Jewish families there. I got fifteen cents a Saturday."

I excuse myself and hurry to the other end of the room, where I extricate Bar-On from a noisy group and bring him to Paul so that he can hear this bit of Diaspora lore.

"It's a bad habit of mine," Paul says after I explain his error. "Again I've wasted a good story on the wrong person. When I turned fifty, which was many days ago, my first wife said to me one morning, 'Look, what in the hell have you done? In fifty years you have gone from Cedar Rapids to Iowa City, twenty-five miles. Half a mile a year.' What do you think of that?"

"That's almost as fast as the Jews move," Bar-On replies. "It took my parents two thousand years to get to the Land of Israel."

Paul Engle abruptly asks if anyone would like a refill and heads for the bar, a man who has twice in a row wasted a good story on the wrong person.

I go over to exchange a few polite words with Paco, the Palestinian, and Billy, the bearded writer from Egypt.

"My dear lady," I hear Piet, the South African writer, say to a woman. "I can assure you from personal experience that an electrical shock to the testicles does not make a man impotent."

Bert, the Dutch writer who has been living in London for several years, stops me. He would like to discuss, briefly, his notion that Bar-On and I constitute a schizophrenia, two faces of a single person. Bjørg, who is standing with him, says, "They haven't decided yet who is the ventriloquist of whom."

"Around here you'll see a lot of pigs," I hear Paul say to

145

a couple from India. "Then you'll go home and write poems. Hogs and poetry, both of them strong supporters of human life."

The rising and falling wail of another smoke detector turns all eyes towards Pedro, my clove-smoking flatmate, who spreads his palms in a gesture of embarrassed innocence. This time it is only a burnt Chinese delicacy. Paco, a charming fellow from Nablus, is telling Billy about the novel he has been writing.

"How many words have you got in it?" Billy asks.

"I haven't counted," says Paco.

"Approximately," insists Billy. When he hears the reply, he says, "It's not a novel that you're writing, my dear boy, but a novella!"

Paco smiles and blushes, his eyes red from lack of sleep.

At the far end of the room, Bar-On is deep in conversation with a young woman whose complexion is like honeyed amber. "That woman is a Jew from France, born in Alexandria," Billy says to me, following my gaze. "She's called Amira. The name suits her, I think: a princess." Amira looks at us and smiles.

A spoon tinkles purposefully against a glass, and Paul announces that he wishes to propose a toast. "Hualing and I would like to welcome our wonderful guests who have gathered from all over the world, the largest group that has ever come to the International Writing Program. And also the largest number of women. But do bear in mind what was written in the welcome letters sent to you: Please, no children! David Lodge once said—and I wish that I had been the one to say it—'Literature is mostly about having sex and not much about having children. Life is the other way round.' Please remember, then, that you are writers above all. In any case, Hualing and I, we're both from the heartlands. She is from the very middle of China, and I lived in Cedar Rapids, the home of Quaker Oats. Every day her father was presented with a bowl of oats by a servant as a sign of status.

God, I had it forced down my throat. . . . Times have changed since then; I love Chinese food and Hualing loves oatmeal. Lucky for you that I was the one who decided on the menu tonight, which is pretty rare around here, so please gather round the table and help yourselves. But first let's drink to the International Writing Program, which has brought you all here tonight, to writing and to the metaphorical children of the future!"

I lay my empty plate on the tea table. The faces of the carved women are flushed and radiant from the wine. They float among the empty glasses scattered about the table and melt into the mixture of languages that envelops the room, and they vanish behind the masks hanging on the walls. Numbed by the wine, I walk out onto the unlit L-shaped balcony. A moonless sky spreads to the horizon, which is sparkling with distant lights. The sky is studded with stars, and I realize that I haven't seen so many stars in the sky since I left the village. Uncle Yusef, at this moment lying on his deathbed, used to say that the only difference between the city and the village is the number of stars in the sky. Somewhere between the folds of the hills flows the Iowa River, in the darkness beyond the Mayflower. "Shlomith, Shlomith," I whisper to myself, as a sort of spell against forgetting. Suddenly the profile of ambered honey is beside me.

"Are you planning a poem to Laylah?" She smiles, with a wordplay in Arabic that refers both to night and to a poet's lady. "My name is Amira." And she leans over the railing and instinctively presses her palm to the top of her blouse. This gesture of modesty, I say to myself, would be lost on Bar-On.

"Yehoshua Bar-On told me that you passed through Paris on your way here."

"Yes, for a day."

"What did you like there?"

"I hardly left the hotel. I visited a cemetery."

"Père Lachaise? We could have met there. I have a friend, a photographer, who's in love with the cemetery. Which tombs did you see?"

Suddenly we were washed in the light of a lantern hanging above us. Bar-On stood on the other side of the glass window of the illuminated, buzzing room, one hand still on the switch and the other waggling at us, and with a sly smile on his face. Then he turned the light off, whipped out his notebook and jotted something down, then smiled again at the spot where he figured we were and retreated into the milling crowd.

"What does he want?" Amira asks.

"I don't know anymore," I say. Amira spreads her arms, clasps her palms to the nape of her neck and stretches her body backward. "It's getting cold. Let's go inside."

Some two months later I will recall this scene, the palms pressed to the nape of her neck, the tremor that took hold of her honeyed skin, under the light brandished between us, and the smile on Bar-On's lips as he abandoned us to the darkness. Something cryptic lingered like the lights gleaming in the endless prairie landscape, the embers that were all that remained of the red grass.

> As I looked about me I felt that the grass was the country, as the water is the sea. The red of the grass made all the great prairie the color of wine-stains, or of certain seaweeds when they are first washed up. And there was so much motion in it; the whole country seemed, somehow, to be running. . . . I can remember exactly how the country looked to me as I walked beside my grandmother along the faint wagon-tracks on that early September morning. Perhaps the glide of long railway travel was still with me, for more than anything else I felt motion in the landscape; in the fresh, easy-blowing morning wind, and in the earth itself, as if the shaggy grass were a sort of loose hide, and underneath it herds of wild buffalo were galloping, galloping. . . .

That same night, in room 821-B of the Mayflower, I move the desk from the narrow entry hall into the room, acting out the delusion common to sojourners who believe that the rearrangement of this or that piece of furniture will grant them the feeling of being home, or at least of settling down for the time being. I take out the papers and books and dictionaries I have brought with me and arrange them on the desk, next to the Hebrew typewriter, acting out the delusion that if you haven't managed to write when you're sitting at your own table, gazing at the familiar landscape of your own books, you will be able to write when you are far from home. I insert some K Mart paper and start to write the first of the many letters to Shlomith destined to fall in a month's time into the hands of her husband.

How to describe a home to someone you love . . . ?

I never tried to describe my home. Because it isn't just the southern window—the *bab es-sir,* as we called it—the chill of which is still in the palms of my hands, nor the *smandra,* the cupboard where we kept the mattresses and the blankets, which towered above our heads like a threatening castle, nor the turquoise-green cat hiding behind it when she was in heat, nor the dappled light dancing on the concrete floor, nor the taste of the salty water dripping all night from the linen sack that held the yogurt for the *labaneh,* the water that our crazy neighbor Ablah would drink, the taste of which rises now from under my tongue, as the villagers say, here in the American Midwest.

My sense of home begins with the spoon knocking against the rim of the pot of lentil soup and spreads like ripples in the village pond and licks at the edge of the *duwara* and limns the view from the southern window and touches my skin from within. All of the houses I've lived in since then have hardly touched me.

Now here I am sitting in Iowa City, more than twenty years after I left the house of my childhood, and for the first time in all these years I feel that I can conjure up the house of my childhood in the village, the smells and the sights and the textures, which now for the first time I describe to Shlomith, who has never set foot there. "I have to come away so far from it," as Amira would have quoted from the *Alexandria Quartet*, "in order to understand it all."

My new home has walls in name only. They tremble at the touch of a hand and seemingly at the touch of a voice. Walls that allegedly give a sense of security and protection, but that could remind Yehoshua Bar-On of a poem by David Avidan:

> The security situation of Israel
> Is like a toilet without a lock
> One hand keeping
> The door shut from within.

For this you must know: On the other side of the kitchen and the bathroom lies another dwelling unit, which is the inverted twin of the one that protects me, and there Pedro dwells, and across the no-man's-land of the kitchen and the bathroom he sends me smoke signals, which seep under my door and envelop me like a saccharine melody that will not relent for four more months. Without advance planning we might simultaneously open our doors to the bathroom—or worse. And since these doors cannot be locked, thanks to some obscure American logic, the situation in the bathroom will always be one of maximum alert, in anticipation of the hand that will suddenly fling open the door and of the mouth that will emit an embarrassed apology in an unintelligible language.

How to describe a home to someone you love?

You could start with the orange drops redolent of cloves, casually sprinkled over the toilet seat.

PART FIVE

THE TALE CONTINUED

"How far away is it?"
"One cigarette."

Conversation between villagers

Father Jurmanus, or, as the villagers called him, Abuna Jurmanus, stood on the lowest level of Uncle Mikha'eel's home, the level intended for domestic animals. On the higher level, used for living and sleeping and entertaining visitors, three watermelons, which had been brought in from the melon patch, stood in a row. Uncle Yusef, then sixteen years old, watched Abuna Jurmanus and then turned away in his skepticism. A few minutes before, the priest had demonstrated to those present his wonderful powers, by flattening with just his thumb the impression on a silver Turkish coin. But this feat was separated from what Abuna intended to do next by a chasm of difficulty that not even the imagination of a sixteen-year-old could bridge. With the steadfastness of a Catholic, Abuna Jurmanus had taken upon himself an impossible trick—to cause the *majidi,* the silver Turkish coin in his hand, to pass through the three watermelons, as if the coin were a bullet. While the *majidi* belonged to the priest, the three watermelons that had been brought in from the patch were the last three of the season, and Uncle Mikha'eel's family needed them to subsist on, literally, for the next three days. But Uncle Mikha'eel's wife's protests were to no avail, and she retired to her corner of the courtyard and muttered between her clenched teeth her thoughts about the whims of men and priests who aren't satisfied with the yoke of Allah but have to go and deck themselves in the harness of worldly male pride. In Uncle Yusef's mouth there was the acid taste of bread made from barley that had not yet ripened. For those were the days of the famine on the eve of the Great War.

Uncle Yusef stood there and thought of his father, Jubran, who had got fed up with the hunger in the village and departed for Argentina. Twenty years before that he was doing *ajir* work, or daily wage labor, for the Freiwat family in Al-Bassa. Em Naser, who had come to the village from Al-Bassa, used to tell Yusef the story of the night when his father, Jubran, was challenged to find out where he stood with his employer, whose daughter he had fallen in love with.

Fifty walnuts were arranged in a line on the upper ledge of the house, and Grandfather Jubran, from where he stood on the lower level, had to crack them with blows of his forehead. The nuts cracked open one after the other, but the heart of the employer's daughter was harder to crack, and he did not win her hand. Em Naser strokes the cat purring in her lap as she sits on her daughter's doorstep in Fassuta and rounds off her story with a commentary on Fate, for the very same girl of Grandfather Jubran's dreams, for the sake of whose green eyes he had cracked fifty walnuts with his love-toughened forehead, as she returned home from her aunt's house one night met a hyena, who laughed in her face and led her bound in the ropes of his laughter to his cave, where he devoured her.

But Em Naser, as she strokes the back of the cat, which is all that is left to her from the chaos of her hasty flight from Al-Bassa in 1948, tends, after the fashion of refugees, to string unrelated stories on a single thread of nostalgia, or to mix up two chronicles from the life of Grandfather Jubran. The hyena belongs to a different tale, the tale of a billy goat that was the bellwether of the flock belonging to Shukri

Freiwat, Grandfather Jubran's employer. When thieves from the Lebanese village of Alma came and took it, Grandfather Jubran went to ransom it. On his way back to Al-Bassa, the sun set and the winter's night surrounded him with its veils of darkness. And suddenly his horse reared on its hind legs and the bellwether gave a bleat of fear. The laughter rolling out of the darkness all around him left no doubt in Grandfather Jubran's heart. It was the hyena who had been terrorizing the shepherds of the area and had more than once "stolen their minds," as the villagers say, and led them to his cave and to their bitter end. The nimbus of clouds covering the face of the moon parted a bit and relieved the panic of the frustrated young lover. He dismounted, took his stick, and stood before the hyena to defend his mind and his horse and his bellwether. The hyena's eyes flickered back at him and trapped him in a bewitched net of laughter and horror. Then the contemptuous eyes drew closer, and as he raised his stick to beat the dark, panting creature, it leapt upon him and sank its teeth into his shoulder. But inasmuch as he was wearing his employer's thick woolen coat, the white teeth stuck in the black wool. He whipped off the coat, and with screams of alarm he attacked the astonished hyena and routed it. But from that night on there was a tic on the left side of Grandfather Jubran's face, which never left him until the day he died, in ripe old age, in Fassuta, in the early 1930s, having voyaged and wandered far and wide.

For ten years Em Naser, small of stature and always with the black *asbeh* tied around her head, after the fashion of the old women of Al-Bassa, would sit on the doorstep of the house of her daughter, who was related by marriage to Aunt Marie, and stroke her purring cat and mourn the loss of Al-Bassa, then console the cat by telling him that the day would come when the two of them would once again wander through the broad spaces of their evacuated home.

Em Naser bore a heavy grudge against Uncle Mikha'eel, the brother of Grandfather Jubran. She would ask him, relentlessly, "Will the refugees return, Abu Khaleel?" Uncle Mikha'eel, whose firstborn son was named Khaleel, would avoid answering her. But his patience came to an end one day in 1951, when a billy goat of his was stolen. He answered her, saying, "Look at me, Em Naser. The day I become a young man again will be a sign that the refugees will return to their homes."

Em Naser tightened the *asbeh* around her head, took her stick and left without saying goodbye. She never came back to his house, even when he passed away, a few months later. "I never shall go to the funerals," she said, "of men of little faith."

Uncle Mikha'eel was a poet, one of the folk poets whose fame spread far and wide during the Safarbalek period, the days of Turkish rule, and his name is still mentioned by the old men of the Galilee. Even though a refined soul was buried within him, the descendants of Khaleel A-Shammas saw him as the bedrock of the family, which not even the famine on the eve of the Great War would move.

It came to pass that during those years of famine the earth was miserly, but Nayef Sirhan, the village's *multazim*—the landlord who had rented the village from the sultan—was generous to himself. Some villagers would return home from the threshing floor with only the winnowing forks in their hands, after Nayef Sirhan had taken his share. So storage bins would empty well before their time, before the new wheat had even sprouted in the fields.

We sat around the low dining table one winter day. Some distance away stood the iron stove, its embers whispering shyly in the space of the big room. A bowl of steaming lentil soup stood in the center of the table, and from it led the paths that had dripped from the full spoons. My mother had spent a long time sifting through those lentils, but a single hollow lentil floated on the surface of the pot, and beside it floated a mite that had been concealed within it. The sight of it pressed upon the silence that filled the big room and spread over the whispering embers. It was the silence of the poor in their hour of togetherness with the meager food on their table. It was not broken by the banging of the spoons against the dish or by the cooling breaths exhaled rhythmically by eight pursed mouths or by the ordinary conversation about the world that spread itself casually around the low table. Then, one by one, the hands halted in their movements toward the dish or away from it, as each pair of eyes locked onto the floating mite. I saw it last, just at the moment the spoon in my hand tapped against the lip of the dish. A cry to my mother escaped from my mouth, a cry no one but me had permitted to escape, one that implied the question: "Why did you leave the mite for us in the lentils?" My father's hand grabbed the spoon from mine, threw it down on the table and slapped my face.

"If you don't like it, then don't eat."

Scolded and slapped, I hid my head between the hard, upholstered backrest and my mother's warm back. I heard the dull tapping of the spoon against her teeth, the hurried sipping and the brief chewing of the lentils of the thin soup, the hollow swallowing sound of the throat and finally, close enough for my ears to touch almost, the sounds made by her stomach, which hunger had incited to be on the alert for the arrival of filling and satisfying food but which received instead a tiny portion of lentils and a great deal of water. I bury my head more deeply into the accumulating sounds and hear the hunger monster in my own little stomach, the sounds growing fainter, receding before the choking in my throat. Mother's hesitant hand strokes, as if in secret, the curve of my back and tries to draw me out of my tightly packed kingdom. I snuggle up to the consoling touch, but immediately draw back into my humiliation, as if I had swallowed the awns from an ear of wheat.

Uncle Yusef went to tell Uncle Mikha'eel that there was nothing more to eat. The corn bread was finished, and apart from a bottle of olive oil, even a visiting mouse would find nothing in the house. The storage bin in Uncle Mikha'eel's house had already been emptied too, and his children were eating certain wild grasses that humans could digest. Uncle Mikha'eel said to Yusef, "Go down to Marj Hlal and see if the barley patch has sprouted and ripened yet." Uncle Yusef knew that the barley was intended for the horse, who in another few weeks would have to do the fall plowing. But God Almighty would most probably not be tightfisted when the time came and would send fodder for the faithful beast. Uncle Yusef picked up a sickle, took the horse's reins and went down to see about the barley. When the shadows had gone from Uncle Mikha'eel's yard, Uncle Yusef returned from the field with his hand holding on to the bridle to prevent the horse from eating the heap of barley stalks. Uncle Mikha'eel brought a broom of thorny burnet and swept the paved courtyard clean, and the barley was laid out for the threshing. The members of the two families gathered, holding whatever came to hand, ox goads and posts and flails and just plain sticks, and began beating the sheaves to separate the kernels of barley from the chaff. And the horse stood by, tied to his empty stall, and filled his nostrils with the fragrance of the barley that would never reach his mouth.

Between the courtyard and the road was a stone wall, and against it leaned a fifteen-year-old girl from the village of Ikrit. Her name was Haniyeh, and she was visiting her relatives. She watched Uncle Yusef threshing the barley. But seeing that he was absorbed body and soul in his task and had taken no notice of her, she smiled to herself and went on her way thinking of threshings in previous years, when she had been visiting her relatives for whom Uncle Yusef was doing *ajir* work.

It was a broiling day in early May, one of those days when the sun could set a bird's tail on fire, as people say. She was alone in the house, she and the horse in the stable. She sat on the roof that looked out over the inner courtyard, watching the shadows of the doves flying over the courtyard and the round stone trough at its center. They were pied doves, who came and went from the dovecote in the attic wall, and the collar of colored feathers around their necks gleamed in the broiling sun and glittered in the watering trough for the girl to watch. She began to sing softly a folk song, "Ya tira tiri ya hamama"—"Fly, fly away, my dove." But she soon left off her tune and smiled, because in the language of children and adolescents *hamama* was the nickname for that bodily organ which boys never missed an opportunity to display to her. Her thoughts are interrupted by the opening of the courtyard gate, and she sees Uncle Yusef passing through the inner courtyard toward the stable. He sees her shadow cast on the watering trough and raises his head and greets her. He has come to take the horse to the field, he says. What are you doing up there? he adds, without waiting for her to reply.

"Come on up here," she throws back at him. "I want to show you something," though she doesn't know what.

My uncle, a maturing boy with time on his hands, can sense in her voice that seductive melody which gives the girls of Ikrit away. He turns away from the stable and goes up to the roof. "What are you doing up here?" he says again.

"Watching a dove," she replies. And even before he can weigh the hint in her word, she looks back and forth between him and the watering trough and then speaks the most daring sentence that my uncle Yusef was to hear in all the eighty-five years of his life. He can't believe his ears. Then, in a voice that has lost the initial embarrassment, she repeats, "Do you want to have a contest with me to see who can piss from here into the trough?" My uncle looks at the girl and looks at the watering trough in the middle of the courtyard, about ten paces from the wall on the top of which they are standing, and the challenge intrigues him. He asks her to turn her eyes away, and when she does so he girds his loins, arches his back, crosses himself, and squirts an arc in the direction of the watering trough. The doves, startled in their flight, rush back to the dovecote, the sunbeams refract as they touch the arc, and the sound of the water splattering on the paving stones of the courtyard makes the horse in the stable neigh. He tries again, but the impetus is lost.

Uncle Yusef used to flavor his stories with the spice of exaggeration, but he swore by all the saints and by Elijah the Prophet, the holy patron of the village, who looked down upon the two of them from the heights of the church belfry, that the girl pulled up her dress, did not ask him to turn his eyes away, rolled down her underpants and sat down on the edge of the roof after the fashion of women, and in a wonderful arc and with peals of laughter pissed right into the trough. As my uncle stood there openmouthed, she came over to him and said, "I won and I can do whatever I want to you." Before he knew it, she had loosened the string of his pants and taken his dove in her hands. He thrashed about like a wounded dove. . . .

And now she leans against the stone wall and watches the awns and the chaff fly from the rubbing hands, to the rhythm of the blowing mouths, and the grains of barley pile up in the burlap sack.

Yusef rose before dawn the next day and loaded the sack on the back of the horse and set out for the mill in Wadi El-Karn, which would eventually become known as Nachal Kaziv. The miller, who was washing his face in the cold water of the stream, raised his head and looked at the young man with the horse approaching him. *"Ya fattah ya aleem,"* he said to himself, invoking the name of the All-knowing, "where have those people in Fassuta found wheat so early in the morning?" After they had exchanged greetings, he repeated his question to Yusef.

"Allah is generous," said Yusef.

The suspicious miller brought his nose close to the sack, and his face fell. "I guess it's better than gathering kernels from the droppings of beasts," he said.

My uncle nodded his head, and he felt as if awns were clogging his throat.

"Never mind, *ya* Yusef," said the miller. "One day we'll eat spit-roasted doves again."

On the way up the path away from the mill sat Haniyeh, on a smooth rock that gleamed in the morning sun.

"Good morning, *ya* Yusef." Her voice echoed through the clefts of the valley. Yusef felt ants swarming up his spine. Her brother had come to take her back to Ikrit, and now he had left the path to find a place among the bushes to relieve himself. Yusef stood there embarrassed and did not know how to continue this conversation. Haniyeh, seeing his embarrassment, hunted around in the saddlebags on the donkey's back until she found the tobacco pouch. She asks Yusef to roll her a cigarette. He finally manages to control his trembling fingers, and with a dry mouth he licks the edge of the paper. She takes the cigarette from him, but the paper opens and the tobacco blows in the wind like her laughter, which wraps itself around the hillside and breaks at the bottom of the wadi.

The two of them will meet many years later in the shadow of approaching death, and he will offer her a cigarette again, and again the cigarette will crumble and she will say to him after her fashion, without blinking an eyelash, that she hopes he has been able to keep it stiff to better avail during all those years. Now she only bids him farewell and continues on her way. But then she shouts after him, "Don't forget our doves." Yusef answers under his breath that doves fly off when hunger dwells in the dovecote.

For three days they ate that bread, and for three days more they could still feel the husks scratching inside their mouths, and the hiccup rising up in the throat, and their bodies shivering. And Abuna Jurmanus, like a pied piper, tries to distract his famished children. He holds the *majidi* between thumb and forefinger, and with a sweep of his arm he flings the coin and it splits the three watermelons.

And deep in Yusef's innards flutter the wings of doves.

PART SIX

THE TELLER: Mayflower II

My best friend, she is bright, her skin is soft
Her eyes even more blue than the sky above
    the apartment house
She takes her chewing gum out of her mouth
    puts it into mine
Says I can have it for five minutes. . . .
Today it is Saturday. The sun is shining.
And the student girls in the Mayflower
Will come in small groups in the evening
Their jeans are clean and they have washed
    their hair
The shampoo smells of herbs and fruit . . .
It is left behind them as an answer
Maybe as a sort of belief.

Bjørg Vik,
"Variations on a Text
by Vallejo, After Donald Justice"

Iowa City, October 3

After the settling in, the days have passed very slowly.

Conversations and meetings and receptions and dinners and readings, trips to farms, arguments and advice, quarrels and love affairs. Words spoken over glasses of wine in the bars in the small, tremulous hours of the night. Forgetting and remembering. Mornings of walking along the east bank. White houses wrapped in the September sun hanging above the trees. Lunches at Bushnell's Turtle, the carafe of white wine leaving a wet ring on the wooden table.

"In case you didn't know," Bjørg says, reading, "the College Block Building, built in 1883, is an excellent example of late-nineteenth-century Victorian architecture. The facade provides an interesting display of richly ornamented pressed tin and heavy bracketed cornice. After several moves, Bushnell's Turtle is now located in the renovated College Block Building as of August 1978."

"And who's this Bushnell?" I ask.

"Well," and Bjørg continues to read from the menu, "David Bushnell, a young Yale graduate, invented the original submarine, the Turtle, for use during the American Revolution."

"Is that what you really want to tell me?" I ask.

"Maybe I'm wrong, and I haven't got any proof, and maybe my Nordic paranoia is playing tricks on my senses, but I can see in people's eyes what's going on deep in their souls. It looks like your Hebraic friend is up to something."

I tell her about the novel Bar-On is planning to write.

"Which means that I have the great honor of eating lunch with someone who before my very eyes is turning into a character in a book. So come on—before you melt away altogether, let's order another carafe of wine."

By the time two weeks had passed, the group had broken up into small cliques, along the tried-and-true lines of mutual affection and conflicting interests. Liam, who had turned out to be an excellent cook, spent most of his time in Bjørg's kitchen, and between meals he worked on his third novel. The Chinese writers, most of whom had spent the prime of their lives in the dark prison cells of the Cultural Revolution, provided the group with a halo of honor, which surrounded us like the ancient wall. They have about them something of the vitality of a dragon who has just burst out of a sealed bottle. Yehoshua Bar-On, he of the open notebook and the inscribing hand, was slowly sinking into depression. Most of the time he shut himself up in his room and refused to share his troubles with anyone. There were rumors about a wife who had left home. More than once I attempted to breach the wall he had erected around himself, but I was always repulsed with a politeness behind which there skulked a hint of hostility. One day Amira revealed to me that he had called her on the telephone, and after elaborate apologies had asked that she clarify the nature of her relationship to me, with the excuse that he needed it for his writing. With the caprice of an Oriental fantasist, Amira told him of the bush that was burning between us with the fire of our newfound love, and that we were planning to live together in Paris.

"And what about the married woman in Jerusalem?" he asked.

"Out of sight, out of mind," she said.

Amira had her own secret, a married photographer of Greek origin, a native of Alexandria, who before she came to Iowa had spent every day for a month with her at Père Lachaise. We would walk through the streets at night, crying out his name, "Dhimos, Dhimos." Perhaps he will hear our cries and save us and pardon us and acquit us and forgive us for the sin we have committed so wholeheartedly. In the wee hours of the night, after a final round of the bars, hoarse from crying "Dhimos, Dhimos" and from this common fate that binds each of us helplessly to a married lover, we would come to the conclusion that we ought to introduce Shlomith to Dhimos and send them both off to a lonely island at the end of the earth. But what we mainly shared was the writing of the first draft of a piece that we called "Père Lachaise" and attributed to Yehoshua Bar-On.

It did not occur to us during these hours of writing together that Yehoshua Bar-On was actually drifting away from us, and that a dark and moldy jealousy was spreading over him in the isolation of his room. Had we not been so wrapped up in the arrogance of young writers, we would certainly have noticed in time the trembling of his hands, the puckers of loneliness on his wrinkled skin, and the disturbed look that would now and then come into his eyes. The relationship between Bar-On and the Palestinian, which had commenced in mutual reservations and progressed to loud arguments, became more and more puzzling to me, until its astonishing turning point in the last week of September, on the upper deck of a yacht belonging to the John Deere Company, which had invited the writers to spend the day on it. Liam and I were sitting by the rail, watching the waters of the Mississippi spread at the touch of the prow and speaking of Willa Cather, whom we both loved, and of John Deere, who was washing our brains with such captivating and Mark Twainian cunning. Amira came up to us and whispered in my ear that I should prepare myself for a surprise that was making its way up the spiral steps. Whereupon from the belly of the ship came Bar-On and Paco arm in arm, the one puffing on his pipe and the other sending into the watery space his liberated laughter. For a moment I couldn't believe my eyes. Liam immediately said, "We should make a poster of this and send it off to the IRA."

Spotting us, Bar-On drew his companion over and challenged me in a tipsy voice: "My dear friend, you are henceforth released from the fear of my open notebook, because I've found a new hero!"

Liam, amused by this twist of fate, asked, "But what has he done to you?" meaning me.

"That's it," Bar-On replied. "He hasn't done a thing to me; that's the problem. His compatriot here speaks much more to my heart than he does. He forces me to respond and take a stand toward him. You have to bear in mind that he is still a pure Palestinian, whose strength resides in his simplicity and his lack of cynicism."

"I think you're just making life easy for yourself," said Liam. "You prefer your enemies simple and well defined."

"Maybe so," said Bar-On, "but my former hero does not define himself as my enemy, at least not in the accepted sense of the word. And that makes it hard for me. On the other hand, I feel much closer to the problems of *this* Palestinian. Perhaps I'll be proven wrong, but my instinct tells me I can make good use of him."

The whole time Paco continues to rock with amused laughter.

"Mabrook." I congratulate him in Arabic.

"Don't worry," he flings back at me. "Your turn will come one of these days."

Later on, Xiao Jun, the Chinese writer who had been an artilleryman, stands with his legs apart on the deck, leaning on his carved stick, and sings an aria from a Chinese opera, with an American flag fluttering above his head. His voice seems to part the waters of the Mississippi like a colorful paddle wheel. By then such juxtapositions look altogether natural to me.

In the bus going back to the Mayflower later that evening, I found I was unable to fall asleep, made restless by the overload of food, wine and new sights. My squirmings in the seat finally woke Amira. "How are you feeling?" she asked. When my reply hung back, she said, "Betrayed?"

"Apparently," I realized. I was now released from the threat of the notebook, as Bar-On had said, and could spend the days I had left here doing whatever I liked. I was no longer concerned that my doings would be preserved in due time in a book, as if they had been confiscated, and thanks to Bar-On's taut style would exist without me forever after. But instead of being happy about my freedom, I was feeling let down. To put it precisely, I *was* feeling betrayed.

"You're right," I say to Amira. "Betrayed."

"Said the bridge after it had been crossed," she added.

Still, it wasn't hard to get used to the new situation. The relationship between Bar-On and Paco took on the look of a close friendship and rose to the top of the International Writing Program's public relations charts. Paco even began to call Bar-On by his nickname, "Yosh" (something it never crossed my mind to do).

Then the stealing began. First the Hebrew typewriter disappeared from my desk. When I told Mary, she suspected that students had done it.

"But who would want a Hebrew typewriter?"

"Maybe one of the writers took it," she said. "Out of jealousy or because the noise of the typing disturbed them."

Then some papers and notes disappeared, among them the first draft of "Père Lachaise." Amira suspected that Bar-On had something to do with it, while I suspected Paco. Then a few days later I found an envelope in my mailbox, and inside it were all the papers that had disappeared. Around the same time, Liam found the Hebrew typewriter in one of the washing machines.

The early evening of the first of October found us once more on the path winding up to the house on the top of the hill for a reception at the Engles', in honor of the anniversary of the Chinese Revolution. The fatigue of autumn had relaxed the squirrels' limbs, and the red leaves scattered along the path on either side rustled quietly under our feet in the drizzle that had begun to fall. Liam quickened his pace. He was dressed in a splendid suit, with a red tie knotted carelessly, and carried a bouquet of flowers in his hand. Bjørg, also bearing a bouquet, laughs and says, "Autumn here is contagious after all." Amira says she misses the sea and the sand and the sun, that she might not have the strength of soul to stand the grim beauty of fall. Paco says that since his childhood he hasn't smelled such an intoxicating odor, because where he comes from the smell of damp earth is buried beneath smells of gunpowder and burning tires. Bar-On, who lingers behind, whips out his notebook and writes. When he notices my look he comes up to me and informs me that several things have disappeared from his room too, but he hasn't found it necessary to tell anyone. I tell him that it never occurred to me to suspect him, of all people. After all, we are still friends. He puts his arm warmly around my shoulder and says that he has thought a great deal about what he said that day on the Mississippi. He feels bad about it, even though he spoke in good faith, if under the influence of drink. Apparently he had touched upon an essential matter in the depths of his soul, which his conscience needed to clarify. I admit to him that I found some lugubrious thoughts of my own surfacing in the wake of the incident, but that it looks as if each of us will have to deal with the problem separately, from his own point of view.

If we may judge Bar-On on the basis of his best writing, he was too discreet to tell me that he didn't believe a word of what I had said and knew that the gap between us would widen until there was no way of bridging it. Just then Amira, who had been walking some distance behind us, lost her footing on the slippery ground. Hearing her thin cry, I released myself from Bar-On's embrace, which was now lukewarm and unconvincing anyway, and went back to assist her. Bar-On turned his head and asked if everything was all right, and when he saw it was, he hurried up the hill to join the rest of the group. I helped Amira collect the scattered contents of her handbag from the wet asphalt slope, and arm in arm we climbed the hill to the Engles' wooden ark, wrapped in the misty drizzle.

The flowers offered by Bjørg and Liam draw warm cries of delight from our hosts. The Chinese writers accept them with a reserved courtesy and a hint of suspicion, but it is obvious that they are surprised by the gesture, which has breached the wall of isolation surrounding them. Xiao Jun even displays the courage of a former artilleryman and fires several rounds of greetings in heavy English at the assembled well-wishers, which elicits applause and cries of admiration.

There is a special savor to evenings at the Engles'. Paul stands head and shoulders above the crowd, a John Wayne of hospitality, always ready to draw from his arsenal a clever remark, spiced with midwestern humor, and be himself the first to respond to it with that rolling laugh of his, which evokes a wonderful mixture of old whiskey and thick, juicy steak. When you're tired of examining the collection of faces belonging to the guests, your eyes can graze among the rare masks hanging on the walls.

Outside, on the balcony surrounding the huge room, the chill of autumn is hanging in the air, waiting politely for the departure of the Indian summer that lingers among the overhanging branches. There is a wooden bench out there, on which Amira and I sit. We gaze at the view spread before us like the ancient Chinese fan in the hand of the dancer who is now performing on the other side of the glass, with her concise gestures and her features frozen into a smile. Among the members of the audience, who only a month ago were strangers and alienated from one another, there is now a different spirit. The last glow of twilight hangs in the western sky, and all the colors of autumn are diffused in the mist.

The dancer finishes her performance; her gestures are gathered up into her limbs like a set of miniature swords returned to their box, padded in red velvet. The fan, which is still open, is laid gently upon the tea table, and there is a polite clapping of hands like puffs of cotton to protect the fragile memory of the dance from breakage. The platters of Chinese delicacies circulate, glasses are refilled and the conversation resumes. Although it's already been a month, Rick still insists on calling me by Paco's name, and I announce that today I have decided to give up, and henceforth I will not correct his error. Bert, the Dutch writer, asks me if I'm still against the discussion of the Israeli-Arab schizophrenia. I suggest inviting Bar-On as an observer. Rick believes that it would be in the best interests of all concerned if I kept a low profile, as I have been doing for the past month.

"I thought you'd never notice," I say.

"I know what your name is," Rick says. "But I know the name of the game, which is why I keep calling you by Paco's name, my modest contribution to the camouflage measures you've been taking."

Bert says he's sorry, he didn't know that things had gone that far, and asks that his comment about schizophrenia be stricken from the record, things being more complicated than he had thought.

Across the room I see Amira's profile, trying in vain to conceal her boredom in the circle into which she has fallen. Dhimos, I say in my heart, Dhimos is the name of the game.

"If you'll allow me one additional observation"—Bert addresses me—"about the matter at hand, I think that Amira's your shield."

"You have no idea of how right you are, my dear flying Dutchman," I say.

Liam approaches the group, his necktie even more awry

and his jacket over his arm. "Your two mates," he says, meaning Bar-On and Paco, "have gone completely bonkers."

"Tell him, tell him," urges Bert.

He says that in his opinion the apparent idyll is just for show, a camouflage, and the showdown is only a matter of time. He does not elaborate, and instead dismisses it all with a wave of his hand. "It was because of this, you see, that I left Ireland. Let's go drink something."

Dramatic thumps on the floor. Xiao Jun waves his stick, and silence reigns. In his hand he holds a sack. Hualing translates that he has just returned from a short trip to the East Coast, but he has managed to bring a present for everyone. The gift is unworthy of being offered to honorable writers like ourselves, but he fervently hopes that the symbolism will compensate for the triviality, and in addition he believes that it is a fitting souvenir of the period we have spent together, a period that will leave us with a pure impression, though transient and temporary, like the autumn leaves on the hillside. Then he spills the contents of the sack onto the tea table, where the fan had lain previously. Miniature bars of soap, from hotels, cascade in a riot of shapes and sizes and colors.

When the laughter dies down, Paul takes the floor. "It's hard to compete with an artilleryman," he says. "And it's even harder to compete with the pure beauty of soap, and it's a thousand times harder than that to give poem-foam as a gift. But nevertheless I would like to present you this evening with the book of poems I wrote on my last trip to China with Hualing."

I leaf through *Images of China*. One is called "Rooster":

> He is the universal male
> from blood red comb to bragging tail. . . .
> He shouts, he rides them, bites their necks:
> Now meet your dear friend—rooster sex.

Amira and I went outside again, to sit on the wooden bench. All of a sudden we were flooded by the balcony light. We looked into the room, and there is Paco trying to hide his face behind a mask he has taken down from the wall, waggling his finger at us. Then he turns off the light and returns us to the darkness. "Well, he's anything but original," says Amira.

"Or else he's smarter than we think," I say.

Later, going down the hill, Liam stops on the path and announces that he is going to perform a Chinese baptism on himself. He strips off his jacket and shirt, peels the paper from a soap, and begins to lather his torso, to cries of encouragement from the group. Bjørg says it was worth coming to the program if only to witness this scene: Liam standing there in the drizzling rain, on a path covered in red fallen leaves, far from Ireland, cleansing himself. Up the hill, on the top story of the wooden house now afloat in the fog, there is a lien on his movements, so that they will be preserved as a copy of an ancient Chinese dance. Even when we leave here, and each of us returns to our own fine and private place, Liam's movements will keep circling in the clear air between the branches of the maple trees.

Bert claps his hands and invites the group to his room for a nightcap. We crowd into the elevator and squeeze up against three students, girls who have been friendly with Liam. They run embarrassed fingers through their wet hair, which has just been shampooed, and the fragrance of the shampoo spreads over us. Liam takes some of the miniature bars of soap out of his pocket, bestows them upon the girls and invites them to the party. As we leave the elevator we notice a naked figure scurrying toward the emergency staircase—a chubby Puerto Rican student whose roommate has played a trick on him. He, too, is swept along with us. We sit him down in the only armchair; someone pushes a drink into his hand. Others try to cheer him up, but he remains silent, as though silence can cover his nakedness. One of the girls from the elevator then takes off her own clothes, climbs up on the table and begins to sing an old Irish song. The ivory down of her young triangle is wonderfully precise in the middle of the small room.

In the morning a herd of white porcelain elephants lumbers across the mahogany desk of the governor of Iowa. Paco insists that this elaborate building in Des Moines is reminiscent of Arab architecture. I tell him that we Arabs didn't get as far as the Midwest. Amira says that the monotony of the cornfields provides the right beat for the blood, that quasi-Arabian beat, for she wouldn't be surprised anymore to see a caravan of camels crossing the yellow desert of the American cornbelt. After the governor responds to the persistent questions of us Third Worlders, Amira slips off her left shoe and writes his name with a pen on the sole near the heel. According to an ancient Greek superstition that Dhimos has told her, the governor will come to ask for her hand before the writing has worn away.

Afterward I take my ease in the inner courtyard of the Des Moines Museum, by the edge of a pool from which a statue of Pegasus is emerging. Drowsy, I look at Nena, a poet from Finland, who is infatuated by a Giacometti sculpture. At the end of the evening, after a banquet in the home of a Des Moines family, it seems possible that Nena will stand before me as tipsy as I am, and will draw my body against hers, simply from the power of that quasi-Giacomettian quality of mortified infatuation which flames up suddenly between two strangers. And on her bed in the Mayflower, in the dim light of the lamp from the hall, I will take off her clothes. Then I will gently slip her nightgown over her head, as in a baptismal ceremony when the priest anoints with the sanctified oil the presumed locations of the infant's faculties. I will insert my hands in the sleeve and slide one of her arms out of it and then the other, and her nakedness scattered about the room will collect itself into the nightgown and wind itself around her sleep, and I will awaken into my solitude, lonely in a strange room, longing for Shlomith.

This morning I went down to see if I had any mail. By the elevator, I ran into Mary.

"What's new on the eighth floor?" she asked in her friendly, caring way. I stared at her and tried to phrase a suitable reply before the elevator closed between us.

"You must come along on the trip tomorrow," she hurriedly added. "Someone called Michael Abyad is interested in meeting you at the Atayas'." The door closed, and I stood there with Shlomith's telegram in my hand.

Great disaster. All your letters stolen. Probably Y. Goodbye my secret. Or shall we fight it? Forever, Shlomith.

Down North Dubuque Street the cars glide silently. Through the double window the red hush of Indian summer in the foliage of the maples, lingering in City Park, pauses over the waters of the river and floats down with the falling leaves. Here and there in the blue sky are cloud strokes. A red hot-air balloon floats on the wind and is momentarily reflected in a myriad of red fragments in the river winding its way behind the trees. Behind the northern wing of the Mayflower the cars disappear, and in a window across the yard, a student with a towel wound about her head makes her bed with slow, easy motions and casts over it a quilt made of patches in a multitude of colors. Then on a corner of the table she scratches her innocent behind.

Michael Abyad? Who is he?

PART SEVEN

THE TALE CONTINUED

The cobbler is barefoot, and the weaver naked.

Village proverb

CHAPTER 8

Imagine, then, a British soldier plummeting from the roof high above the third floor down into our courtyard, landing in a puddle of water from the early-December rain. The water splashes on the gas mask over the face of a boy playing by the puddle and blurs his vision. But first imagine a shot, just a single round from among the hundreds that had begun with the gray dawn, whose trajectories crisscrossed the skies of Haifa, in the warp and woof of the war between Jews and Arabs. Then imagine this one bullet hitting the soldier standing watch on the roof. He falls, and behind him the sharp spire of St. John's Church rises toward the brightening sky. The boy, who is about seven, freezes to the spot where the thud has caught him trying to frighten a neighbor's daughter with the gas mask he has bought from a peddler of military equipment. Now imagine the long second that passes between the thud and the scream: the silence that falls on the courtyard and is cast over the body, and then is lifted by the scream, which hangs in the air until the silence wraps itself again around the still body.

After the fashion of a villager who no longer takes any notice of the gunpowder lurking in the air, Father had come to Haifa a few months before, in the summer of 1947. It was just when the end of the British Mandate began to appear on the horizon, and with it the possibility of prosperity, because Fassuta was already becoming a depot for smuggling from both sides of the Lebanese border. To Father's credit, he was never tempted to participate in the smuggling operations run by my uncle Yusef—who was moving tobacco, arak, and other, even more elevating goods from the north to the south—even though these operations were handsomely remunerated. He was not by nature a sharp man of business. He was an artist at walking the tightrope between wealth and poverty, between safety and danger, and if in times of crisis he might skirt the edge of catastrophe, he somehow managed to lead the family to a safe haven.

I think about the two of them: the one brother a man of the soil who knew by heart both volumes of the chronicles of the Hlal tribe, the volume of the homeland and the volume of the wanderings, and who in his soul yearned to be a folk poet, like Uncle Mikha'eel, whom he might even have exceeded in talent; the other brother a craftsman so exacting that every pair of shoes he made continued to walk even after their owner died, as my uncle Yusef used to say, and who never acted without forethought and calculation, though in his large endeavors he always came out middling, neither at the top nor at the bottom, and whose life's work lay at the two poles of the body, the head and the feet. But when I think about the two of them now, I realize that the real man of the earth was my father, and that my uncle was a prisoner of the enchantments of the air, fire and water of the world.

Be all that as it may, in the summer of 1947 my father took his savings, one hundred Palestinian pounds, and invested most of them in a year's lease of a house on St. John Street in Haifa, in the very heart of the neighborhood that in only a few weeks would become one of the strategic areas in the fight for the city. The village cobbler's dream was to own a shoemaking shop in Haifa. But his dream proved to be like an honored guest at a village wedding, who makes his entrance just when the hosts are pressing their guests to take second and third helpings of all the delicacies that the women of the house and the neighboring women and the related wives and daughters and daughters-in-law have prepared late into the previous night. And now the honored guest takes his place at the head of one of the tables in the full knowledge of his own importance, and he waits for a skewer of the succulent liver of the fatted calf that had been slaughtered, or a lavish portion of the kid seethed in its mother's milk, only to find that the cooking pots have already been emptied and their bottoms scraped for the last morsels, and the cooking fires have died out.

Uncle Yusef tried to persuade my father that the future is in the hand of an *afreet,* a quick and mischievous *djinni,* and that there is no telling what will happen when the country is seething and quaking. But the sharp-eyed can see the sparks spraying out of the air vent of the *mashhara,* the apparatus for making charcoal, and knows that fire has seized hold of the insulated wood within, and that this batch will yield nothing but ashes. My uncle Yusef's images were like that, and my father, who did not like the meandering arabesques, replied with the proverb "Every man has his own Laylah." Whereupon Uncle Yusef drew himself up to his full height and said, "You go first to see what the situation is and then bring your family." My mother's nod of agreement left my father only one course of action.

But my uncle couldn't tell that my father would bet his shirt and lose it on the State of Israel. For when the fall of 1947 came, it was with storms of bullets. By then he had already bought and set up his shoemaking machines in the cellar of the house, acquired a pile of lasts and even found a stitcher. The first clients came to inspect the quality of his work and to ask about prices, and inquisitive neighbors expressed amazement at the daring of the enterprise at such a time. All of which made my father all the more sure of his venture. But then the sparks my uncle had already noticed began to burn holes in the fabric of the dream. And on that one gray December day everything collapsed and fell apart with a great thud, and my father stood there by the body with his hammer still in his hand and thought that this was not how he had imagined his dream might come crashing down.

The soldier was lying on his back with his eyes open. One arm was flung over his head and the other protected his chest in a sort of belated embrace. Blood seeped from the corner of his mouth and dyed the muddy water with the crimson of ancient palaces and glowing hearths and velvet armchairs. My brother Jubran, the boy in the mask, drew close to Father and did not take off the mask, as if it were the last line of defense between himself and the dead soldier, and the neighbor's daughter ran for her life to her mother, because she didn't know what else these villagers had up their sleeves for her. Father looked at the hammer in his hand. Someone could come into the courtyard, take in the scene and ask the wrong questions. So he hurried to put away the hammer before he called the police.

That was at the beginning of December. And like the dreamer who is shaken awake and tries to close his eyes again to return to the chambers of illusion, my father closed his eyes and soothed my mother, saying these were but transient episodes, and the skies would clear soon, and the battle would be decided for one side or the other, though of the other side he knew nothing. The next morning he began to prepare a hiding place in the house, just in case. It was a dark little room, a forgotten pantry of sorts, the doorless entrance to which was easy to conceal behind the kitchen cupboard, and like everything else in the world, it waited for its hour of glory, which was soon to come.

In January the feeling took hold that what could not be settled by shooting could be settled by car bombs; what would not be settled by "concerts," as the shooting was called in the suburbs, could be settled by the solo performance of shock waves in the air. Those were the days my father regretted he was a cobbler and not a glazier, though in his heart he already knew that he had to pick up whatever pieces he could and go back to the village.

One evening in January, Uncle Yusef came to stay with us, he and Khaleel, Uncle Mikha'eel's son, after having transported one of their cargoes to Nazareth. They were still sitting around the sparse supper table when all the windows flew open with a whoosh and the walls trembled.

"I am your eldest brother," said Uncle Yusef to my father, "and tomorrow I'm taking your family back to the village, and you can pursue your crazy dreams all by yourself." Father looked at him and said nothing.

In the morning they all set out, except Father, on the long and devious journey to the railroad station at Faisal's Column in the lower city. Whatever they could carry they took along with them. On the way they stayed close to the walls and went by way of every little side alley they encountered. In her heart my mother offered up a prayer of thanks to the Virgin for granting her the wisdom to oppose my father's wish to bring to the new house the mirrored wardrobe and the wooden bed and all the rest of the furnishings from the *jhaz* that had been brought on the backs of two camels from Rmeish to the village eight years before. She thought of the long journey she might have to make back to Lebanon, and about the embarrassing moment at the end of it when her brother Elias would stand at the entrance to his home in Beirut and accept her and her children and her husband, and what remained of their worldly goods. What would he think of his sister who had been sent as a bride to a Galilean village with wide-brimmed and colorful *chapeaux* in her suitcases and now had come back as a refugee, bare of head and despondent of soul? Thinking of their small private tragedy, she wondered if she had turned off the fire under the pot before they left, and if my father would remember to put out the kerosene stove.

It had begun to rain again when Jubran noticed the man in the gas mask who stood at the end of the alley. He stood with his legs apart, like someone who knew exactly what he was doing, his hands in the pockets of his British jodhpurs, indifferent to the rain falling on his head and on the gas mask covering his face.

"It's the English soldier that fell into our courtyard," said Jubran. Uncle Yusef told him to keep quiet. And they, too, stood there in the rain. Behind them stretched Allenby Street, crisscrossed now with bullets and the sounds of explosions, and before them stood the man in his gas mask.

"Since we're getting soaked," said Mother, "let's get going."

They went forward a few steps. The man stood still. The end of the alley behind them was filled with smoke.

"He has a gun in his pocket," said Khaleel, and suggested to my uncle that he give the man the money they had gotten in Nazareth instead of bringing it to the connection in Rmeish. My uncle pulled the packet of money out of his pocket and held it out in front of the eyes that he had to assume were behind the gas mask. Still the man wouldn't budge. It became clear that he wanted everything they had. My uncle stuffed the bank notes into the pockets of the mysterious man, and then he set down beside him the suitcase and the bundles of clothes.

"*Khawaja,* we are not from here," said Khaleel to him in Arabic. "We are simple villagers, and this is not our war."

Later, in the crowded train that was taking them to Akka, Khaleel broke into a burst of relieved laughter. The people in the crowded compartment had broken the spell of the nightmare. My uncle boiled with rage at him and at all the nations of the earth and particularly at the fact that in a moment of weakness he had taken Khaleel's advice, he whom the whole village came to for advice.

184

"Well," said my mother, "let's hope that Hanna hasn't scorched the pot." My uncle shook his head and said, "When the camel's gone, don't cry over the reins." And after that they didn't say a word the whole way back to the village.

But the pot, as it happened, did get scorched.

The next day my father went to his Armenian stitcher, to ask his advice. The latter offered him two hundred uppers in return for his machines. Heavy iron in exchange for light portable leather. "I don't belong to your war," said the stitcher, "so I don't need to wander all over the place and be light of foot. But you have to be ready and alert all the time, prepared to set out on your way the moment anything bad happens. For if it is your destiny to be a refugee, you must always be prepared to accept it. So put your home into a suitcase, and your trust in your feet, as a cobbler should."

For a man to be able to walk a long way he needs a sturdy sole sewn correctly to the upper of his shoe. Though my father was not to attain full refugeehood, ever since then he took care that every pair of shoes that came out of his workshop would serve its owner for many long years of walking, in rain and in heat, over stones and through mud, in their going forth and their coming hither, for if the decree of wandering passed over you the first time, no one will swear to you, upon the head of your little daughter Catherine, that it will the second time.

For three weeks he turned the exchange over and over in his mind, until he came to a decision. Then for two whole months he shut himself into the house and devoted himself body and soul to the creation of his life's masterpiece. In his mind's eye he saw the Idea of the Shoe, the all-purpose universal shoe, the shoe for attending receptions in the homes of the Khayat and Khoury and Karaman families, and for trudging to the last of the tents in the most godforsaken refugee camp in the world.

During the day he would sleep a troubled sleep, and at

night he would sit down to the tools he had brought with him from the village. After dipping them in high-grade gasoline, he would wipe and polish them until they gleamed in the lantern light in the forgotten pantry. He handled them like ancient ritual objects as he prepared them for the task that he had taken upon himself. Then he sat down at his table, and with his thick carpenter's pencil he made plans and specifications for the Shoe—how it would look and of what materials it would be made and what uppers and what soles and what color and what laces. Then he would erase and go back and redraw every detail from all its angles. When finally he visualized the perfect pair of shoes standing before him on the table, he set to work on the execution of the plan. He selected the best leathers, the best threads and the best soles he could get his hands on. Apart from hasty trips into the smoky streets to buy a bit of food, he remained in the forgotten pantry. Each evening he would move aside the cupboard that covered its entrance and go into his dusky kingdom, and the cupboard, as if in response to some unheard command of "Close, Sesame!" would return to its place and seal the door behind him.

One morning he ventured out of his enchanted cave and found that the door of the house had been broken in during the night and several items had disappeared. But he did not grieve over the loss or permit himself to worry about the rest of his possessions. From that morning on he no longer shut the front door at all, and he allowed the winter winds to overturn and rifle through the few things that remained in the apartment.

In the middle of April, as he later realized, the work was finally done. The *djinnis* came and sat around his table and examined the pair of shoes from every angle, as their gleaming white beards brushed gently against the leather of the uppers, and the uppers shone in the light of creation. Their ivory fingers caress the two soles and the soles tap on the wooden table like the hoofbeats of the hind let loose. And in the same way the *djinnis* had appeared in a burst of light, they also vanished in a burst of light. As his eyes became accustomed to the dimness of the quaking lantern, he saw a flash on the other side of the cupboard, but by the time he had pushed the cupboard aside and stepped out into the kitchen, the light had faded as if it had never been. He collapsed onto the last stool that remained in the apartment and leaned his back against the wall the rest of the night. At dawn he saw a splendid crimson feather in the first light on the windowsill.

He was shaken awake by an uproar in the courtyard. He rushed into the pantry, still in the grip of his dream, and pulled the cupboard closed behind him. He heard footsteps, and from the depths of his weariness his practiced ears managed to distinguish three different pairs of shoes.

The owners of the shoes spoke Hebrew, a language my father did not understand, and he strained his ear to interpret their tone and cadence. Soon they went on their way, and the house fell back into its silence, into the sounds of distant explosions. Father emerged from his hiding place. And the feather that in his dream was on the windowsill had vanished.

That was on the morning of Friday, April 23, 1948. Haifa had already fallen. My father put the shoes in a burlap sack and set out on his way. In the port a boat was taking on some of the fleeing Arabs who would come to be known as Palestinian refugees in the course of time and their wanderings. When my father heard that the boat was heading for Akka, he climbed aboard and squeezed in among them, because from Akka he could get to the village. A man who was standing next to him asked him if the burlap sack was all he was planning to take along on the journey. My father stuck his hand into the sack and pulled out the pair of shoes, as if he were pulling a *djinni* out of a sealed bottle. The man stared at them, enchanted. "I'll give you everything I have in exchange for them," he said, and pulled out a dank wad of bank notes and stuffed them into the pockets of my astonished father. Then he opened his own burlap sack and took the shoes from Father's hands and slipped them inside. A dull thud was heard.

"What did he have in his sack?" Uncle Yusef was to ask him. "Why didn't you look to see whether he had a gas mask?"

CHAPTER 9

Time would pass, and the man in the gas mask would continue to flicker in the family's memory like the male firefly flickering his love on a summer night as he alternately twinkles and floats and dives yet again into the darkness. His pallid light is reflected on the shoes of Mahmood El-Ibraheem as he sways in the cold November wind and his eyes begin to close on the sight of the courtyard of his house, and his hands, which had known better days than these, now tighten around the sides of his Arab breeches, to prevent them from loosening the noose of the rope around his neck. And now his eyes close and their shine dims and fades, and only the shoes will keep on shining by the light of the fireflies hovering around the body that is taking leave of the soul they are accompanying on its final journey into the darkness.

The last memory that passed through Mahmood El-Ibraheem's mind was the memory of his old grandmother telling him and his brothers as they lie down to sleep on a midsummer's night, on the roof of the same house that is now offering him its final mercies, about how the fireflies come from the ends of the earth, even on the stormiest of winter nights, to accompany those who put an end to their own lives on their final journey. As she recited this, she looked straight into the eyes of the youngest of her grand-sons, and a shiver snaked down his back and his little hand unconsciously fingered his throat. He hung on to his grand-mother's look, like a boy hanging on to the rope that is tied around his waist and is pulling him in regular jerks out of the depths of the cistern. His feet recoil from the touch of the new shoes, as if the soles and the uppers were made of the briers from the threshing floor prepared for the suspects investigated at the Tarbeekha police station in the summer of 1937.

That year the spirit of the Arab Rebellion began to seethe in the villages, after the passage of the first great enthusiasm that drove the villagers to offer food and help to those who had raised the banner of revolt. But as the grain bins became emptied of the 1936 harvest, out of the sealed bottle burst the *djinni* who was to drown the rebellion in a turbid outpouring of corruption and weakness. And Abu Shacker, who had lavished on the rebels of nearby Deir El-Kasi quantities of bread and olive oil, now held back, for he began to see the clouds of hunger and anxiety gathering on the horizon.

Then the murders began. A red seal stamped on the flap of his *qunbaz,* the long-sleeved garment worn by men, told the owner that his days were numbered. A hired assassin from Tarsheeha was the executioner of these sentences. The *mukhtar* of Ikrit, the *mukhtar* of Suhmata and the *mukhtar* of the western quarter of Deir El-Kasi paid no mind to this red seal, and they paid with their lives. Then came the turn of the common people.

On October 30, 1936, as I have written, Abdallah Al-Asbah sat in my father's barbershop and abandoned himself to the pleasure of getting shaved, and with eyes closed he sank into a deep torpor after several sleepless nights. But Al-Asbah was to see something unseen by my father, whose train of thought had unwound and gone out of the barbershop and trailed after the hem of Elaine Bitar's dress, so that he didn't see, or maybe he saw but without noticing that he saw, a man passing now in front of the window in the opposite direction to Elaine. The man sends a quick glance into the barbershop, his one hand shading his eyes. He doesn't pause for long, but Al-Asbah, in a piercing moment of sharpened awareness, rises to the surface of his doze and instantly takes in the scene outside the window, and his instincts carve it in his memory. Then the relaxed body stretches out again, hanging there in the noose of his drowsiness. Only the whizzing of the bullets will remind Al-Asbah, in the darkness of the goatshed, of what his eyes had seen, and he would add Rasheed Karrarah to the long list of names of those his vengeful arm would one day reach out against.

It was from Bethlehem that he came, and like the famous Galilean before him, he came in the shadow of the cross, which he was to carry almost to his death. Karrarah was what everyone called him, a distortion of his real name, which no one remembered. Just as the villagers were satisfied to have no good explanation why Elaine Bitar had come from distant Beirut to show off her wide-brimmed *chapeaux* in this obscure Galilean village, so they refrained from inquiring into the motives of this man who came to the village one morning in the summer of 1936 and said that he wanted to establish a high school, which would offer a broad education to youngsters he believed to be thirsting after knowledge in this illiterate world where guns and rebellion were beginning to raise their ugly heads.

He did establish a school, and to the handful of students who enrolled he spoke for long hours about someone named Marx, word of whom had not yet reached Fassuta, and with enthusiasm about socialism and religion and society and saving the world and virtue and marriage and free love. On Sunday he was always the first to kneel when he had only to sit comfortably on the pew in the Church of Elijah the

Prophet, and the first to cross himself when he had only to bow his head. But in time the villagers came to respect him less and to suspect him more, for his words rushed from his mouth like an endless waterfall. Then came the time when all the veils of mystery fell from him and the real reasons for his coming to the village began to be clear.

It began with his nightly searchings outside the village, his questioning the elders about the 1860s and his probings into matters the villagers dared touch upon only in stories and legends. He kept mentioning to them a Crusader document from 1183, which told about the fortress of Fassove, as the Saracens called it, and another document, from the year 1220, where the name Fasole was mentioned, and which told about the golden treasures that were hidden away in the broad cave over which the fortress was built. So it became apparent that he was after the gold, and the villagers began to regard him as a foolish hunter who has stumbled into an alien forest.

In those days Abu Shacker was a young and impulsive bachelor, and he volunteered to guide the teacher from Bethlehem through the byways of the village and the twists and turns of its legends. He would lead him to presumed entrances to the cave and spend moonlit nights with him awaiting the appearance of Ar-Rasad, who would lead them to the magic word which would open the entrances that had been sealed since the days of the Crusaders and would reveal to their eyes the glitter of the Crusaders' gold. But the days went by and Ar-Rasad did not appear and the entrances to the cave did not respond to the magic words that they took from ancient texts and whispered at the sealed rocks. Gradually the idea began to pierce their minds that the secret was sealed and hidden to them because certain powers were present that were determined to banish Ar-Rasad far into the depths of legend, that is, those same rebels who arose to defy the authorities and to tamper with the fate forged in the celestial chambers, which no human hand could change.

Thus they came to perceive the Arab rebels as the enemy of Ar-Rasad, who was wary of them and did not show the tip of his tail in fear they would attempt to take control of his treasures by force.

Once the villagers knew what Karrarah's aim was, they encircled him with a ring of polite distance, in addition to the ring of forbearance with which they had already surrounded the foolish hunter. Then the rings multiplied and tightened, for his avowed purpose now took on an explicit political stance against the tyranny of the "gangsters," as he called them, and against the submissiveness of the villagers before those who had arisen to oppress them.

The "gangsters" might have ignored this teacher with a wrinkle in his brain had it not been for a sequence of events in the summer of 1937, the "threshing summer," as the villagers call it. An idea took root in Abu Shacker's mind, and he told it to Karrarah, saying they should compose a letter in which they exposed the sufferings of the villagers at the hands of the gangsters, who had filled the empty measure with bitterness instead of wheat, and they should send the letter to the British command post located in the police station at Tarbeekha. So they secretly composed the letter in English, insofar as their modest knowledge of this language allowed them. With all the rashness to which youth is prone, Abu Shacker took the letter and headed north to deliver it himself. But the farther he progressed from the village, the weaker his knees became and the thinner his courage. By the time he reached the Northern Road he stood on the banks of his own little Rubicon. If he was to return to the village with the letter still in his pocket, the trust that the teacher had placed in him would be lost, and if he was to pluck up his courage and take it to the police station, the rebels' spies, planted in the ranks of the British Army, would report him, and the man who had sent him, to those gangsters who had not a shred of mercy in their hearts. Whereupon he shook off these thoughts and found himself standing in the middle of the road. Without further deliberation he brings a few stones from the side of the road, arranges them in a pyramid and lays the letter at its vertex and another stone on top of it to keep his words from flying away on the summer wind and reaching the alert ears of the evildoers.

As it happened, Abu Shacker's eldest brother was herding his flock of goats along the edges of the Northern Road, and he saw the pile of stones standing there in the middle of the road. Out of a herdsman's curiosity, he approached and saw the paper lying under the stone. He took it and examined the peculiar letters scattered along the length and breadth of the page. Then he said to himself that only the *mukhtar* will be able to decipher such strange Arabic.

At that very hour the *mukhtar* was sitting with Mahmood El-Ibraheem and several rebels under his command. Al-Ibraheem took the letter from the *mukhtar*'s hands and passed it on to one of the rebels, who served as a spy against the British and regarded himself as a master of their language. He read the letter and his face fell. It proved to be of no help at all to Abu Shacker and Karrarah that the *mukhtar* explained that this letter was nothing more than the youth's ignorance triggered by the teacher's well-known foolishness. But the rebels, with Mahmood El-Ibraheem at their head, saw this as a golden opportunity for teaching a lesson to all those hesitant villagers who had begun to have doubts about the justness of the Arab Rebellion, and to show them what happened to traitors who dared to speak ill of the rebellion to those who were its greatest enemies. And in less than an hour the two of them were brought to Al-Balat, a meeting place outside the *mukhtar*'s house. First they cursed them, then they beat them, then they kicked them. Then they took them to a place on the outskirts of the village, and the men took turns riding on their backs. Then they tied Karrarah's hands and feet and lowered him into an abandoned well.

Abu Shacker was brought to the courtyard of Al-Ibraheem's house, and there he was questioned the whole night about his connections with the British enemy. The next day he was released. Not so Karrarah. Through two endless nights, when silence enveloped the houses of the village and the wild beasts in its fields were mute, Karrarah's wails rose from the depths of the abandoned well and surged through the air until they broke against the walls of the villagers. But no one dared go to him, not even under the cover of darkness, until the wails carried to the doors of the police station at Tarbeekha and the British Army came and pulled him out of the darkness and brought him to his birthplace. In the years that followed, when his name came to be spread far and wide because of his great wealth, the villagers would say that the dark pit where he had been cast was the entrance to the eastern tunnel leading to the cave over which the village is built, where the golden treasures of the Crusader knights lie buried, and Allah alone, may his Name be praised, knows the truth of the matter, unless indeed it is all another creation of the village's imagination stirred up by the tailfeathers of the fabled Ar-Rasad.

Once the British had heard of the letter, they decided that the time had come to introduce some English calmness into the Galilee. So they sent troops to the villages and rounded up everyone suspected of belonging to the rebels.

About a dozen men in Fassuta were involved in the rebel cause, to some degree or another. Among them was Kareem Mikha'eel, who had lost his heart to a beautiful Muslim woman from the village of Jdaideh and had abandoned his wife and his home, converted to Islam, taking the name Muhammad Mikha'eel, and married the woman from Jdaideh. To his wife in Fassuta he explained that he was now numbered among the warriors of the rebellion. Not many years later he was to abandon his new wife as well and enlist in the British Army and be sent to fight in Greece, and there he would take a Greek wife. In time he would abandon her, too, and travel to Argentina, and there, as was his habit, he settled down and raised a family. When he returned in the fullness of his days to the village, he recounted how he had tended Uncle Jiryes on his deathbed, and brought with him the Arabic translation of the Old Testament that had accompanied my uncle on both his journeys, in this world and the next, and a small notebook, purchased in Beirut, in which were copied from memory, in his ornamental handwriting, Syrian revolutionary songs from the 1920s.

On that day in the summer of 1937, the "summer of the threshing," Kareem Mikha'eel had come to the village on one of his rare visits. He was among the men brought to the center of the village and commanded to strip to their waists. A reddish mark on the shoulder was sufficient to implicate its owner as belonging to the rebels, for the mark was taken to be the welt left by a rifle strap. So they took all those with red shoulders, and Muhammad-Kareem among them, to the command post at Tarbeekha. There they separated the men of Fassuta from the men of Deir El-Kasi and began to interrogate them. The pink-shouldered men of the village, whose habit was not always to shoulder their rifles but to carry them in their hands, an act of village boastfulness, were sent home except for Muhammad-Kareem. On their way out they managed to catch a glimpse of the inner courtyard, where British soldiers were covering the floor with briers. In their frightened imaginations there was no room for doubt as to what the briers were for, and they hastened to inform the *mukhtar.*

Muhammad-Kareem and the men of Deir El-Kasi were first ordered to remove their shoes, and then they were tied together in twos like yoked oxen and led to the inner courtyard. There they saw that the floor had been covered with briers, which they were ordered to thresh with the soles of their feet.

When the *mukhtar,* a cousin of Muhammad-Kareem,

came to the police station he tried to persuade them to stop the threshing. He said the rebels were only naive hardworking farmers who had been incited by urban rabble-rousers and pushed into a rebellion that had so little to do with them that they couldn't tell their enemies from their friends.

When Muhammad-Kareem came back home, he told his wife and children more than the British had been able to make him confess: that he had converted to Islam, married another woman and joined the Arab Rebellion. His wife neither wept nor reviled him, for she loved him with a great love; even when in the fullness of their days he returns from distant Argentina to the village she will tell him that she forgives him and absolves him and has never harbored ill feelings toward him, and will remind him how she sat by him and with her nails and her teeth pulled the thorns of the briers from the soles of his feet.

Despite the November chill, the summer's threshing burns now in the soles of Mahmood El-Ibraheem's feet as he hangs from the rope, his feet which are encased in the shoes that several days earlier he had taken off the feet of a dead man he had encountered in a ravine near the Lebanese border. He recalls that day of threshing in the summer of 1937, and the rope tightening around his neck suddenly brings to his mind the sight of that strange mask he had found in the burlap sack that lay at the feet of the corpse. He sees the firefly twinkling its tail in front of him and sees a man holding a pistol hiding in the shadows. Then he is a little boy on the roof, on a night when the moon was full, listening to his grandmother's tales of the fireflies who come to accompany those who take their own lives, to mitigate the final darkness.

And the shoes, which had been intended for endless wanderings, dance on the cold wind.

PART EIGHT
THE TELLER: Mayflower III

At three o'clock he breaks in their hands like a tender twig, ready to suggest the Arab, as a solution of sorts.

A. B. Yehoshua, *Facing the Woods*

Iowa City, December 4

Snow: no Shlomith, no Michael Abyad.

The day after the meeting with Michael Abyad I went for a walk, though I was exhausted, along the riverbank. The strips of sod that the workmen had laid a month earlier were now withered with frost and squeaked underfoot. The bare branches of the trees on either side seemed pocked with the scabs of some disease. The greenish water was streaked with darkness. Winter shows the first signs of its coming, then lurks in ambush behind the thinning foliage. The October days that were to follow would no longer be what they once were. A blue soberness was in the air: the clarity of the skies burning like frost despite the warming sun. Fewer squirrels scurried along the grass-edged sidewalks. Then heavy rains fell during the nights, no longer the twilight drizzle of September but whipping down with a sort of restrained vengeance. The smell of the sodden earth aroused in my memory musky scents from the village and hooves beating in the mating season. And when finally the snow came, there was a pervasive sense of missed opportunity.

Michael Abyad was called back to Beirut the day after our meeting. But tomorrow he is due to return to Iowa City.

Two months have passed since that day at the Atayas' house, also the day Paco threw the beer can into the lake. Two months during which I have chewed Michael Abyad's gum, as Bjørg would have put it, and seen the world through his eyes. I saw the workmen taking away the strips of sod that had been rejected by the black earth, and Bar-On trying to strangle Amira, and the first snowflakes at the end of November, big as an infant's hand, carpeting Iowa City, after most of the writers had departed.

Shlomith does not leave me in peace, though my future is now empty of her. What is she doing, what is she feeling right now? Meetings with a lawyer, finding an alibi for the love letters, shoring up the defense against the ethnic issue. Are her days utterly lonely? Does she weep like a hunted beast while I stand and watch from afar, if that's what I'm doing. Neighs of longing are all I can draw from my Arab lungs.

This Michael Abyad has silently woven himself into my life, where the magic thread of Shlomith has come undone and unravels in my hands: like a rope slipping through one's hands following the full bucket, whipping against the throat of the cistern and sinking into the depths. And the surface of the water ripples for a while, until it returns to the mute language of mirrors.

From the day that Paco cast the beer can into the Atayas' lake, the chasm between him and Bar-On gaped open again, though both of them continued to behave as if nothing had happened. One morning we found Bar-On was gone. He had left at dawn to return to Israel, as he had wanted to do that first night when he stood at the back entrance to the Mayflower and the smell of midwestern carpets hit his nose. Some of the writers heaved sighs of relief and even congratulated Paco for now being free of him. As for me, I felt as if I had missed something, and even felt a few mild pangs of conscience, for perhaps I should have gotten closer to him—however unlikely that was—instead of spending my time trying to match my life with that of Michael Abyad, who had appeared and vanished like a flash of lightning. But then the bitter taste Bar-On left in my mouth would arise again and overwhelm everything he had left behind, even the taste of the meal in Kalona, the Amish village.

I was waiting in the bus that would take us to Kalona that Friday morning, when Bar-On sat down next to me. I told him that I was saving the place for Amira. He nodded in a hurt way. "I've been wanting to talk to you," he said. With a rudeness I still don't understand, I told him that he knew where he could find me. Just then Amira appeared in the door of the bus, and Bar-On got up and went to look for a more welcoming place. When I told Amira what had happened, she said that for the last week she, too, had been unkind to him, to say the least, because she had no patience anymore with his childish behavior. We decided we should get together with him and try to reach an understanding.

Paul Engle asked for silence. He explained to us the Amish community we were going to visit, and asked that we try not to offend them, especially to avoid smoking in their homes.

At the entrance to Kalona, a sign said "Courtesy, Service, Progress." We took in the black horses trotting along, harnessed to a traditional buggy, the little girls with black bonnets, a few women in gray, wearing scarves. We then visited the workshops of craftsmen in the middle of the village, lingering in the shop of a local potter, who turned her wheel with her bare foot. The clay pots scattered on her shelves looked as if they, too, were barefoot. We were served a midday dinner at the home of an Amish family. Bjørg drew our attention to a piece of wood hanging on the wall, on which was inscribed a four-line poem in praise of the beautiful home. The daughter of one of the Chinese writers was singing a folk song, and as Amira began to remark about the poem on the wall, Bar-On, who was sitting opposite us, hushed her. But at the end of the excellent meal Bar-On pulled his pipe out of his pocket, tamped in tobacco and began to light it.

As I try to reconstruct what happened next, I recall only the scene at the Engles', at the first reception, when I stood with Amira in the darkness outside on the balcony and suddenly we were flooded with light and Bar-On stood there on the other side of the glass, with one hand still on the switch, shaking a chiding finger at us. Now it's Amira's turn, and she says in Hebrew to Bar-On: "You know, it's really an act of *chutzpah* on your part to smoke here." Just then the singer finished her song, and in the applause Bar-On didn't understand what Amira was trying to say. He leaned across to her with the lit match still between his thumb and forefinger and his other hand cupping his ear. She repeated her words in a louder voice.

Now that the applause has ended, everyone turns to look at her. Then, as in a dream, Bar-On's face swells with fury as he reaches across the table and grabs Amira's neck. He shakes it so forcefully that his hair falls away from the pate he has concealed. Only then do I understand what my eyes are seeing. With a strength I didn't know I had, I grabbed both his hands and pushed him back into his chair. Amira covered her face with her two hands, placed her elbows on the white tablecloth and breathed deeply. The silence that had fallen upon the table was broken by Paul, who came over to ask her if he should deal with the situation. Amira shook her head and said there was nothing wrong. Bar-On pushed his chair back and hurried outside, followed by Paul. Bjørg whispered, "It's time we all realized just how much violence can be aroused in people by songs in unknown languages, in the most unexpected places." Amira burst out laughing, and all the guests turned their attention to the dessert.

A huge bouquet of flowers arrived the next day at Amira's room, accompanied by a long letter of apology and an invitation to drink coffee. But ten days after these events happened, Bar-On left the Mayflower without saying good-bye to anyone. "Just when I was beginning to fall in love with him," said Amira.

Last night I read some of my poetry in the Selected Works Bookstore, at the southern end of Dubuque Street, despite Rick's recommendation that I keep a low profile. Though it was the last of the readings by members of the International Writing Program, some of whom had already returned to their own countries, a large audience filled the shop, despite the falling snow that had begun to accumulate outside. A sense of ending was in the air, for in a few days the rest of the suitcases would be packed and ways would part, and promises to write letters and keep in touch would be made. Iowa City would be packed away in the suitcases of memory: the red autumn leaves spread out before the nose of a tiny squirrel as it runs, a hot-air balloon floating silently in the blue sky, shampooed coeds in an elevator, the Engles' balcony at twilight, Liam washing himself in the drizzle. And wine, lots of wine.

Amira draws my attention to five students sitting cross-legged on the floor, their backs against the wall and checked *kufiyas* wrapped around their necks. I smiled at the concern in her voice and went on talking to Bert, but my eyes kept straying to the five students. Then Rick comes over to ask me if I had invited them. I begin to worry.

"Do you know why they're here?"

"I don't know who invited them," I say. "I hope there won't be any trouble."

"What kind of trouble?"

"Maybe the combination of 'Arab Poet' and 'from Israel' that you put on the announcements was not to their liking. The word 'Palestine' is missing."

"Whoever makes any trouble," Rick says with his American bluntness, "is gonna find himself outside."

I want to go over and talk to them and find out what

their intentions are, but Rick hurriedly begins the proceedings by asking everyone to sit down, and the way over to them is blocked.

First a Polish poet reads from his work in clipped, whispered Polish, as though to say, "I'm not the one who wrote this." Pedro, who has been sitting next to the quintet, pulls a pack of clove cigarettes out of his pocket and shares with them. I notice a smoke detector concealed among the bookshelves above their heads. I sit there, waiting to see what will neutralize them first, the smoke detector or the Polish poetry. But the detector fails me, and in the intermission they flee for their lives into the white night, stunned by uncomprehended poetry, to Rick's satisfaction and to my disappointment.

Before I begin to read some of my Hebrew poems translated into English, Amira leans over to me, her palm pressing the top of her woolen shirt. She suggests that the next day we go out and buy ourselves some checked *kufiyas*. "No," I say to her. "Tomorrow I'm going to meet Michael Abyad."

PART NINE

THE TALE CONCLUDED

People say telling tales is good for sleep, and I say it's meant to keep people awake.

> Rabbi Nahman
> of Bratslav

CHAPTER 10

In 1940 Aunt Jaleeleh had began to approach the end of the third decade of her life. My mother was already pregnant with my eldest brother, and all eyes turned anxiously to Jaleeleh, the youngest of the girls, whose hand no one had yet come to request. Rada Mikha'eel, who came to be known as Abu Jameel, the village carpenter, stood off to the side, absorbed in his courtship, and observed the arabesques in the minds of the Shammas family, worried that the hand he sought would be knocked out of his grasp and fall to the lot of some other suitor. Indeed, he was never to get a clear answer.

Aunt Jaleeleh, who still lived with her brother and her new sister-in-law, would encourage him with promises but make everything depend upon the family's consent. And the family, though small and shrunken compared to the rest of those in the village, behaved like a major clan with many branches, all of them comprising enough contradictory opinions and cross-purposes and qualifications and second thoughts to drive the average suitor out of his mind. Too many cooks, as the proverb says, burn the food. To the main cooks were added all the brothers-in-law and sisters-in-law, each stirring the pot with his or her own ladle. And Aunt Jaleeleh is in the middle, her mind whirling.

My father was the only one who supported Rada Mikha'eel without doubts or qualifications, and he acted as a one-man delegation to bring about the hitching of my aunt's carriage to the carpenter's horse. He found nothing wrong with him and quite liked the man's "light blood," that is, his sense of humor. But Abu Ibraheem, Aunt Marie's husband, regarded it as a major flaw in the suitor's character. "I will not agree to my sister-in-law marrying a man who wastes his time imitating animals and amusing children with silly songs," he said. My father, who not long before had been a fobbed-off bridegroom himself, became impatient and demanded an immediate decision.

When she heard that, Jaleeleh upped and packed her things and went off to live with her sister Marie. Marie's house was near Abu Habeeb's house. This neighbor was also her brother-in-law and godfather to Zaki, who eventually became Aunt Jaleeleh's husband.

On a stormy December night in 1948, Uncle Zaki is summoned to the house of his godfather, Abu Habeeb. He stands before the door soaked to his skin, like the *tatamus*, the bird that warns of approaching snow and that is frightened by his knocking and flees into the driving rain from the shelter it had found at nightfall in the doorway. The door opens a crack and Abu Habeeb bids him come in. By the lantern light that flickers in the wind that accompanied him through the door he sees, huddled in a black *abaya*, Mahmood El-Ibraheem sitting by the fire in the corner. He is blowing on the embers, trying to get the damp kindling to ignite. Zaki El-Aasi, even though a man's man, feels his knees turn to water and tries to make his dry mouth say good evening, though it's hardly the greeting to use at such a late hour; but his voice is inaudible and it comes out as if he, too, were trying to stir up a fire from dying embers. "They say that you've been hanged," he finally said. "Or that you'd hanged yourself."

210

Mahmood El-Ibraheem grinned in his corner and turned his head toward him and said, "I've stopped trusting ropes."

"Do you trust me?" asked Zaki El-Aasi.

"If not, I wouldn't have sent for you," said Abu Habeeb.

In the late 1950s, Abu Habeeb, Uncle Zaki's godfather, would come to Sunday Mass riding on his donkey, swathed in an *abaya* the color of honeycombs, a proud elder bathed in honor and glory. I remember his bristly white mustache, and his broad fingers, which after he would sit down on the pew behind me would pull his *iqal* off his head and toss it nonchalantly at the foot of the pillar to the right of the altar. When Mass was over he would lay his hand on my shoulder and say, "Boy, get my *iqal."*

This was a few years after the first public school had opened in the village, after the closing, at my father's initiative, of the school that had been under the auspices of Archbishop Hakim. To Hakim's surprise, Abu Habeeb, the trustee of the *waqf,* believed in public schooling and supported my father. When things got heated and the priest locked the school, Abu Habeeb went up to the door after Sunday Mass, inserted his cane under the hasp of the lock and pulled it out with its nails and screws. Then with his sturdy eighty-year-old shoulder he pushed in the door, and its two halves opened wide and nearly came unhinged at the sound of the applause all around. Throwing a few parting words in English, he went on his way, followed by awed looks from the assembled villagers. From that day forth, the village children blamed him for having invented school.

In 1926 Abu Habeeb traveled all the way to New York, to turn over a new leaf. His wife and his firstborn son were left behind in his parents' house, and his wife was soon to discover that he had also left behind his second son. She was a sickly woman, and she knew she was carrying an orphan in her womb, but she told no one. When the time came for her to give birth, her father-in-law went to Bent Jbeil to bring Dr. Mgheizel to deliver the baby. These were the days of the *mustaqradat* at the end of February, the days of rain that spring lends to winter. Dr. Mgheizel, whose soul was still wrapped in the gloom of winter, said he couldn't travel in the rain, and sent the father-in-law away. He trudged through the rain as far as Ein Ebel, where he met Mahmood El-Ibraheem, who asked him why he was looking so downcast. He told him what had happened at Bent Jbeil, and continued on his way.

At midnight, after she had gone into labor, there was a sudden knocking at the door. The father-in-law got up to open it, and there stood Mahmood El-Ibraheem, dripping and shivering but with the doctor firmly in hand. At dawn the doctor came out of her room and announced that he had managed to save only the child. The news reached New York three months later, but Abu Habeeb did not have enough money for the trip. Three long years later he came back to the village, during the Great Depression, and he married his wife's sister, but he did not forget what Mahmood El-Ibraheem had done for the sake of his first wife. Now he was about to pay back that twenty-year-old debt, which is why he has sent for his godson Zaki at this late hour.

Uncle Zaki had once been a student of Rasheed Karrarah. It disturbed him that the man he so respected was the victim of maltreatment by the inhabitants of Deir El-Kasi, led by Mahmood El-Ibraheem, who was now huddled by the fire in the corner like a wounded lion. In addition to which, Abu Shacker was his cousin, and only two weeks earlier Zaki had got him talking and had heard from his own mouth the story of that night in the courtyard of Al-Ibraheem's house.

Here, on the one hand, sits that hanged man who about ten years earlier had led his cousin and his respected teacher in the humiliating procession to the abandoned well, and on the other is his respected and beloved godfather. How can he not help Abu Habeeb repay his debt to the man who brought the reluctant doctor all the way from Bent Jbeil by force? But now the tangled past seems to him irrelevant to the main point: the figure of this rebel huddled in his recent defeat, rubbing his hands together above the embers, an old English gun and a scimitar leaning against the wall next to him, both covered in drops of black rain.

I went outside; it was so dark you could hold up your finger and not see it. Luckily I was wearing my boots. I went to my house, and Jaleeleh was standing outside shivering, unable to sleep because she is so worried. "I hope you bring good news," she said. "Allah is generous," I said. I hid the gun under my coat so she wouldn't see it, then I went over to the cupboard and found a few candles and stuck them in my pocket. I stopped at the children's bed and covered them. Jaleeleh is watching and she doesn't believe it. "You're not going anyplace now," she said. "Woman," I said to her, "put your trust in Allah. There's something that must be done before morning. I'll be back soon." She said, "What does your godfather want you for?" "A twenty-year-old debt," I told her.

It's a good thing the rain has stopped, I said to myself. Just the wind now. If only I don't run into the army.

Whom should I believe: my cousin Abu Shacker, who saw him hanging, or what he says himself, that Al-Asbah happened to have followed Abu Shacker and cut the rope at the last minute? What do I know about hanging? Where are the marks on his neck, and how did he manage to elude the army that caught Abu Shacker? But why should I endanger myself and my family for the sake of a murderer who took care of a lot of personal grudges in the name of the rebellion? Why should I get involved in wars that aren't my own? Not my war? Maybe it is my war and I didn't know it, and the time has come for me to know it.

Isn't it too late? It's probably two o'clock now. Half an

hour to get to Deir El-Kasi. In the dark, maybe an hour. I'd better be careful. I know the house. Too bad I didn't take along my spade, because who can guarantee that the Jews didn't take everything that was in the houses? Will the storm hide the sounds of digging? Maybe they've posted sentries around the village. They're like cats with nine lives, those Muslims from Deir El-Kasi. They'll be back. Too bad I didn't eat a good supper. My stomach's complaining. Maybe it's fear? Of whom? What's it compared to Mahmood El-Ibraheem's fear when he kicked the stool away, or Al-Asbah's fear when he discovered that the corpse he was carrying on his back began to move? I'll probably never know fear like that in my whole life.

Here's the well where they left Rasheed Karrarah for two whole days, and no one came to save him. He screamed for two days and no one came; everyone was afraid of Mahmood El-Ibraheem and of his long arms, which could reach out and grab them even from the end of the world. Is it the end of the world that he should need me now? The hero needs the ordinary man, the rebel needs the collaborator. Collaborator? But he's the one who's supposed to have been the collaborator. Maybe this whole story about Abu Shacker and Al-Asbah is nothing but another smoke screen to hide the simple truth that the man has been collaborating with the Jews since '36, so they kill him and resurrect him again and again. Maybe this whole story is nothing but a trap. Come to think of it, what was the connection between Abu Habeeb and the rebels between 1936 and now? And why me, of all people?

Better hurry; this drizzle is going to turn into a downpour any minute. I wonder what my brother-in-law Yusef would say about this whole story. If he were to find out that I went there at the bidding of Mahmood El-Ibraheem on such a rainy, stormy night, when the whole world is in the hand of an *afreet,* he'd never speak to me again. He hates them so much, a blind and implacable hatred. What have they ever done to him? If this rain keeps up I can forget about plowing for a while. Then what will we eat this spring? The cows are dry; they barely give a liter of milk. All this walking, and I haven't even reached the school yet. Someone must have been crazy to think that this was the best place for a school, halfway between Fassuta and Deir El-Kasi. Nice stone, though. What will happen to it now? Maybe some smart goatherder will turn it into a shed.

There's a light flashing on and off. No, maybe I'm imagining things. There it is again, flashing on and off. Probably in the western quarter. If it were from the eastern quarter I would turn back right now and forget it. I'd tell him that the village was crawling with soldiers and it was impossible to get close to the house, that he should forget about the jewelry and the money. After all, Mahmood El-Ibraheem didn't work very hard for them. Who would have thought that the Jews would draw such a line between the past and the present, and between both of them and the future, which lies in the *afreet*'s hand. The jewelry is probably the treasure that was collected over the years from the local farmers who tried to bind the mouth of the beast of the rebellion and save themselves from it. How do I forgive myself for that? And the money—is it really from the Jews? the English? Maybe I'll take it all myself and say that the wall had been broken in and that the army had probably taken everything. It's possible to fool an old fox, especially when he has no teeth. But you mustn't hit a dead man. And the man looks dead to me, even though he managed to slip through the noose. It's like being dead to lose a home overnight, a black night like this one, and be condemned to wander Allah knows where.

That light is flashing again like a gigantic firefly. Another refugee come back to dig among the ruins? A soldier trying to scare away the darkness and the fear? Or maybe just my crazy imagination? How could I have not noticed the moon until now? Even with this rain, it's peeping out from behind the clouds now and then. A full moon in the middle of winter. When will I see a full moon in the middle of winter again? Why am I still hiding this gun under my coat? I hope it's still working. Too bad I didn't dig up my own pistol from the garden. Who has already been killed by this gun? Against whom has it fought? From here on better move very quietly, try to muffle the suck of the mud against my boots as I walk. Here they can even hear your thoughts. I'm beginning to feel that this whole journey is to pay off a debt to myself. Not to anyone else. All right, let them catch me. Now I'm going to raise the rifle, and it's going to glisten in the light of the moon peeping out from behind the veil of clouds. The veil of clouds! Fear makes pearls out of rusty language. So my studying with Karrarah hasn't gone to waste.

Well, here's the house. . . . And here's the courtyard. . . . And here's the western wall. I'll touch it, tap it to discover the hollow places.

He was right. Exactly where he said. I hope the spade is where he said it would be. The Jews don't need it at the moment. They're still shooting. Also, the noise of the storm will muffle the noise of the digging in the wall. The plaster is falling, and here's the opening. But the darkness makes it difficult. I'll light a candle. Good, I can see that this room has no windows. But snuff out the candle. Even in the dark you can feel silver and gold. Mahmood El-Ibraheem didn't need candles when he looted all this. He did it in broad daylight. The candle smell lingers in the room. Another smell penetrates my nostrils. A presence! Someone else is in the room now. . . .

A hesitant flame licks the damp logs. Abu Habeeb urges me to eat. Two white globes of *labaneh* lie in the mirror of oil, and bread freshly warmed over the fire. It's been months since I've tasted *labaneh* like this. I could kill for it, but it seems like my appetite, which used to be insatiable, was left behind in Deir El-Kasi, along with everything else we didn't take with us in the chaos of flight. I wonder what became of that jar where the *labaneh* floated in the oil, on the cupboard in the kitchen. When the camel's gone, there's no use crying over the reins. Many camels have gone. And I take it all calmly. I gaze into the oil and wait for my *mandal* to appear. Two white globes of *labaneh,* that's all that I see for me.

Allah is my witness; He looks down from there and determines fates. If you're fated to wander, you wander, and if you're fated to stay behind, you stay until it is His will and the wheel of Fate turns once more. Their luck is good, these Christians from Fassuta. They've always hunkered down at the end of the road, where the warrior comes to rest. The victors always spare some village at the end to remind themselves of what they have destroyed. What would have happened if it had been Deir El-Kasi at the end of the road? We would have been spared, for sure. But these Christians always knew how to stay off to one side, at that back door where the conquerors linger and ponder all the doors they have broken into. The Christians know how to keep the embers glowing so the fire never goes out. Not obvious embers, but a continuous dying, so that you can never tell if the fire is alive or dead.

That doctor was also a Christian, a good doctor, they said, but he couldn't keep the mother alive. A false doctor, that's what I say. Abu Habeeb thinks that's why I came to him, to call in the debt. But who remembers that? The only reason I knocked on his door is that his house is the one at the northern end of the village, the first house I came to. And when he told me that he would do whatever I asked, I remembered that doctor and that rainy night. And it wasn't only gratitude that I heard in his voice but also an apology of sorts, that I had wandered and he had remained behind, a sort of tardy acceptance of the fate that had toyed with us all those years and put us on opposite sides of the barrier.

Those people from Fassuta were never wholehearted, even when they gave us a bit of help here and there. The rebellion and everything that came in its wake passed right under the upturned noses of those Christians, and they didn't lift a finger. And when they were kind enough to help out, they did it with a lot of fuss and far too much show.

Abu Habeeb was not like them. He had something else in him—American, maybe. Bits of English sentences rather than songs of rebellion in Arabic. He doesn't belong to this place. He's a temporary guest, so he did all he could to leave a good impression behind. That young man he brought, Zaki El-Aasi, I remember him from back then, he was a student of that apostate Karrarah, and two years later I ran into this Zaki while he was out with his flocks and he said to me, maybe threateningly and maybe in jest, that we would meet again someday. And now here we are. He could help himself to whatever he finds there and run away. But he won't do that. You don't take revenge on victims of the times, for after all their religion speaks about forgiveness and mercy, so they say—well, let them prove it. He is going to enter my house, the house I'll never see again.

They tell me we will return, but deep in my heart I know that we're grasping at a flimsy and rotten straw. Refugees is what they've begun to call us, and whoever has that name stuck to him will never be able to rid his flesh of it. Like a birthmark. How much more fitting it would have been had Abu Habeeb sent that child who was born at the price of the mother's life twenty years ago. But it was a girl, apparently, perhaps the age of my youngest daughter. What will become of you now, my little love? I nearly betrayed you and left you alone to face hunger and poverty. The rope is still around my neck, even though the hero Al-Asbah undid it that dark night. I was already at my grandmother's gate, I was already knocking at the gates of her mercy, surrounded by the twinklings of fireflies, like a bridegroom on his wedding day, no longer walking barefoot and naked on that threshing floor of briers. . . .

I thought that I had put out the candle, for the smell of its extinguished wick hovered in the room. But no. An elusive light flickered in the room, a dazzling light that alternately flared and dwindled. Someone is in the room with me, but my eyes can't see him. The wall gapes open and the plaster falls off it and in the wall there's a niche and out of the niche falls a small tin box with a clunk on the floor.

The niche seals itself up again and the wall returns to its previous state as if nothing had happened. The light sweeps over me and over the room in a final wave of brightness and ignites the candle. The candle flickers in the wind and the room once again is shrouded in dimness and my knees are shaky and the tin box is sealed. All I want is to get out of here and go back out into the black night, to the full moon, to the drizzling rain, to the darkness. I pick up the tin box, it's almost too hot to hold, and I flee for my life into the night.

Darkness all around, and in my hands I juggle the box. . . .

He's late. When I was his age I could get to Deir El-Kasi in the time it took to smoke two cigarettes, even on the darkest nights, and here it is my seventh cigarette. Does the way home get longer when it's no longer your home and it's strangers who are doing the walking?

I look down at the wonderful shoes I took off the feet of that poor fellow, and I wonder where they will lead me. I'm certain that I'll never take the road home again to Deir El-Kasi. But I won't tell that to my little love. I can no longer tell her that when spring comes we shall see the anemones flowering at Tal Hlal, as red as the blood shed by the fighters for Palestine. But in my own veins flows different blood now, blood diluted by defeat, by concession, and in the veins of the treacherous earth different blood is already flowing and the anemones will be another color, Jewish red. *Rahat Phalasteen.* Palestine is lost and will never return.

Whenever I lost something when I was a child, I would spit into the palm of my hand, point the forefinger of the other hand and mutter, "Satan, Satan, mighty Other, where oh where can the lost sack be? Half for you and half for me, and the rest goes to the bridegroom's mother." And then I would flick the spit with my finger, and in whatever direction it flew I would search for the lost object. But now everything is lost except for the spit, except for the shame of having lost.

"We thought something had happened to you," said Mahmood El-Ibraheem to Zaki as he walked in and slammed the door behind him, pale as the fire that guttered in the corner. At once he thrust his hand inside his shirt and extracted a corroded tin box and held it out to Mahmood El-Ibraheem. Abu Habeeb watched him with admiration and told him, "We knew you wouldn't disappoint us. Take off your coat and come sit down by the fire."

"The fire is out," said Uncle Zaki, "and Jaleeleh is waiting at home."

"Sit down," Mahmood El-Ibraheem said to him, and he sat. Mahmood El-Ibraheem stretched out his hand and grasped the scimitar and presented it to Zaki and said, "This is for you for being so brave, but I'll give you something else, too, as a gift."

Zaki said to him that the sword belonged to its owner and was not intended for his hands. Mahmood El-Ibraheem said that a sword always seeks to return to its scabbard, and the scabbard of this sword was Palestine and not the refugee camps. "Trust in Allah," said Abu Habeeb, "and the sword will certainly return to its scabbard." Mahmood El-Ibraheem gazed at him for a long time, his eyes moist, and then turned to Uncle Zaki and said to him, "If this is true, then take it in trust." Uncle Zaki held out his chilled hand and grasped the sword, which was icy too.

Now Mahmood El-Ibraheem took the corroded tin box and tried to remove the lid, but could not. He stuck his hand into his pocket and pulled out a small penknife. He opened the blade and slipped it between the lid and the box.

All of a sudden a tempest of flame rips through the fireplace in the corner and the room fills with its glow and the corroded tin box burns gold for a moment and the lid falls into the fire and goes up in a great flame through the chimney and cracks appear in the chimney. All three men fling themselves flat on their faces and cover their heads, waiting for the four walls of the room to collapse and for the ceiling to fall on their heads. The light goes out, and the room is dim once more and cold in the light of the flickering lantern.

Forty golden coins were in the box, and a folded paper, yellowed and crumbling. Zaki gazed at the coins in the box and hoped that one of them would find its way to his hand. But Mahmood El-Ibraheem grabbed the coins and distributed them among his many pockets. Then he took the paper and began to unfold it. When the paper was spread out by the pale light of the lantern they saw that mysterious red letters were inscribed upon it. "It's the amulet that was found on the body of Karrarah, your teacher," said Mahmood El-Ibraheem to Zaki. "And those are the magic words that if uttered at the right place in your village are supposed to open the door leading to the cave where the Crusaders' treasure is hidden. But the dervish who saw this paper said it's only half of the whole paper, and the door will never open unless the other half is found and the Word is completed. Therefore this paper is worthless by itself, but if Fortune smiles upon you and you find the other half of the paper, you will never lack for anything."

Zaki took the paper, folded it gently and thrust it into

his shirt, trying to conceal his disappointment. Only when Mahmood El-Ibraheem finds himself back in Deir El-Kasi, Zaki thought, will this paper find its missing half.

The days went by. The scimitar was given to Abu Shacker, who had seen its outline on the wall of Mahmood El-Ibraheem's house. In time Uncle Zaki forgot all about the matter of the folded paper. Had it not been for the cows that were lost at the Lebanese border some ten years later, it is doubtful whether the paper would have ever again risen to the surface of his memory. It came to pass that in 1959 the herdsman who tended Uncle Zaki's cattle in the pasture near the Lebanese border came and reported that two armed men had attacked him in his sleep and tied him up and led the cows across the border. There were thirteen cows, which constituted almost all of Uncle Zaki's worldly goods. He went to the police station at Tarsheeha and filed a complaint about the two armed men, but the police were in no hurry to track them, especially since their trail would lead across the border. In desperation, Uncle Zaki went to see the sorcerer Sheikh El-Bi'nawi, the grandson of the famous Al-Bi'nawi from the days of the Turks, whose name was spoken among the villagers with great respect.

Al-Bi'nawi was seventy years old and a grandfather when he married Hadla, Abu Habeeb's aunt, at the turn of the century. In the fullness of his days, the forces of darkness came to him to demand what was coming to them. He gave them a sack made of black goats' hair and commanded them to go down to the seashore and wash this sack until it turned as white as snow. They went and did not return for many years. When his strength had dimmed they returned and tried their luck once more. He gave them a sieve and asked them to bring him water in it. Their wisdom stood them in good stead, and they plugged the holes of the sieve with their fingers and brought the old man water in it. They had come to admire his cunning and they granted him another extension, even though the tendons of his lower jaw hung loose. So Al-Bi'nawi continued to write his amulets in cryptic letters and send them forth on the waters flowing in the imaginations of the villagers, until Death finally came and swept him away and his amulets helped him no longer.

For three days Al-Bi'nawi, the grandson, sat in Uncle Zaki's house, and all his attempts to conjure the *djinnis* came to naught. It vexed him mightily. "Some presence in this house," he complained to Uncle Zaki, "is preventing me from summoning my forces." At the end of the three days he closed his eyes and described to Uncle Zaki and to all those present, among them my father, the half of the amulet that had been hidden in a corroded tin box. Uncle Zaki remembered Mahmood El-Ibraheem's gift, and extracted it from the depths of the *smandra*. Al-Bi'nawi unfolded the paper with great trepidation, and when he saw the red letters he immediately asked whether there were any relatives of Jiryes A-Shammas among those present. "He's my brother-in-law, and this is his brother," said Uncle Zaki, pointing at my father.

Al-Bi'nawi said to them, "Jiryes A-Shammas visited my grandfather, may Allah have mercy upon him, in the village of Tarbeekha in 1926 to have an amulet made that would soften his mother's heart and remove the obstacles from his love for a certain Almaza. But my grandfather sensed the presence of a dark force in his room, and when he asked Jiryes A-Shammas to empty his pockets he pulled from an inner pocket a carefully folded paper. My grandfather took the paper with fear and trembling and spread it open. It was the other half of this paper. But my *djinni* is whispering in my ear that the half that was in the possession of Jiryes A-Shammas is on another continent, far, far away from here. Nevertheless the place where the door to the great cave will open has been exposed quite recently, not very far from here."

My father spoke and said, "If there is any truth in what you say, please be so kind as to take us there."

Al-Bi'nawi said to him, "Indeed, I shall take you there, but a half-complete amulet is not enough to release the shackles on the tongues of the *djinnis,* and it is not enough to cause Ar-Rasad to turn his enchanted key in the keyhole of the years. And what is more, he can bring great trouble down upon our heads if he sees us showing interest in an incomplete and imperfect reality."

My father said, "To know a thing by halves is better than complete ignorance."

Al-Bi'nawi nodded his head and said, "I just wanted to warn you. Let us go."

At that time Abu Hilmi, Uncle Yusef's good friend, had been digging the foundations for a room he wanted to add to his house. He was greatly astonished one night when he awakened to a tremor of the earth. He took his lantern and went outside to see what was happening to his foundations. The earth was sinking, and he saw a ring attached to a smooth stone that was slightly exposed among the clods of earth. He hadn't told a soul about it. Now the group approached his house, led by Sheikh El-Bi'nawi.

"This is the main entrance," the sorcerer said. "But I have only half the key. Seventy years must pass until this ring is once again revealed." And before he finished speaking the ring had sunk again between the clods of loose earth.

Twenty years passed before I heard this story from Uncle Zaki, at the beginning of August 1978, at the memorial service for my father. I asked him why he hadn't written to Uncle Jiryes to ask about the amulet. He answered that my father had dissuaded him from doing so, because he had never believed in such things, and besides, the connection with Uncle Jiryes had been broken at the time. Also, it was very doubtful that Jiryes would have remembered some secret paper from more than thirty years before. If so, then why hadn't he himself asked Almaza about the amulet? I probed. Indeed, he had asked her when she came from Lebanon, he said, but she didn't remember a thing. The only amulet she could recall was the one her husband had put around the neck of his son Anton before he set out on his journey. Probably a verse from Psalms or something like that, after the fashion of village amulets.

I asked Uncle Zaki to give me that paper. "I'm very attached to that paper, as you call it," he said. "It's all that remains of a time past. Furthermore, in my heart I know that it can bring only misfortune to those who possess it."

"But you failed," I threw back at him, as if I were driven by the spirit of the younger generation. "Why don't you give me a chance to complete the treasure map?"

Uncle Zaki smiled and said, "Come, I'll tell you what we'll do. If you find the other half of the amulet, I'll give you the half that I have." I smiled too, to the chagrin of my mother, who had been standing there the whole time among the women dressed in black who had come to condole her.

A few years later Kareem-Muhammad Mikha'eel would come to the village bearing that Old Testament in Arabic translation which had accompanied Uncle Jiryes in all his travels, and a small notebook purchased in Beirut, in which he had copied down from memory Syrian revolutionary songs from the beginning of the 1920s. I looked for the lost amulet between the pages of the Old Testament, but I didn't find a thing.

O noble and mysterious Ar-Rasad, though I walk through the valley of the shadow of death, I will fear no evil, for Thou art with me.

CHAPTER 11

Once again I stand at the gate that is ajar. Now that my life has followed the course of this winding arabesque, I find myself once more at the place where I started, as if that flight from the village of Khabab in southern Syria back in the 1830s had been a foreshadowing of the real journey that awaits me now.

Clearly Uncle Yusef would have derived no pleasure from these words. He would surely have employed a less obvious and more politely arrogant style. When he finished telling one of his stories, he would flip with his right hand the left tail of his pure white *kufiya* behind his back with a swift, charming gesture and raise his head, nostrils flaring and a satisfied smile playing around his eyes. He would throw a quick glance at the faces of those present to see what impression the story had made, and then devote all his attention to his worry beads.

His stories were plaited into one another, embracing and parting, twisting and twining in the infinite arabesque of memory. Many of his stories he told again and again, with seemingly minor changes, while other stories were granted only two or three tellings during the whole of his lifetime. All of them, however, flowed around him in a swirling current of illusion that linked beginnings to endings, the inner to the external, the reality to the tale.

Whenever I recall that day on the enchanted boulder in the center of the *duwara* and see him pruning the shriveled branches of the grapevine to make way for the rising sap of the approaching spring, I tend to believe that it wasn't by chance he passed on to me the story of my name. The scene came to my mind the day Uncle Zaki told me about the lost half of the amulet, and I realized it was Uncle Yusef who had ensnared me that day as he was pruning—because were it not for him, it is doubtful whether the family memory would have continued to exist.

So here I am standing at the entrance of the cave, without a key or rather with only a flawed key in hand. Uncle Yusef, in his great cunning, gives me a tiny key to use to find my way through the winding chambers of the arabesque, where I stand at the gate, ajar, behind which lies another story that will invent itself in a different way. Then, with his charming gesture of the right hand, he flips the left tail of his pure white *kufiya* behind his back and devotes all his attention to the pruning. But I know very well that he foresaw it all, down to the smallest detail. He knew that I was destined to retell his story one day. That's why he so graciously granted me the key that let me into all the corridors but kept the master key in his own hands.

Now the tale brings me back to that scene on the boulder. There is someone else, whose name is the same as yours, and half your identity is in his hands, half an amulet, which, if joined with the half the family holds, will open the door of the cave for you so you can reach the golden treasure. But though there is this promise, there is also a threat, for you are as likely to come upon the magical formula that will unbind the mouth of the wild beast, and all of a sudden you will realize that the glittering gold is nothing but the flickering tails of male fireflies in the black night.

That's how Uncle Yusef was. On the one hand, he was a devout Catholic, who like Saint Augustine was utterly certain, as if the Virgin Mary herself had assured him, that the years of his life were but links in a chain leading to salvation. On the other hand, as if to keep an escape route open for himself, in case the only reality was dust returning to dust and the jaws of the beast of nothingness gaped wide, he still could believe that the circular, the winding and the elusive had the power to resist nothingness. However, he did not judge between these contradictory beliefs that dwelt back to back within him, and he even conceived of them as a single entity in which the *djinni*'s Ar-Rasad was one and the same as the cock that crowed at dawn when Saint Peter denied Jesus thrice. And here I am, his nephew, who served as an altar boy until I was twelve and since then have trod among the alien corn, here I am trying to separate myself from Uncle Yusef's circular pagan-like time and follow the linear path of Christian time, which supposedly leads to salvation, to the breaking of the vicious circles.

However, before I even get a firm foothold in the tale, I find myself snared on the boulder. Uncle Yusef's whole attention is upon the work of pruning, and his lips are parted in a tolerant smile: "I've given you all the tools necessary for a weaver of tales and I've sent you out into the world with many stories in your pack to keep people awake nights, and now you're coming back to me, like a bird into the hands of the fowler, to escape from the snare I had set for you when you were still a child. In what direction would you like to send the red horse of the tale?"

Rebuked, I stand before my uncle. I have not managed to rescue him from the maze of his stories, nor have I enabled him to feel at peace with the meaning of his experience or even mine. He was well aware that his being was flawed and incomplete, like my own, and the tale, in either of its versions, does not have sufficient power to restore the earth pulled from under our feet. This he knew, but he decided to hold his tongue until it was my fate to stand before the entrance to the cave. I would need to utter the complete

Word, and he would see to it that I did not lack for a single syllable. But he did not live to do so. So here I am back at the entrance again, a mute turtledove instead of the crowing rooster.

The priest's dovecote stood opposite the window of the first-grade classroom, and the cooing of the doves sneaked into the reciting of the alphabet, as did the disappearance of Ameen, Uncle Yusef's youngest son, on the Friday of the last Eulogy to the Virgin Mary in April of 1957. I sat by the window and thought about the bicycle he had promised to bring me from Nazareth on his next visit, that day I had sat in the southern window scribbling a thick tangle of red lines on pictures of horses in the Egyptian journal *Al-Hilal* in order to avenge the treachery of my uncle's red horse. A bicycle made of candy, which I could ride on and nibble at to my heart's content. But now the candy bicycle had become only a dream.

Twenty-five years were to go by before Ameen came back from Lebanon for his next visit, empty-handed, as Uncle Yusef had expected. He did not live to see him and suffered from his absence all those years. Nineteen eighty-two was the same year in which, on the twenty-seventh of September, the picture of Michael Abyad riding on his bicycle and looking at two corpses in the Sabra camp appeared in *Time.* I hold the magazine open in front of Ameen, after having filled him in on my speculations about the fate of our lost cousin. His indifferent eyes do not even take in the changes in the landscapes of his childhood and mine, and with his measured fluency of language, which I've always envied, he tells me, "There's another problem beyond the picture, beyond those two slaughtered corpses lying exposed to the eyes of the man on the bicycle, behind the identity of the bicycle rider who only in your wild imagination is your long-lost cousin, beyond your fantasies of slipping a ring onto his finger and shoes onto his feet, and slaughtering a fatted calf in his honor as Saint Luke tells us in the Parable of the Prodigal Son. The problem is that it's the Lebanese Christians who have been slaughtered far more often. For a hundred years, since the 1860s, they've been suffering at the hands of the Muslims and the Druse. And if this Michael Abyad, whose face looks so pitying, identifies with the Muslim corpses lying by the sidewalk, well, it's better both for him and for us that we not be related."

It was Hilweh, all tearfully, who came from Nazareth that Friday during Lent to tell Uncle Yusef that Ameen had run away. On Good Friday, two weeks later, they brought his things to the village, including his books and his notebooks. Among them was a notebook into which he had copied poems by a famous Lebanese poet. "To the fair homeland, where the clouds are the color of the doves' cooing," was a line in one of the poems. Since then that line rises to the surface of my memory every time I come to the village, for the cooing of the doves that the priest kept in his dovecote, opposite the window of the first grade, also infiltrated my alphabet of longing.

Ameen has other longings now. He longs for the days when these savages who don't ride bicycles return to the desert they have come from, so that there would be no need to slaughter them. I closed the magazine. The cooing of the doves we shared had vanished.

It was I who went to call Uncle Yusef from the field, from Uncle Nimr's land, as we called it. Even though Hilweh had made me swear not to say a thing, I told him from across the field that Ameen had run away, even though I had no idea what it meant. Uncle Yusef stopped the horse in the middle of the furrow, took the plow out of the earth, set it down near the furrow, came over to me and said, "Where is it he's run away to?" It was as though he had been certain that one of these days Ameen would run away, and all he wanted to know was the destination. I said again that he'd run away. He said, "All right, but where?" I said, I don't know. Now I see us both as two small and helpless figures beside the horse and the furrow, but at the time I was slow to grasp what the news meant, that I would never see Ameen again. I buried my face in my uncle's khaki pants and cried. My uncle patted my head with his hand, which smelled of the earth, and told me to go home, he would follow me shortly.

Halfway back along the path I found myself standing frightened in front of a lizard who had come out to bow to the April sun, and it seemed to me as if he were summoning me to come to him. I stood there stunned, weeping silently, until my uncle's hand grasped my shoulder and brought me home.

"Ameen has run away to Lebanon," Hilweh told him.

"I'm hungry," he said, and sat on the doorstep to untie his shoelaces. For the next twenty-five years he was to untie his shoelaces and wait for Ameen. In October 1982, when Ameen returned to the village, he went to visit his father's grave, and there he saw a lizard, out of season, bowing on the tomb.

Many of our neighbors had passed away during Ameen's twenty-five Lebanese years, but the figure he missed most from the local scene was Ablah, the neighbor's crazy daughter, who slept in the hayloft with the animals and all through the year wore a black rag, which protected her neither from the winter's cold nor from the cruelty of the children, despite all the efforts of Em Ramzi, her mother, to dress her in the clothes her other daughters had cast aside. More than her mother wished to protect her from the cold, she wished to appease the women in the neighborhood, who saw Ablah's white nakedness peeping through the tatters, little *djinnis* setting seductive snares for their husbands' eyes.

Ablah came to the village as a young woman early in

1949 from the Haifa orphanage that had been named after the archbishop. No one knew where her wide-brimmed black hat had come from, or the black satin dress that made all the wives' eyes pop out. Until the moment Ablah opened her mouth and rolled her eyes around in their sockets and sent her loud laughter somersaulting through the air of the village and beat her breast and held her breath, as she always had, her mother thought a genuine princess of the blood royal had crossed her threshold. When she realized her mistake, she raised her voice in an agonized wail. The disaster she thought she had got rid of forever had come to her with the coming of the Jews, and she would never be free of Ablah until the day she died. So she cursed the Jews: "Damn their memory, for bringing down upon our heads this plague of insanity."

Her neighbors got together and came to Em Ramzi's house and stood in a circle around the princess in black. As if they couldn't believe their own senses, all the women began to touch the body trapped like a *djinni* of lust inside the satin vessel, and Ablah released all the loud somersaults of laughter that had been bottled up inside her during the years at the orphanage. She kept on laughing even when her mother, wailing and beating her, dragged her to the hayloft, where her place had been before she went to Haifa. Ablah, like a new bride in black, raised her voice in a trilling ululation, which woke up all the sleeping *djinnis.* The elders shook their heads and muttered and said, "May it be God's will that our sanity stays stuck to us with carpenter's glue."

The days went by and Sabha the cow ate the black hat and the satin became tattered and filthy, but Ablah's body, somehow still white as snow, kept the women awake nights and visited their husbands' dreams. Then her belly swelled, and it was little help to the infant who emerged from the depths of madness into the manger that the Savior had been born in Bethlehem that same night. Em Ramzi took him away under the cover of darkness and a storm and she laid

232

him under the rock where I would eventually stand and weep at the sight of the lizard. Ameen, who at that time was still a teacher in Nazareth, came home for the Christmas holiday, notified the archbishop and asked him to intervene. The archbishop sent a woman from the orphanage to collect the infant, who hovered between life and death, and she took him to Haifa, to the same place his mother had come from several years earlier.

Then great melancholy descended upon Ablah. The somersaulting laughter became a hollow wail, and her body went to ruin and sank into her rags with a kind of heartbreaking surrender. No one paid attention any longer to the sight of the children surrounding her and offering her a bite of bread if she would lift what was left of the black satin. And she, with an indifferent hand and empty eyes, would raise the hem of her dress and reveal to their cruel eyes a wonderfully precise triangle, which would be etched forever in the children's memories.

Ameen asked what had happened to Ablah. They told him she had been sent to an institution. And what had happened to her son? They told him nobody ever bothered to find out. Then Ameen told them that several years earlier an attempt had been made on the life of the Patriarch Hakim, as he made his way in his luxurious Mercedes from Beirut to Damascus. The young man who had been arrested and accused of the attempt told the investigators that he had grown up in an orphanage in Haifa. When he had insisted on trying to find out who his natural parents were, it was Archbishop Hakim who had him sent away to Lebanon, where he was adopted by a Muslim family. The picture that had appeared in the newspaper was like a male version of the young Ablah. Those who heard Ameen's story were embarrassed by this skeleton in the village's closet and hastened to change the subject.

As we return from our visit to Uncle Yusef's grave, I tell Ameen about the day of the lizard. He now tells me that he

233

made up the whole story about Ablah's son out of some impulse that isn't entirely clear to him. I told him that Uncle Yusef wouldn't have liked that story, as he was a great admirer of the Patriarch Hakim.

"He wouldn't have liked your story either," said Ameen. "Your story about a nephew of his who went to give comfort to the slaughtered Muslims in Beirut."

"I think you're wrong," I told him. "That's the difference between you and him."

Khaleel, the family's patriarch, who had been sent to the village by his father before the latter met his death at the foot of the minaret, found shelter in the home of his cousin Abuna Elias, who was the village priest. Later, at the end of the 1860s, Archbishop Domani had excommunicated this Abuna Elias, because of his excessive leniency in his dealings with his flock, and because of the many friends he had made among the Muslims of the region. Among these was Mahmood El-Haj Kasem, from the village of Tarsheeha, the great-grandfather of Al-Abed Fathallah, who was Uncle Yusef's colleague in the smuggling business.

The priest and this Mahmood were bosom friends from the time the latter found out that the Ottoman sultan had granted him the title of Aga, but it was necessary to bring the document certifying this from far-off Beirut. Abuna Elias went to congratulate his friend for the honor that had befallen him, and asked permission to ride Mahmood's noble mare, whose fame had spread through all of Galilee, to bring the document back for his friend. On the next day, before the shadows of evening fell, the rider returned from Beirut and delivered the title of Aga into Mahmood's hands, and shortly thereafter Abuna Elias felt an incredible pain in his groin and the wonderful mare urinated blood until her spirit left her body three days later.

Thus, it was by virtue of ancestral friendship that the Christian Uncle Yusef found the Muslim Al-Abed Fathallah to be his partner in smuggling on the Rmeish-Tarsheeha route. In the spring of 1929, a few months after Uncle Jiryes had left for Argentina, Uncle Yusef borrowed my father's camel, tied it to his own and set out with one of his relatives for the Lebanese village of Rmeish, to transport some crates of arak to Tarsheeha, where his partner, Al-Abed Fathallah, would take it from there. A certain Saleh, also of Tarsheeha, helped my uncle load the crates of arak on the two camels at Rmeish, and on their way back Saleh waited in ambush for them on the Northern Road to turn them over to the authorities. But the relative slipped away and summoned Al-Abed Fathallah from Tarsheeha, and he managed to wrest the goods away from the treacherous Saleh. However, the shots were heard as far away as the police station at Tarbeekha, and some policemen came and apprehended everyone. First they were held in detention at Atlit, and when they were sentenced they appealed to a higher court in Jerusalem, but there they had the bad luck to come before a judge who, explained my uncle, hated all Arabs and sentenced him and Al-Abed Fathallah to a year in prison, which they spent in Al-Kishleh in Jerusalem.

There was an Armenian convict named Hagob in their cell, who was serving a term for having tried to murder his Muslim girlfriend's brother. My uncle, an indefatigable wordsmith, composed poems of love and longing for this Hagob, which were smuggled out of the prison right under the noses of the jailers to the girlfriend, but not before all the prisoners had memorized them.

Many years later, when my uncle crossed into Jordan through the Mandelbaum Gate, which was the custom every Christmas until 1967, he was to meet this Hagob in the Armenian quarter of the Old City and be introduced to his children and to his wife, for whose eyes the poems had been written. Uncle Yusef was to say to her that had he been aware of how much beauty Allah had bestowed upon her, he would have taken refuge in silence and not insulted her beauty with his shallow rhymes. She told him that it was only because of his poems that she had kept faith with Hagob, and were it not for him it was doubtful whether they would have married. Uncle Yusef told her that she should be grateful, then, to the arak of Lebanon, without which he and Hagob would never have met.

That year Ameen did not make it to Jordan, which was the only way he could have met his father. Or the following years either. When he finally was able to travel to see his father, after the invasion of Lebanon, all he saw was the lizard bowing on the tomb.

After the visit to the tomb, Ameen and I went to visit the family of our late uncle Nimr, Grandmother Alia's brother.

In the fifties I would accompany my mother on her visits to Georgette, Uncle Nimr's daughter. Uncle Nimr had gone with Grandfather Jubran in his first voyage, and when the boat that brought them back anchored at Alexandria, Uncle Nimr debarked and vanished into Egypt. Twenty years later he came back to the village with a Freemason's ring on his finger and a great deal of money in his pockets. He bought Tal Er-Rweiseh, the hill at the eastern end of the village, and on its top he built the most beautiful house in the area at the time.

My mother and I would climb the marble steps rising to the main gate, which was made of iron and stained glass. Uncle Nimr's voice called "Come in" from the other end of the huge entry hall. My mother pushed open the heavy gate and I would lose myself in the hall surrounded by two upper galleries that were reached by gleaming wooden staircases. Uncle Nimr would be sitting at his table, nursing a glass of arak, with the bottle and a dish of hazelnuts before him. Life tiptoed in his presence. From the day he moved into the house he never left it or showed the slightest interest in what was going on in the village beneath.

Now I sit with Ameen in the entry hall. The stained glass

has long since disappeared, replaced by cardboard and old newspapers. The wooden stairs are worn down, the walls cracked and moldy. Uncle Nimr passed away in the mid-fifties, on the day the threshing floor burned down because of a spark from the exhaust of the first threshing machine that had been introduced into the village. In his funeral procession walked farmers whose world had been destroyed by this fire, two months after Ameen had run away to Lebanon.

That same year, during the ceremonies marking both the completion of my first year of primary schooling and the first anniversary of the founding of the public school, whose lock had been forced by Abu Habeeb's cane, we were sent to bring laurel branches to decorate an enormous Star of David that one of the teachers had built from six planks. Our principal wished to make a good impression on the Jewish inspector of schools whom he had invited to observe the achievements of the new school.

The Star of David covered in laurel branches was hung carelessly above the front of the stage, where it frightened the children in the program and the people in the first row of chairs, as they thought it might topple down upon them. Seven boys came onstage to open the ceremony, each of us holding in his tiny hand a heart-shaped piece of cardboard on which was inscribed one of the seven letters of the Arabic greeting *Ahlan Wasahlan.* Each child in turn shouted a rhymed couplet about the letter that had fallen to his lot, looking up at the threatening Star of David. When the last child had finished his recitation about the letter he was holding and the two words were complete and had brought a smile of satisfaction to the inspector's face, Ablah leapt from out of the blue onto the stage like a tempest. She cupped one hand over her mouth, producing her wild ululations and trills, and with her other hand she began to lift the hem of her dress.

CHAPTER 12

The village butcher, Abu Ramzi, the father of crazy Ablah, drew the blade across the throat. Blood spurted, nostrils flared, skin shuddered and was still. He took a special reed and inserted it through a cut just above the hooftop through the leg. The flesh separated from the skin with a soft rustle. Then he pulled the reed from the scabbard of flesh, put his mouth to the slit, filled his lungs with air, and blew and blew again until the belly swelled. Then he tied each of the legs to the fig tree near the enchanted rock where I stood, openmouthed.

My uncle's wife knelt before the icon of the Holy Virgin hanging on the western wall and begged the Savior's mother for mercy. Such a thing had never happened in the village on Good Friday. Meanwhile outside, on the *duwara,* the knife blade pierces the membrane of skin between the thighs with purposeful and pitiless strokes. Abu Ramzi's hand grasps the lip of the opened skin, and following each knife stroke he peels it away from the glowing, steamy flesh, quivering in the noonday sun. First along the thigh, then along the slopes of the tender belly, the flesh is ripped from the confinement of the skin. The limbs are carefully pulled out as if from the sleeves of a nightgown.

It was two weeks after Ameen's disappearance. From Sa'sa', far to the east, his oldest brother, who served in the

Border Police, had brought back a roe which had been hit by the military vehicle that brought him to the village. Uncle Yusef, who was still withdrawn and refused to believe that his son had disappeared, seemed indifferent to the sacrilege. But my uncle's wife, who had never permitted meat to enter her house on Wednesdays or Fridays, as we were commanded by the holy church, viewed the butchering of the roe on Good Friday, of all days, as an act beyond the daring of even the basest infidel. To her it was an omen that her son Ameen would never return to the village. His things, which had been brought that morning from Nazareth, shrank into a corner of the room and silently joined her prayer. Her eldest son said to her, "My brother has disappeared, so what difference does it make anymore if there's meat on Good Friday or not?"

Everyone was always very busy during Passion Week. The women, including my mother, would shut themselves in their homes, both from solidarity with the Holy Mother, who was alone during the week of the Passion, and in order to bake the date cakes of this holiday. However, because of Ameen's disappearance, we didn't have any date cakes that year, and we didn't even eat hard-boiled eggs, as was the custom, at Easter. On the morning of that Friday, we children were sent to the fields to gather flowers for decorating Jesus' coffin. Narcissus and cyclamen and quantities of yellow calycanthus . . .

It is the flowers of yellow calycanthus that infiltrate my memory on the way to the village of Silwad in the spring of 1983, when I go to visit Surayyah Sa'id, the village's Laylah Khoury. I come armed with the photo of the bicycle rider looking at the victims of the slaughter and with my cousin Ameen's denial, which I take as actual evidence for my hypothesis. I'm on my way to feel with my own inquisitive hands the stalactites of doubt that I had forbidden myself to touch.

For two years now I have been obsessed by the story

Surayyah Sa'id has passed on to me, through my friend the journalist, about Michel, the adopted son of the Abyad family in Beirut, about his Palestinian mother, who belonged to the Shammas family, and about Michael Abyad, who in the late seventies had returned to Lebanon and joined the PLO's Palestinian Center for Research in Beirut.

On my way to Silwad, I think about my brother's friend Sami. I used to wake up at sunrise and take the largest pot in our house and go to Abu Sami's goatshed to bring milk. Sami himself, his father's firstborn, his pride and joy, who had been the leading man in the school play *Merciful Is He in Whose Hands Lies the Power,* was at that time studying law at the Hebrew University in Jerusalem. The journey back home was both backbreaking and nerve-racking: for I had to keep the milk in the pot as still as possible. In those days Sami moved through Jerusalem holding a different pot. He had to keep the Al-Ard, a group dedicated to Palestinian self-determination, from overflowing the boundaries of the law. Which it eventually and inevitably did. By then Sami had married Hanneh, Aunt Marie's granddaughter, and after years of harassment by the authorities the couple moved to Beirut, where they both joined the Palestinian Center for Research.

Early in February 1983, two months before I went to visit Surayyah Sa'id, a car drove into the parking area of the Palestinian Center for Research. Hanneh had left her husband in his office on the seventh floor, said goodbye to him and walked down the staircase. In Fassuta her grandmother Marie lay on her deathbed, thirty days before she was to meet her Maker, wrapped in the shroud that she had purchased years ago in Jerusalem. Hanneh had grown up in her grandmother's household, her father having been killed at a wedding in Fassuta by a stray bullet fired by a Jewish resident of Elkosh, formerly Deir El-Kasi. The car in the parking area exploded. Sami rushed out of his office and ran down the stairs. On the fourth floor he found Hanneh, lying dead.

She left a nine-year-old daughter, the same age she had been when her father was killed.

"So here we are in Silwad," said my friend the journalist, as he parked his car in the village square. He told me how to get to Surayyah Sa'id's house and went about his business. A group of curious children gathered around me, as village children will. "Who are you looking for?" "Thank you," I said. "I know how to get there." However, they didn't give up and accompanied me, a retinue of inquisitiveness, until I reached the house.

A woman in her fifties stood there, dressed in black, and her disheveled hair, the color of ashes, fluttered in the light wind of early spring, which also fluttered the smoke rising from the oven improvised from an oil drum in front of the house. The woman was snapping twigs and throwing them into the oven. I am gripped by the feeling that it would have been better if the story had remained curled up like a caterpillar in the cocoon of silence forever. But now the cocoon has hatched and the butterfly of the story, with a magical flick of its wings, has shaken off the webs of years of forgetfulness and the way backward is blocked, both for me and for the butterfly.

A black goat wandered up and gently butted against the woman's legs and bleated and wagged its tail.

I greeted the woman and asked if I was speaking to *Sitt* Surayyah Sa'id.

"Yes," she replied brusquely, as if impatient to go about her business.

I introduced myself.

She stopped snapping the twigs and gave me a long look. Then she smiled.

"Yes, your friend the journalist was here two years ago. How is he?"

"He brought me to the village."

"Why didn't he come here with you?"

"He has some business of his own. He'll come and pick me up here."

First mistake, for how could I be sure that this woman standing here would invite me into her home? "I mean, we agreed that he would look for me," I added.

"You don't have to apologize. After all, we're from the same village. But come inside; it's not comfortable standing outside like this."

"I see that I've come at an inconvenient time," I said, looking at the oven.

"It's nothing, and anyway the dough hasn't risen yet. I just wanted to keep busy."

We walked up the path. The smells of the house hovered in the entrance shaded by a vine that sent its tendrils out in all directions. The door was open. "Come in," she said.

You can still turn around and leave, I said to myself. Surayyah Sa'id's hand gently touched my arm, as if she were prodding me to go through my partly open gate. A white spring butterfly flew out of the house with a graceful flicker and disappeared. "There goes a *bashoora*," she said. "I wonder what it's brought us. Come in."

I went in. A large sitting room furnished with beds covered with flowered cloth was revealed in the dimness. A faded old wardrobe hugged the wall on the left, and opposite it was a closed door, which apparently led to another room. I sat down on the only chair in the room, and through the doorway to the kitchen I noticed the twins, about thirty years old, sitting at a battered table and eating heartily from the plates before them. On the other side of the table were piled layers of pita, with cloth folded between the layers, ready for baking. Surayyah Sa'id sat down on the edge of the bed closest to the western window.

"How is your uncle Elias?"

"He died of cancer years ago. Aunt Rose too."

"*Sitt* Rose died! May Allah have mercy on them."

Sitt Rose! As if she were still Laylah Khoury, a little girl in the Bitars' house in Beirut.

242

She sat silently. Perhaps she was thinking about her dead. Then she asked, "Did you know them?"

"No. And even my mother saw them only once since '48. At Christmas, at the Mandelbaum Gate."

"Forty-eight . . ." She repeated the date, indifferently, as if it had led a life of its own in her memory. One of the twins noisily laid his spoon down on the table, and came over to me. I rose to greet him and shook his hand. A smile of happiness lit his face. I mumbled a few words, and he went into the other room. His brother remained seated at the table and stared at me.

"My sons," she said with the same indifference, the same concession.

"Yes, I read about them in the newspaper, that time when the Border Police were in the village." Another blunder, I realized.

"And that's how you tracked me down!" She smiled. "So what do you want me to tell you?"

Up until this point our meeting had gone as I had imagined it. But now the great adventure began, and I have no say in what direction it will go or into what territories it will lead.

"Not much . . . Just until the dough rises," I said blindly.

"My husband wouldn't like me telling you stories of my past while he's sitting in jail. They call him a security prisoner."

"How long has he been there?"

"What matters is how much longer he has. A lot. Who's going to live that long?"

"You're still young."

"If I'm still young, then suppose I offer you a demitasse of coffee." She rose gracefully.

"Thank you. Maybe later."

She sat down again. She did seem younger, more at ease.

"Sometimes I can't believe that I've managed to live through all this, that I really am that little girl who was orphaned in Fassuta and passed through Beirut and then

243

returned to her village and from there was expelled to Jenin and then from there to here." She looked out through the window, then went on. *"Sitt* Sa'da, damn her, taught us about the guardian angel who stays by our side from birth to death. Sometimes I think it's the angel who has gone through all this instead of me, and I who stood off to one side and watched my own life going by."

"That's why I've come to see you. So you can tell me about some of the things you saw while you stood aside and watched."

"Where do you want me to begin?"

"Wherever you want."

"Let's begin with the story I kept bottled up for thirty-three years until your friend the journalist appeared. It's strange. I just remembered that Jesus was thirty-three when he was crucified."

"You still remember that?"

Another blunder, but she went on. "Yes, there are things that *Sitt* Sa'da taught me that I've never forgotten. By the way, my husband never asked me to convert to Islam. But after what the Christians did to me, he didn't need to ask."

"I'm thirty-three now," I said.

She laughed and said: "You could have waited another week, until Easter. But you're still too young for this; let's not talk about the dead. It's for the living that you came."

"I don't know anymore."

"Where do you want me to begin?"

I took out the issue of *Time* and opened it and gave it to her.

"Is this the man?"

She took the magazine and held it to the light from the window. As she studies the photograph her face softens, then becomes more alert. "It's been thirty years since I've seen him, and the picture isn't so clear. But judging from the profile . . . There's also something about the shoulders—how shall I put it?—that movement when he looks sideways and

244

his shoulder seems to want to look, too, and lifts a bit. It's him, all right. And who knows, maybe one of the people lying there is my father-in-law. Is your father still a barber?"

"No. I mean, he died several years ago. In the end, he was a cobbler."

"You know, sometimes I think about the touch of his hand, when he took me from Fassuta to Beirut. Till we got to Bent Jbeil he didn't let go of my hand. My hand fell asleep and he didn't let go of it, so I wouldn't get lost. But I surely got lost afterwards." She looked out the window again. "The fire has also gotten lost," she said, "but never mind, the dough hasn't risen yet."

She looked through the doorway into the kitchen, where her son was still sitting near the unbaked pita. She raised the magazine again to the light, put it down with a sigh and began her tale.

"I was happy to go back to the village in '48. You're always happy to go back to a place, especially back home, even though I didn't have a home there. I mean, my sister was there, but it wasn't as if I'd come home. My parents died in '35. Sometimes I think about my father, dream about him. About my mother—I don't know. As if she had died on purpose, died and abandoned me and my sister, two orphans. As a matter of fact, I didn't think at all about the whole period until I got to the Abyads' house. There I had a lot of time to think. I began to forget *Sitt* Sa'da. But I couldn't forget one thing, the thing that won't leave me in peace as long as I live.

"Many years passed before I understood what it all meant. I haven't mentioned this to a soul. Even now, I hope I'm not speaking falsely of the dead. Allah forbid. When *Sitt* Sa'da took me from your grandmother's house in Beirut and brought me to Mary Sursuk's house, Mary told her that my room was downstairs, and *Sitt* Sa'da led me there down the steps. I was only ten years old. I was shaking all over. She closed the door and came over to me. Even before I knew what was happening I began to cry. She took both my cheeks in her cold hands and kissed me on the mouth for a long time. All the years I worked there I remembered her hands inside my clothes, and her lying on top of me on the creaking bed and her heavy breathing. Three times a year I lived through that, somehow. Then I began to run away from the house whenever she came from Fassuta to collect my pay. When I returned to the village I found out that she had told my relatives that she was keeping me in a good boarding school.

"I was sixteen when Mary Sursuk began to pay attention to what her sons had in mind for me. My blond hair drove them crazy. But since she liked me and didn't want to throw me into the street, she spoke to the Abyad family. They took me in and gave her their old servant instead.

"They had one son, Michel. The first thing I noticed was that he didn't resemble his parents at all. But wealth doesn't leave any room for question marks. It doesn't leave any marks at all. No one noticed my existence there. Except for Michel, sometimes. We were the same age. He wore white clothes all the time, shirts, pants, everything white. I spent half my days there washing and ironing his clothes so that they would always be immaculate. He was like a cloud in a summer sky. He hardly noticed me at all. I would look at him for hours. Even when he slept. I don't know if that was love. Maybe because of that, because I used to look at him while he slept, I didn't tell your friend the journalist that I had known him.

"You don't look like him a bit. It's strange that he is your cousin. I'd say he looked more like his father, Jiryes, who was apparently a good-looking man. And the whole time something inside me whispered that somehow Michel doesn't belong to them, that he's different. I didn't have any parents, and I can always tell when they're missing. So I watched over him all the time, like the amulet that hung around his neck, which he never took off for a moment.

246

"That morning in '48 I found it in my room, on the dresser next to my bed. They told me he had gone away. During the night he had come into my room, as I had dreamed dozens of times, and left the amulet on my dresser instead of a farewell. When I saw the amulet, I knew that he had gone, before they told me.

"Then they came and told me that my sister was looking for me, to bring me back to Fassuta. After he left, there was no reason for me to stay on in Beirut. Then the other servant, the laundress, told me about the man who had suddenly appeared in the house and threatened to reveal the truth about Michel-Anton. I never met Almaza, even though we were from the same village and I was the same age as her son. She worked at the other end of Beirut and wasn't fond of company. So I came to the village, and then the soldiers came. I didn't even have time to get to know my sister again. In the truck they told us that it was Almaza's brother-in-law who was the informer. I said to myself, Well, you've lost a son and I've lost a home. Nobody owes anyone anything. Then I married Al-Asbah's son, and we had the two sons that you saw. Deaf-mutes, even though all during the pregnancy I wore your cousin's amulet. Look what came of it."

"Do you still have it?"

"What do you think?"

"Do you know what's inside it?"

"You mustn't open amulets!"

"If you only knew what is inside it!"

She rose from the bed. Her black-garbed body stretched and glowed in the window's square of light. The son who had sat the whole time by the kitchen table got up and followed her. Both of them went into the other room. I sat there looking out the window. I thought I'd better leave.

And now she comes out of the room and closes the door. She comes toward me. I see the black leather thong around her white neck, and I see it disappearing behind the buttoned collar of the dress. She moves closer to me. I can feel her breath making my eyelashes tremble. Take the amulet, she says. And my hands undo the buttons, one by one. Each button that's unbuttoned seems to release another strip of beaming flesh, stunning virginal flesh. Now before my eyes the amulet lies sheathed in the black leather triangle, and my hands pull her two arms out of their sleeves and two wild nipples lift themselves before my eyes, and two ivory arms draw my head to the ivory gleam, and the black dress falls in folds, and the room fills with light. This is the body that should have visited the dreams of the other Anton in Beirut, this is the body that should have covered him with its virginity. I go down on my knees and cup my hands around the two white buttocks, I bury my face in her triangle and breathe in the chill of the mildew, the ancient odor of the stones and the dark scent of the silt rising from the bottom of the cistern, suffusing the space around me with the feeling of porous ground, waiting to touch the soles of my feet. I am dropped farther and farther down. I breathe in the narcissus and the cyclamen and the yellow calycanthus flowers and slowly the scraping sound ebbs away and I seem to be closer to its echo that rises from beneath me and wraps me in dim solace. Suddenly a cry is heard, and the cry shatters into a myriad of fragments, and the body of Laylah Khoury, the body of a woman who is not yet twenty years old, is cast over me, and my body is caught on the hook of the amulet, with great reconciliation and with infinite compassion that tell me the triangle of the black amulet will remain between her breasts forever.

PART TEN
THE TELLER: Mayflower IV

The narrator of the story is the story itself.

John Barth

Iowa City, October 5

It's been several days now since I've slept. Since the Chinese party, I suppose. The truth is that I have fallen into a doze now and again, but it gets shaken off as if it hasn't happened. Like a tablecloth that is pulled away in a single easy sweep, leaving the crystal vase standing there on the exposed wood, on top of its reflection, as if it had always been there. That's how I've been waking up, into crystalline alertness, a reflection within a reflection.

Yesterday in the afternoon we went to Larry Ataya's country house, sequestered from the world in the lovely deep woods on the way to Kalona. It used to be a farmhouse, and now it is a place of solitude and relaxation. The pot of chili stood outside, by the door, on a hearth improvised from three stones, and Tanya Ataya, her hair the silver of ashes, stirs the pot and with her hand waves away the smoke from the twigs. The guests walk into the house to look for a can of something cold to drink and then sit around on the porch, exhausted from the heat and the bus trip, and sip from the cans.

Mary introduces me to Tanya, who says, "Michael Abyad will be late, I'm afraid. He called us from the airport at Cedar Rapids a few minutes ago. His flight was delayed. But he's on his way here."

"And who's Michael Abyad, if I may ask?"

"You don't know him. He's a friend of ours. My husband, Larry, and he—they're both of Lebanese origin."

"Why does he want to meet me?"

"I've no idea. But you'll like meeting him, I think. Why don't you go inside and get yourself a drink?"

I went into the house. A generous-sized living room, with a few pieces of heavy wooden furniture scattered about on an amazingly large Oriental rug. Worn wooden steps leading up to a gallery with two rooms. Bar-On, puffing at his pipe, stands entranced by a picture hanging on one of the walls. A woman holding a tuft of yellow chamomile flowers in her right hand, her body in a long turquoise dress, and beneath its hem a hesitant step. Her eyes warm and full of light, like the sun shining on brown pools in the wood. A glow of rich, dark color in her cheeks. Her brown hair curly and wild-looking. Bar-On sees me and smiles affectionately.

"You're looking very depressed. What happened?"

I remembered that during the flight to Chicago he had asked me the same question. But at that time I was in high spirits.

"You remember the story I told you in the plane?"

"About breaking up with that married woman?"

"In the plane, I made the whole thing up. The day before yesterday I got a letter saying that it's really happened."

"I'm sorry to hear that. But how did it happen?"

"Seven of the letters that I had written to her fell into her husband's hands."

"And he wants your head on a silver platter!"

"Now that you mention it, his name does happen to be Yohanan."

"And what are you planning to do, if you don't mind my asking?"

"Nothing. It's all over with, I think. Six months ago she

252

filed papers in the civil court, asking for a separation from him. There's also a child. Her lawyer advised her to break off all contact with me, at least until the trial is over."

"Please forgive me for what I'm about to say, but I'm sure you'll understand. I have the impression . . . and believe me, I really do sympathize, if that's the right word, but personally—how shall I put this?—I have the distinct impression that I've given up on a really terrific story. By the way, I haven't seen Amira today; where is she?"

"She wasn't feeling well. She stayed in her room."

Tanya Ataya stood in the doorway and asked if we wanted to join a tour she was about to lead around the farm. "What if he comes and I'm not here?" I ask.

"He's waited for so long, he'll wait a little more."

Bar-On pricked up his ears.

It was a neglected farm. Wild bushes had taken over the pastures and hid the tree trunks and threatened to invade the paths as well. We walked along the path leading to the lake, at the far end of the farm, a winding grassy path that bent through the undergrowth. Paco, a beer can in his hand, says it reminds him of the homeland. Swarms of mosquitoes signal that we are approaching the lake, and several people announce their intention to relinquish the sight and to head back to the shelter of the house.

Then we found ourselves under the sun's golden net, which hung suspended from the treetops reflected in the lake, but this was no dream of easy gold. A quiet, hidden light seeped through the branches and gently sprinkled the surface of the lake. "The surface of the Pool," Bar-On would've corrected me, invoking a poem by Bialik. Then the pool withdrew in intense stillness, as if the silence and the splendor of the wood were redoubling in the mirror of the slumbering waters. We gazed at the dome of blue, and a lone bird glided silently across the quiet mirror.

Suddenly a splash shatters the stillness. Amid the ripples, a beer can sinks into the water.

"It's a pity you did that," said Tanya to Paco.

Bar-On, his face red with fury, muttered at him: "Why the hell did you do that? Why?"

Paco muttered a few words of self-justification, saying he couldn't control his urge to break the silence.

"You know," Tanya added sadly, "ten years ago a friend of ours talked us into letting him organize a rock festival on the farm. The festival lasted for several days, and when it was all over the organizers cleaned up all the garbage on the grounds. A few days later I'm standing here by the lake watching the herd of cows that had come to drink. Suddenly I see the water turning red, and one of the cows collapses and falls in. I didn't know what was happening. Then another cow fell in, and another. There were cows collapsing in the pastures too. The vet's examination revealed that the cows had been losing a lot of blood because of cuts in their digestive systems. Thousands of metal tabs from pulling open the beer cans were scattered all over the pastures. We invited a group of kids from a nearby school to come and pick up all the tabs, for a nickel each. But it was already too late."

On the way back, Bar-On and Paco didn't exchange a word, even though they walked next to each other. I kept seeing the beer can landing on the surface of the mirror and the circular ripples rustling on the face of the water and distorting Bar-On's face into profound rage. It seemed as if he could forgive Paco his support of Palestinian terror as a last resort, or at least understand it; but there was no way he could forgive the throwing of the beer can. Liam, who was still troubled by the fate of the herd, kept asking Tanya about it and wanted to know every detail about that day on the shore of the lake. Every now and then he would look significantly at Paco and Bar-On, and then at me, as if to say, "I told you so."

At the house Larry Ataya tells me Michael Abyad is waiting for me in a room upstairs. My mosquito bites are now swelling, and I scratch them as I climb the stairs. I knock on the first door, and when no answer comes I open it and peep hesitantly inside. The room is empty. I look down at the big room. Tanya smiles up from the bottom of the stairs and points to the second door.

I open the door. He is sitting by the table, a silhouette against the background of a flowered curtain drawn so that only a small amount of daylight filters through, and the window frames the whole of it. A table lamp casts a pale ring of light, which falls only on his hands, clasped on a reddish cardboard file. In the brittle shadows is the dim face of a man from the East, in his fifties. He rises to meet me, all in white, and asks me to come in. He shakes my hand warmly and introduces himself, apologizing for the dramatic setting.

"It's the American in me," he says with an apologetic smile, and gestures to me to sit down, on the other side of the table. "You're probably wondering why I asked to meet you," he adds in English. "Does the name Abyad mean anything to you?"

"As far as I know, there was an Abyad family in Haifa, until '48."

"Good. We've already gotten hold of a thread. Do you know of any connection between your family and them?"

"I believe my uncle's wife worked as a maid in their house."

"Almaza," he said, a simple statement of fact. "She was like a second mother to me," he added in Arabic. "Third, to be precise. My name is Michel Abyad, and Almaza worked for us in Haifa. In '48 she fled to Beirut with us. A year later I came here, to America. I was twenty-one."

"She's died in the meantime. You most probably know that."

"Yes. I mourned for her more than I mourned for my mother. It was Ameen, your cousin, who told me."

"Ameen?" I said, surprised.

"I knew him in Lebanon, of course. Sami told me about her too. . . ."

"In a minute you're going to say that you know Shlomith as well?" This slipped out, and I immediately regretted it.

"Shlomith! No. Is that someone I ought to know?"

"Look, I haven't slept for a few days now, and I'm not sure this isn't some kind of hallucination. Maybe you'll tell me what this is all about?"

"What this is all about"—he went back to English and tapped on the reddish file—"is the story of my life."

"And where do I fit in?"

A knock on the door. Without a pause for an answer, the door opens wide. Bar-On stands embarrassed in the doorway. I look at him in astonishment. He apologizes and asks if we have seen Paco. Then, without waiting for an answer, he apologizes again and slams the door behind him.

"Who's that?"

"A friend of mine, a Jewish writer from Israel."

"An Israeli writer! He looks like a man who is capable of anything. In any case, the story is this. . . . Do you think he reports back to the Shin-Bet?"

"You mean Bar-On?"

"If that's his name. Yes."

"Maybe," I say distractedly. I can already see two detectives waiting for me at Ben-Gurion Airport at Lod, requesting me with dry politeness to accompany them. Contact with a foreign agent.

"You're not getting me involved in anything, are you?" I ask with a smile but with some concern.

"No. Not unless having a past is a serious crime."

"I was expecting a more reassuring answer," I say shortly.

He spreads his palms in a gesture of hopelessness and leans back.

"You're right. I didn't pay sufficient attention to that possibility."

"In other words, I'm in trouble already."

"That's not what I meant. The worst that can happen is that they could ask you a few questions, but trust me, that'll be the end of it."

"I suggest we put an end to it now." I get up to go. "I'm delighted to make your acquaintance, but I'd prefer that you allow me to make my own decisions about when to contact a foreign agent." I held out my hand, but he clasped it with both of his, as if to plead with me.

"Please sit down, I beg you," he said in Arabic. "Nothing bad will happen to you because of our meeting. Please stay and listen to what I have to say. . . ."

I sit down again, ashamed. At myself, at having allowed Bar-On to invade my life once more. Here I am sitting with someone who has recently met with two people who are dear to me, whom I'd like to see face to face and talk to, and instead of asking him about them, I panic and worry about whether Bar-On is going to think that there's an attempt here to recruit me into the ranks of a "hostile organization." And I ask myself how I would have responded if Bar-On had not been breathing down my neck, and whether the situation of Bar-On not breathing down my neck is at all possible, for better or for worse. Michael Abyad's voice overlaps the end of my thoughts.

"My parents, as they would say in Israel, belonged to the founding fathers of Arab Haifa. They had no children. In January 1928 they go to Beirut, where they adopt an infant only a few days old. A year later they return to Haifa and pass him off as their son. That was the year that Almaza, Jiryes Shammas's wife, came to work as a maid in our house, after Uncle Jiryes—if you will pardon me calling him Uncle—had sailed for Argentina and her son, Anton, had died. You probably know the story. I'm raised by Almaza, and during my childhood I hear about Anton, the baby who died before he was a year old. I hear about him, and sleep on his pillow, and even have his dreams. In '48 we escape to Beirut, and Almaza comes along with us.

"A year later a woman dressed in black appears at our house, claiming that she is my mother and demanding that I be returned to her. I have a nervous breakdown and the doctors advise my parents to send me away, to a distant country; at least that's what my parents said. Money was no problem. Here in America I become Michael instead of Michel, with all that this transformation implies. I didn't want to look back, especially after my so-called parents passed away.

"Many years later, in 1978, I go back to Beirut and join the Palestinian Center for Research. At this point you might begin to get worried again, but let me reassure you that you have no reason for concern. There, I tell my story to Sami, who introduces me to Ameen, Uncle Yusef's son.

"At that time I was thinking about trying to find my mother, the woman in black, but Beirut wasn't exactly the best place to do that then. I wasn't even sure she was still alive. The story of little Anton came up again. He was such an important figure in my childhood that sometimes I used to imagine that I was he. In Beirut this desire took hold of me again, to the point that I put myself entirely into his hands. Why shouldn't I be the son of Almaza, who raised me and loved me as much as if I really were her own little boy?

"Ameen told me about you, and that you were named Anton after the child who had died. I decided to write my autobiography in your name and to be present in it as the little boy who died. A piece of the Palestinian fate that would confuse even King Solomon. I didn't tell Ameen what I had in mind, but during the days of forced leisure during the civil war, in Beirut, he patiently told me in great detail everything I wanted to know about you and about the family. You were still a child when he left the village, so I filled the gaps from my own imagination. Sami also provided me with information about the history and about the village.

"I came back to America and I began to write my fictitious autobiography. I didn't tell anyone about it. I locked it all up in the closet again after I'd come out of it myself, you might say. And then a few days ago Larry told me that the members of the International Writing Program were going to be visiting him. I glanced absently at the list of members, and I saw my fictitious name there. Which is also your name. Take this file and see what you can do with it. Translate it, adapt it, add or subtract. But leave me in. I didn't take time to arrange the material. I haven't even found a title for it. . . ."

If Michael were the teller, he would have ended it like this: "He opened a drawer and took out a pencil and wrote on the file: My Tale. He frowned at this a moment, then he used an eraser, leaving only the single word Tale. That seemed to satisfy him."

But maybe, out of polite arrogance, he might have finished with a paraphrase of Borges: "Which of the two of us has written this book I do not know."

EPILOGUE

Because of what Michael had to tell me, I did not come home until mid-January. Uncle Yusef died on December 31, New Year's Eve, before my return from the States, which was two weeks later than I had originally planned. Our Savior's Mother loved him, after all, and she also shed her grace on me, but I was not ready to accept it.

Forty days after his death there was a memorial service in the village church, held by his friends and acquaintances and their children, who had inherited his friendship. When the ceremony was over and the clouds of incense had dispersed, we walked in silence to the old house, to honor his memory. I passed through the inner courtyard and saw the child that I had been coming out of our house, dragging after him his little pillow, and going to sleep in Uncle Yusef's bed. Uncle Yusef would now sleep soundly until the Virgin Mary came to open his eyes on Judgment Day, as he believed.

When the last of the people who came to condole us had left, Hilweh, Uncle Yusef's daughter, mentioned that the next day they would be coming to blow up the rock in the middle of the *duwara.* Yusef, Uncle Yusef's grandson, had reached manhood and found a bride, and he wanted to build a house for himself. He chose to build it on the plot of land we called the *duwara,* and they'd already begun to dig the foundations. But the boulder that had gleamed nights when the moon was full was an impediment to the excavations. Yusef the grandson went to the authorities and asked for their help. They gave him permission to employ a *hablan* to blow up the rock.

One of the relatives pricked up his ears upon hearing the Hebrew term for "licensed demolition engineer" and asked whether that wasn't what a *feda'ee* is called. When he was told that the two Hebrew words *hablan* and *mehabbel* sounded similar, he told about something that had happened on the morning of the day Uncle Yusef was buried, not far from the cemetery. Two *feda'ees* were killed there, and they looked exactly like each other, like two halves of a lentil. He could see them lying there by the roadside that morning before sunrise, when he was on his way out to the field. The soldiers told him to take a different route. All those present agreed that there was something strange here, that twins should meet their death under such circumstances. Then the conversation turned back to the licensed demolition engineer who was to come the following day.

Aunt Hilweh was now very worried about her nephew. Even though she can no longer see the rock gleaming on nights when the moon is full, as her life sinks away, year after year into her twilit fate, she is still possessed of a certain amount of concern lest the royal Ar-Rasad be stirred from his rest and bring down a spell upon all who have a hand in the explosion of the legend. But the whole matter only brought little smiles to the faces of those present. They immediately covered their lips with their hands, appropriate behavior for mourners on the fortieth day. Abu Mas'ood's name came up, as he had been the first to offer to blow up the rock.

The next day, when David the licensed demolition engineer had completed the work of setting all the fuses and had hidden himself in the shelter of the *bab es-sir*, Hilweh took herself to the corner of the room where the icon of the Holy

Mother hangs. She crossed herself three times and prayed silently, just to be sure. *"Wardah! Wardah!"* my lips whispered. David pressed whatever switch it was he pressed, and the sound of a dull explosion shook the earth under our feet. We hurried out through the *bab es-sir* to the *duwara*. Tiny fragments of rock from the spill of detritus hovered in the air and drifted down on our heads. A cloud of dust rose from the place where the rock had sat ever since the day the *djinnis* had put it there to seal their cave.

And now the dust disperses in the cold February wind, revealing a gaping white mouth and clods of earth. Relieved laughter escapes the lips of the witnesses to the scene, and even Hilweh smiles in embarrassed disappointment. But very quickly the smile freezes on her lips, her eyes are fixed on the sky, her hand points upward and a sharp scream escapes from her:

"Look! Over there!"

And a feather, a crimson feather, turns round and round, dizzily descending in slow circles over the gaping white mouth, and lands caressingly upon the clods of earth.